MANNING
A RAPTOR

MANNING A RAPTOR

AA Freda

ISBN 978-1-957582-93-1 (paperback)
ISBN 978-1-957582-92-4 (eBook)

Printed in the United States of America

CONTENTS

CHAPTER 1

BAD NEWS COMES IN THREES

Miles Cornish, the new controller for Coppi Enterprises is opening his apartment door late Friday night. He and his wife, Jennifer, moved to Colorado Springs two weeks ago from Lowell, Massachusetts because they wanted to give their two-year-old daughter, Elizabeth, a cleaner and healthier lifestyle. These first two weeks of work have been hectic for Miles, the company is in the midst of updating their IBM 360 to the newer 370. He has been working until past ten every night and is really looking forward to the weekend.

The Cornish's have not had time to start looking for a house of their own and rented a small, one-bedroom apartment in a transient community. A lot of their neighbors are soldiers from Fort Carson who live off the base. That night when Miles gets home, a chocolate cupcake with two candles is on the kitchen table.

Jennifer walks out of the bedroom, smiles, and comes over to give Miles a kiss. "You're home at an almost normal time for a change."

"Yes, things should be less crazy the next couple of weeks. The IBM crew needs to make some adjustment to the main frame. Where's Liz?"

"She's sleeping," Jennifer says, and walks into the kitchen, picking up matches and lighting the candles on the cupcake. "Happy second anniversary."

Miles gives her a side glance. "Are you doing this every week that I'm on my new job?"

She smiles slyly. "No, when you get to one month, I'm changing to monthly and then to yearly. Blow out the candles."

Miles blows out the candles. "There, are you happy?"

She comes over and gives me a kiss. "Yes, very happy. So, how do you like your new job?"

"Yes, I like the job. I just wish I had my own office. My cubicle is so cramped."

"Why don't you speak to your boss?" She walks over to begin setting the table. "You're in management; you should have an office."

"Jack says that I should speak to Kathy. She's in charge of the offices." He walks over to give her a hand.

Jennifer stops what she's doing. "Kathy is that attractive blonde assistant for James that you were telling me about?"

"Yeah, she's the one. Kathy is one of the people that interviewed me for my job. Kathy is not only drop-dead gorgeous, she's smart as a whip. I had to be really on my toes to be able to answer her questions during the meeting."

Jennifer looks over at Miles. "Is she the one that you were telling me is having an affair with James?"

"That's just a rumor."

"Are you going to ask Kathy for your office?"

"To tell you the truth, Jen, I'm a little frightened of Kathy. Everyone in the office is afraid of her. The other day, I was walking down the hall with two of my coworkers and she and James were walking by. I said, 'Hello James.' Kathy comes walking back and pulls me aside."

"'Is James a personal friend of yours?' she asks me. 'No, why do you ask?' I said. 'Because you called him James,' she said sternly. 'Only his friends and the higher echelon at the company call him James. Since you are neither, you will refer to him as Mr. Coppi.'"

Jennifer looks at Miles. "Wow! That's one tough gal."

"Yeah, you're telling me. Let's forget about her. What do you have planned for the weekend?"

"I was planning on going house hunting. Would you mind babysitting Lizzy?'

"Not at all. I'd like to begin my new writing project."

"That's the book that you're writing on the Coppis?"

"That's right! I'm going to the library to do research. I'll take Liz with me."

Jennifer laughs. "Good luck trying to keep a two-year-old quiet in the library."

It is Jennifer that suggested the idea to Miles to write a book on the Coppis. Writing is a side passion of his. He has written two novels, which he submitted to agents and publishers, but has had no luck attracting any interest in his works.

Jen told him, "Why not try your hand at non-fiction? I can't imagine anyone that you can conjure up in your imagination that would be more exciting than the Coppis." And, with the research that Miles has done so far, Jen is absolutely right: the Coppis are a fascinating couple.

Samantha and James Coppi are living the good life. A massive horse ranch in Colorado Springs almost as big as the Island of Manhattan. A sixteenth-century chateau in Lyon, France. A business global empire that has a worth larger than most countries. An empire so powerful that it can overthrow governments. Now the Coppis are embarking on a new venture: the expansion of a railroad. This is why the company is upgrading to a bigger computer.

And not just any railroad, but a behemoth that encompasses the entire Southwest, from the Mississippi to the Pacific Ocean. Not bad, for a confused couple that met by chance in a country honky tonk. The Coppis future back in 1968 looked bleak—she was pregnant with someone's child, not James's. He was assigned to an infantry brigade headed to a war in Southeast Asia. It appeared that all the odds were stacked against the young duo back in 1968.

But now it is 1981. Sam is pregnant and is expecting their fourth child. From what Miles can gather from the little that he knows about the Coppis, is what they desire most is an unexciting and routine lifestyle, an existence that will allow the couple to enjoy the fruits of their labor. But you really cannot turn back the wheels of time, can you? With so much wealth, can the couple ever hope to find a peaceful, ordinary life?

You do not get to their status without overcoming obstacles on the road to riches. A fortune cannot be made without eliminating threats that want to take it all from you. And you don't get to the top without creating enemies along the way.

Miles's story about the Coppis begins in Los Angeles, continues to Africa and South America, and eventually reaches Washington, DC.

• • • • • • • • ● ● • • • • • • • •

Mendoza steps off the bus and, hit with an unusual cold blast, zips his jacket way up. This April morning is unseasonably cool for Los Angeles. Daylight is still a few minutes away. There is no one around as he makes his way to work. He looks up at the wall, with its familiar graffiti. Yesterday he received some great news—Old Man Sanchez is retiring and has agreed to sell him the bodega.

Not only that, Mendoza won't have to come up with any money up front. The old man agreed to take payments over time.

It's the first real break Mendoza has caught since returning from Vietnam 12 years ago. His involvement in the fragging of Sergeant Camby in 'Nam came back to bite him in the ass. The police threatened to charge him and three other soldiers with the murder unless they agreed to testify against a fifth soldier. It was this fifth man, James Coppi, that the police were really after. The authorities offered Mendoza a pretty good deal in exchange for his testimony against James—a dishonorable discharge and ten years' probation, no jail time. It was an offer he could not turn down.

The result of his agreement with the feds did not turn out to be as good an outcome as he had hoped—he avoided jail for his part in the murder, but ended up with a criminal record. The criminal record messed up his ability to find a good job and make a decent life for himself. As far as potential employers were concerned, he was a felon, and that was the end of any interview discussion.

What really stuck in Mendoza's craw was that the guy he had ratted on, James Coppi, beat the rap and did not serve any time. Mendoza's testimony was for nothing.

He finally caught a break when the owner of his neighborhood bodega, Sanchez, agreed to take a chance on him and give him a job. Not that Mr. Sanchez had much choice— finding good, honest people willing to work in the Barrio is slim pickings. The South-Central Los Angeles neighborhood is filled with Mexican gangs. Turf wars between the gangs went on constantly. There is a shooting almost weekly; the bodega itself had been robbed several times.

The robberies of the store had stopped when Sanchez shot a would-be robber in the face with his buckshot shotgun last year. News of a shooting spreads fast in the Barrio. A thief walking through the hood with a face full of pockmarks is a good warning to anyone who might have an itch to hit the bodega again.

Old Man Sanchez is visiting his daughter in Tucson this week, and Mendoza is opening the store. After a few blocks, he notices a lone walker coming his way. He warily eyes the hooded stranger. Mendoza has never had any trouble in the Barrio—still, he watches the fellow guardedly.

"Mendoza?" the stranger says when he gets to him.

"Who wants to know?" Mendoza answers, looking into the man's face.

"Death!" The stranger answers, and pulls out a gun.

Mendoza turns and starts running. The shooter chases, firing wildly at the fleeing Mendoza. One of the bullets finds its mark in the middle of Mendoza's back. Mendoza stops and recoils from the impact for a moment. He starts back to running, but halfway up the block, he collapses.

The shooter puts the pistol to Mendoza's head and pulls the trigger. The gun lets out a click, but doesn't discharge. The weapon is out of bullets. No matter. The gunman glares down and spits at the lifeless body.

· · · · · · · ● ● ● ● ● ● ● · · · ·

Major Pator wipes the wetness off his face. The rain is so heavy, it is hitting him sideways. Reaching under his poncho, Pator pulls out the case containing the field glasses. He is trying to locate the remnants of the rebels that he's been chasing through Zaire for the last six months. Pator points the binoculars across the river, but nothing is moving. A fog is beginning to develop in the jungle valley below him.

As he's looking across the river, his top sergeant climbs up the crest and comes alongside. "Do you see anything?"

Pator puts down the lenses. "No, nothing."

"What happened to the rebels?" the sergeant asks. "They weren't that far ahead of us. I can't believe the entire unit just simply disappeared into the boonies."

Pator shrugs. "It's easy, I guess, when you're on foot and don't have to move heavy vehicles."

"Now what?" the sergeant asks. "Do we keep pursuing?"

"No," Pator says as he puts the glasses back in the case. "We're too far ahead of the rest of the corps." He lets out a sigh. "I'm afraid they've slipped away. Round up the men—let's report back to the main unit. Let's see what the colonel wants us to do."

Pator looks up at the sky. "If it wasn't for this fucking rain, we would've caught those bastards!" He turns to the sergeant. "Hurry, round everybody up. I'd like to get back before dark."

Back in the main unit's camp, Pator looks around. Shelters have already been erected. Soldiers are filling sandbags and building defensive works.

Pator looks over at his sergeant. "I guess we're planning on being here awhile." He stops one of the soldiers walking by. "Where's Colonel Bauer?"

The soldier points. "That large tent over there, sir!"

Inside the tent, men are setting up communication equipment. Pator looks to the back of the shelter, where Bauer is sitting behind a table littered with maps.

"What happened to you?" Pator asks when he gets to him. "We had the rebels in a complete rout."

Bauer looks up and smiles wryly. "It's this damn storm. We couldn't move our equipment any longer. The mud must be a foot deep—we kept getting stuck. How far did you get?"

Pator pulls up a chair and crosses his leg, wiping the caking mud off his boot. "The border." He looks up at Bauer. "What now? Do we wait for better weather and continue our chase?"

Bauer forces out a laugh. "Now we call in and wait for further commands—our orders were not to cross into Rwanda."

Pator asks, "How long do we camp out here?"

"I don't know," Bauer answers. "James is on his way, he should be here in two days. We'll see what he wants us to do—he's running the show."

• • • • • • • • ● • • • • • • • • •

Dalrymple leans back in his office chair and clasps his hands behind his head. A wide smile forms on his face as he enjoys one of the few moments of serenity. As the Chief of Staff and closest aide to the President, he doesn't get too many moments of peace. It's been three months since the inauguration and the action has been non-stop, at least twelve hours a day.

The result of the 1980 election had been a surprise— everyone expected the Democratic incumbent to pull through, but those hostages at that embassy was just too much for the voters to swallow, and they voted for change.

Dalrymple eyes the conference table across from his desk— papers are strewn over the top from last night's late meeting. He turns to his right. The coffee table, surrounded by the sofa and wing chairs, still contains remnants of the food that had been brought in.

Another crisis in South America was the subject of last evening's discussion. Castro was acting up in Bolivia. The Chileans and Argentinians were freaking out about having a communist regime next door. These calamities are non-ending. Just three months into the job and Dalrymple had already faced more than a dozen crises. But he loves every minute of the action.

There's a knock at the door and his assistant Marvin looks in. "Jack, you got a minute? There's something important that I need to discuss with you."

Jack nods. "Yeah, come in. What's up?" he says after Marvin sits.

Marvin clears his throat. "There's a serious problem that's come up. I received a call late last night from a close friend, Irvin Rothstead. He's a senior loan officer at the El Paso Community Bank. Irvin called to give me a heads up. Apparently, the bank is about to call a loan on one of the bank's customers, Phil Eisley."

Jack sits up, and a worried expression comes over his face. "Who?"

"Phil Eisley! Irvin called me as a courtesy, to warn me. He knows the close association between Eisley and the President. Eisley is behind on payments of a loan he has with El Paso. The bank is getting ready to declare a default."

"Default? Why? Are you sure? Eisley is filthy rich. He contributed nearly a million to the President's campaign."

Marvin nods. "Yeah, I was shocked, too."

Jack looks at the clock. "It's 8:15. Is this guy Irvin in his office?"

Marvin looks at the clock too. "No, I don't think so. Remember; his office is in Texas. They're an hour behind us, but I have his home number."

"Let's give him a call," Jack says.

Getting the officer on the line, Jack demands, "What's this default all about?"

"Eisley owes us, and three other banks, 350 million dollars," the banker says. "He's six months behind on the payments. Eisley used oil wells that he owns in Texas, and oil that's on two tankers, as collateral for the loan. We can't understand, with gasoline prices at record highs, why Eisley can't pay his bills."

"If you have the collateral, why are you worried?" Jack asks. "Work out a deal with Eisley to sell off the assets in an orderly fashion and pay back the loans. Isn't that better than declaring a default and having a forced liquidation?"

The voice on the other side gets louder. "That's just it. Eisley isn't cooperating. We think he's stonewalling us. Since he's not helping us retrieve our money, we're getting concerned about the collateral."

Jack starts tapping his finger on the desk.

"Are you still there?" Irvin asks.

"Yeah, I'm still here." Jack lets out a breath. "I'm thinking." After a few moments: "What if we validate the collateral? We can send someone down to make sure that the assets are there. Would that appease the banks and hold off declaring a default?"

"I can't make any promises," Irvin answers. "But that would certainly help. The person that will be conducting the examination must have an impeccable reputation, to satisfy the banks. This guy Eisley is very shifty."

"I've got the perfect guy in mind," Jack answers. "James Coppi."

"Who?"

"James Coppi!" Jack affirms. "He's out of Colorado."

"Yeah, I know the name."

"Would that work?" Jack says.

"Yeah, it certainly would help," Irvin says. "If a guy with Coppi's reputation for integrity attests that the assets are there, it would certainly make the banks a lot more comfortable."

"Okay, I'll make the arrangements." Jack hangs up and stands up.

"Where are you going?" Marvin asks.

"To speak to the President," he answers. "He needs to call Coppi and have him drop what he's doing and conduct the examination right away."

"Isn't it early? The President is probably still eating breakfast."

"I'll have to interrupt; this is important."

Soon, Jack is sitting across the table with the President. The warm, welcoming, fatherly smile that was across the President's face when Jack first walked in has all but disappeared. There's a period of silence as Jack is allowing the President to process the information he just revealed.

"Is this fellow Coppi the right man?" The President finally speaks up. "Can he be trusted to keep this quiet?"

"I don't know too much about the fellow," Jack answers. "But his firm gets millions in government contracts, so it's in his best interest to not upset the apple cart."

"I met this fellow Coppi and his wife Samantha at the inaugural ball," the President says. "They seemed nice enough folks."

"He has a great reputation," Jack says. "No one will dare question his findings."

"I hope you're right and that Coppi can be trusted," the President adds. "My good buddy Eisley plays fast and loose."

"We don't have much of a choice, Mr. President. If we don't send in Coppi, the banks will declare a default. Who knows what will turn up if that happens? The press will have a field day reporting on your association with Eisley. Please call Coppi and ask him to get involved."

CHAPTER 2

SAM AND JAMES GET INVOLVED

Sam waddles her pregnant body down the long hallway toward James's office. Kathy, James's longtime assistant and her dearest friend since she was a toddler, looks up from her desk, smiles, jumps up, and runs over to give Sam a hug.

"How do you feel?" Kathy asks, and pulls away from Sam, staring at her up and down. "You look great!"

"And you need your eyes checked," Sam answers, pushing her strawberry blonde hair away from her face.

Kathy smiles broadly. "The big day is almost here. What is it, about two months?"

"Two months and ten days, according to the doctor," Sam answers. "I've had it! This baby better not be late. He's having a good ol' time in there." Sam looks down at her stomach. "Look! His foot is sticking out. What's he doing in there, anyway?"

Kathy's eyes widen. "He? You said he—it's a boy?"

Sam shakes her head. "No, I really don't know the sex. The doctor wanted to tell us, but neither James and I wanted to know."

Sam looks around. "Are the people that I was supposed to meet here?"

"Yes, everyone is waiting for you in the conference room."

The phone rings on Kathy's desk. She lifts the receiver and takes the call. Kathy puts her hand over the phone and looks over at Sam.

"The President's secretary is on the line," she whispers. "The President wants to speak to James."

"Who?"

"The President!"

Sam furrows her brow. "Of the country?"

Kathy laughs. "Yes, that one!"

Sam gulps. "I'll take it in my office," she says, and hurries away.

Sam takes a breath and tries to collect herself. "Hello," she says in a shaky voice after picking up the phone.

"The President would like to speak to James Coppi," the woman says. "Is he available?"

"This is his wife Samantha, James is out of the country. Is there anything that I can do to help?"

"Let me find out," the lady says, and puts her on hold.

"Mrs. Coppi, it's so nice to speak to you again," the man says. "How've you been?"

"I'm just fine, Mr. President, thank you. Your secretary said that you wanted to speak to James, but unfortunately he's out of the country and won't be back for a few days."

"Is there a way to get in touch with him? It's very important."

"Unfortunately, where he is, communication is unreliable. Is there something that I may be able to help you with?"

"Maybe so." The President proceeds to tell Sam what he needs.

When he finishes, Sam says, "So, you would like for our firm to verify Mr. Eisley's collateral and report back to you?"

"Yes, to me first, and then to the banks. The banks will be footing the bill. I'll have my chief of staff arrange to get the contract and send it over to you. Will your firm agree to do the work?"

"I don't foresee any problems, sir. It sounds quite routine."

"Good," he says, and after a pause, "Mrs. Coppi, I would appreciate you keeping this very hush-hush. Please tell your men to be very discreet."

"Yes sir, I understand."

When she comes out of the office, Sam walks to Kathy's desk. "I'm heading into the meeting, but if James calls, come and get me. I need to speak to him about the call I just received."

"Who are you?" Sam asks the man standing outside the conference room.

The man smiles. "Miles Cornish. I'm the new controller. Jack couldn't make the meeting and asked me to attend."

Sam sticks out her hand to shake. "Oh, yes, I've heard about you. Welcome aboard, it's a pleasure to meet you Miles." She opens the door. "We better go in and get started."

"I'm sorry to keep you waiting, gentlemen," Sam says, walking into the conference room. "Unfortunately, there was an important call that needed my attention." She looks around the room. "Who wants to begin?"

"I guess I'll start," says one of the men. "I'm Colonel Chase." He motions to a man sitting next to him. "And with me is General Farnwell."

When Chase is finished making his presentation, Sam looks at the man in the neatly pressed full dress army uniform. Cleanshaven, buzz-cut hair—nothing is out of place with the guy. "So, let me recap, Colonel Chase, and see if I truly understand what you're proposing. Our company is to assist this Bolivian rebel group, the Guerreros, in their fight against the Federales who are now running the country. We're to provide the rebels any assistance that they require, without limitation. Am I correct?"

"That's right," the colonel answers.

Sam sits back in his chair. "May I assume, Colonel Chase, that you have documentation from the US authorizing this undertaking? It's my understanding that Congress is considering passing a law forbidding the use of American funds to arm the Guerreros. Since Vietnam, Congress isn't about to let the Executive Branch get involved in any more overseas excursions. There's no appetite for these adventures any longer."

Chase looks over at the man sitting next to him. "General Farnwell knows more about the legislative side of this arrangement than I do. I'm a field man."

The general takes a pack of Marlboros out of his jacket and looks over at Sam. "Do you mind if I light up?"

"No, go right ahead." Sam pushes an ashtray toward the man. As she does, she takes a closer look at the man dressed in civvies, not military attire. The gray hair and the wrinkle lines on his face give him the appearance of being much older. But Sam has done her homework and she knows the general is no more than seven years older than the colonel. Maybe the stress of doing four tours in Vietnam aged the general.

The general lights up and takes a drag. "We don't have anything in writing sanctioning the project." He lets out a puff of smoke. "However, Samantha, I can assure you that the Secretary of Defense gives this mission his wholehearted endorsement, and so does the Secretary of State. I've spoken to both men personally. Those gentlemen are the ones that sent me out here for this negotiation."

Sam smiles. "With all due respect, General, we need a little more than your say-so. We won't move forward with just your word."

"Mrs. Coppi, we can't put anything in writing," Farnwell says. "Your husband, of all people, should know how this works.

This contract is between your firm and the Guerreros. The US government can't be seen as having an official position."

Sam looks away from the men for a moment and stares at the wall. After she reaches a decision, she turns back to the men. "I'm sorry, fellows. I'm inclined to advise James to pass on this proposition. There's just too much risk to our companies."

"May I know why?" Farnwell asks. "You've done these types of arrangements before, with the previous administration. Why won't you do this one for us?"

When Sam doesn't respond, the colonel chimes in. "Mrs. Coppi, it's not complicated. You can have one of your foreign enterprises do the contract. Call it a consulting agreement. Nothing that sounds too nefarious. Your company will just be supplying advice."

"Where's the money coming from?" Sam gets a little louder. "Can you guys explain that to me? Congress will want to know who's footing the bill. And where will the rebels obtain the money for the arms, if not from the US?"

"Samantha, I can assure you that the money will not come from the United States," the general says. "The financing is from foreign sources. The funding will not be in violation of this act that's being put forward. Which, by the way, I want to remind you—hasn't passed yet. And may never pass."

"I'll tell you what, Samantha." The general places the cigarette in the ashtray. "I'll have both the Secretaries of Defense and State give you a call to assure you personally that they've got your back if something goes haywire. Although I'm quite certain that nothing will go wrong, and that we're all perfectly on the right side of this affair."

"What's our cut?" Miles gets into the talk.

The general turns to Miles. "That's the beauty of this arrangement: there's no accountability. Your cut is 25—maybe 30 percent." The general leans forward. "That's 25 to 30 percent of a hundred to two hundred million. And there's no one to account to. It's not American money, and it's not subject to audit."

Sam shrugs. "I'm still not clear. Who pays us? Who do we send the bill to?"

"The Guerreros," Colonel Chase cuts in.

"How?" Sam's voice goes up a notch. "It's my understanding that this is just a small, unorganized group of guerrilla fighters."

"No, Samantha, you're quite wrong. The Guerreros are well organized and quite formidable," Colonel Chase says. "We wouldn't be backing the outfit if we didn't believe they could win. We need your company to provide the rebels with the logistical support to carry out the war."

The colonel looks over at Sam, who is shaking her head.

"Here's the deal, Mrs. Coppi. Here's how it works. The Guerreros have a shell company headquartered in Chile. One of your overseas companies will bill the Chilean firm for your services, supplies, and any equipment that you provide. I'll personally walk through the invoice and make sure you're paid."

Sam leans forward. "I'm still troubled about the money trail. Why can't you just tell me where the funding is coming from?"

"What do you care?" Colonel Chase shoots back. "Where the Chileans are getting the money isn't anyone's concern as long as it isn't US taxpayer money. There's nothing in this affair that puts us in violation of any act that Congress might pass."

Colonel Chase leans forward and gives Sam a sly look. "And by the way, let me remind you, there is no way of auditing this Chilean enterprise. The US doesn't have jurisdiction."

Sam looks over at one of her men in the room. "What do you say, Rodney? You handle the government side of our business. You know something about these affairs. Weren't you behind the coup in Guatemala?"

Rodney smiles. "On Guatemala, I have no comment. As to this affair—yeah, it's doable. It can be done. Quietly and under the radar—I don't foresee a problem."

Sam turns to another. "How about you, Ian? You're in charge of international. This project will be your baby if we decide to move forward."

"Yeah, I agree with Rodney. It's no problem. We've done these types of covert operations before. Many times, and without a hitch."

Sam smiles at the youngish-looking, freckled-faced, redheaded Englishman, who gives the appearance that he should be hanging out with friend at a pub, not at a corporate meeting. Indeed, Ian is one of James's must trusted advisers and runs the entire international operation.

"What about all the other matters you've got on your plate? At last count, there were eleven."

Ian shrugs confidently. "We can fit this project in without much of a problem."

"What about the African project?" Sam asks. "That's one massive program. James is on his way to Zaire right now. You can squeeze this assignment in without affecting that venture?"

"No, it can be done," Ian answers. "Ernie and Gary have a good handle on Zaire. They're hunkered down, and not on the move. And, besides, neither of those men are needed for this matter."

"How about you, Vernon?" Sam asks the last and the oldest man in the room. Vernon, out of all the participants, gives the appearance that he belongs at a corporate meeting. A touch of gray in his hair and moustache, a dark blue suit with matching blue tie, and always a white handkerchief in his breast pocket. "You're the president of the company; you get the final word. Should we proceed?"

Vernon clears his throat. "There'll be problems, Samantha—I don't care what these men say. Any time you have politicians involved—you'll have trouble. This is the eighties, not the sixties, when these activities weren't being scrutinized. No matter how well you plan, something unexpectedly always creeps up. And you can bet that when the unexpected pops up, the politicians who say they got your back will run for cover, and we'll be the ones left with the mess."

"So, what are you saying, Vernon? You don't believe we should do the deal?"

"No, I'm not saying that we don't do the deal. I'm suggesting that we be very careful. Dot all of our Is and cross all of our Ts. I'd like to be there when we take the call to the Secretaries of Defense and State. Fully document what those men have to say. It's important for us to know exactly what 'they got our backs' means.

"How far will these politicians go to protect us? With that being said, if we can work out those details and be satisfied with their response, I'm all for the project."

Sam stretches and smiles. "All right; now that we're in agreement, we'll move forward." She looks at Vernon. "Subject to that last conversation, of course, with the Secretaries of State and Defense."

Sam turns to Ian. "Ian, you'll be in charge, but you'll report directly to Rodney, not Vernon, me, or James."

She looks over at Miles. "Miles, you'll handle the monetary aspect of this project. I want you to handle this directly—don't involve any of your staff. Let's minimize everyone's participation. The less people in the know the better."

Sam turns back to the military men. "Make arrangements for that call from the secretaries."

• • • • • • • • ● • • • • • • • •

When Miles gets home late that night, the television is on and both Jen and his daughter Liz are sprawled out asleep on the couch in the living room. He walks into the room, leans over and kisses Jen on her forehead.

Jen's eyes flip open and she smiles. She reaches up and pulls Miles down to her giving him another kiss. "You're home late."

"There was a lot going on in the office today," he says.

Jen stands up. "Let me put Liz to bed and I'll warm up your supper."

She reaches down and lifts up Liz. As she is about to go out of the room she turns back to Miles. "Your brother Jeffrey called earlier."

"Okay, thanks. I'll give him a call while you're getting dinner ready."

"How's everything in sunny Colorado," Miles's brother Jeffrey greets when he's on the line.

Miles laughs. "To tell you the truth Jeff, I've been so busy at work that I've hardly had time to enjoy the beautiful area."

"What have you been working on?"

"Oh, just financial stuff. You wouldn't be interested."

"What about those visitors you got today?" Jeffrey brings out. "Those military guys."

Miles shakes his head. "How did you know about that?"

Jeffrey laughs. "Let that be a lesson to you little brother. You can't hide anything from old Jeff." After a pause he adds. "Senator Hartley called and told me. What was the meeting all about? Hartley suspects that it was about Bolivia."

"Jeff, I don't think we should be talking about this. If you called me because you wanted to know what my company discussed, you wasted your time."

"So there was a meeting about Bolivia?"

Miles gets louder. "Jeff, I told you that I'm not going to talk about it!"

"Miles I hope you remember that it was Senator Hartley that got you out of that mess years ago. Hartley was the one that got involved and cleared up your problem. You might want to show Hartley some gratitude if he should happen to call you."

The phone goes quiet. "I hope you know that Hartley is getting ready to pass legislation that forbids Americans getting involved in Bolivia," Jeffrey says. "Hartley thinks that the administration is hiring your boss James Coppi to get around this regulation."

"Jeff, can we change the subject, please?" Miles answers irritated. "I don't really feel like talking about any of this stuff."

"All right, let's drop it. Just be careful that you don't get dragged into the mess. How's Jen and my niece?"

"Both Jen and Liz are doing fine."

"How about you? Aside from work, what do you do to pass the time?"

"I've been doing some writing."

Jeffrey laughs. "You're still writing? I thought you gave that up?"

"No," Miles replies. "I still write to pass the time, it keeps me busy."

"What are you writing about?"

"I'm actually writing about the Coppis. I've done some research and those two sound quite fascinating."

"The Coppis?" Jeffrey yells out. "Do the Coppis know that you're writing about them?"

"No," Miles says. "My writing is probably not going to amount to much, and it'll probably never get published. I'm just writing to pass the time. Doing the research on the Coppis gives me something to do. If when I'm finished, and I like my work, I'll present it to the Coppis for their approval."

"All right, I've got to go," Jeffrey says. "Give my regards to Jen and a kiss to the baby for me."

CHAPTER 3

AFRICA

James is sitting at the Sabena terminal of Zaventem Airport in Brussels while Sam was conducting her meetings. Once again, there is an announcement that the flight will be delayed. It is now scheduled for 10:30pm. The flight was originally to take off at 5:00pm. He is beginning to resign himself that he may have to spend the night in Brussels.

The delay is really screwing up his plans. There's a private plane that he chartered to take him from Kinshasa to Kivu, where he's to meet Ernie Bauer. He's hoping that his plane is still waiting in Kinshasa when he finally gets there.

Max, his bodyguard, walks over, takes a seat next to him, and hands him a bottle. "Here's your water, Boss."

"Thanks." He twists off the cap and takes a sip.

"Do you think we'll make it out tonight?" the big man asks.

"Who the fuck knows?" he forces out. "Sabena is such a shit carrier; they're on the verge of bankruptcy. The airline probably doesn't have enough money to buy fuel—we may not get out for days."

"Why didn't we take your jet?"

James takes another sip. "My plane doesn't have the range. We would've had to make a stop to refuel. Besides, I didn't want to keep my plane in Kinshasa, what with the political turmoil and all."

Max sits up. "There's the announcement, we're boarding in twenty minutes—I guess we're getting out tonight after all."

James stands up. "Don't be so sure. The airline could still change its mind. I need to find a phone and call Sam. There was an important meeting today, and I want to know how she made out."

The first news Sam tells him when she's on the line is about the call from the President.

"This sounds awful strange, don't you agree?" he says when she's finished. "The President not giving the assignment to an underling? He made the call to you himself?"

"So, what are you saying? That I should've turned him down?" she says.

"No, no, of course not, how could you? It was the President. Tell Charlie to send the Sarge to conduct the examination. The Sarge can be trusted to keep his mouth shut. I've got a strange feeling about this job—something doesn't sound right. Tell Charlie to get the Sarge to Texas right away. I'd like to have a report on the Texas oil wells on my desk when I get back. Tell me about the other meeting with the military guys. What did they want?"

Sam proceeds to tell him about the Bolivian affair.

"You did good," he says. "I'm glad you insisted on getting the secretaries to verify the authorization. The whole assignment sounds kind of suspicious. It could come back to bite us. I'd like to be there when we make those calls."

"How long will you be in Africa?"

"I should be home in three days. I'm meeting with Ernie tomorrow morning and I'm coming straight home after that."

"OK, be careful. You know I can't sleep when you go on these dangerous trips."

"There's nothing dangerous about this trip. It's in and out."

"So you always say! Anyway, be safe. I love you!"

"I love you too!"

• • • • • • • • ● • • • • • • •

James looks out his window as the plane makes its final approach to the airport into Kinshasa. The morning sunlight shimmers over the water of the Congo River. The second longest river in Africa—second only to the Nile. And just like the Nile, the Congo is a life source for millions in Central Africa, whose inhabitants from time immemorial described it as "the river that swallows rivers" and which Portuguese explorers translated as "Zaire." James looks on in awe at the river's power; a river which crosses the Equator twice on its route to the Atlantic and reaches depths of over 700 feet. James reflects *how formidable the land must be.*

Next to the runway there are rows of shanties inhabited by the refugees who have made a home in Kinshasa. There are sandbagged foxholes alongside the runway. In the middle of each hole, a 50-caliber machine gun is mounted on a tri-pod. Soldiers are milling around the pits, looking bored. *A good thing,* he reasons. If there was any action in the area, the soldiers would have been on alert. The 707 brakes hard after it hits the runway. Moments later, a large, one-story gray stucco building comes into view. A metal ladder is pushed against the plane, and James and Max disembark. More soldiers with Tommy guns are in front of the terminal.

Max comes alongside. "All these soldiers with weapons—do you think there'll be trouble?"

James smiles. "No, I don't suppose so—at least, not here in Kinshasa. Look at the building: there're no bullet holes in the walls. There's hasn't been any action in this area."

"What kind of trouble are you anticipating?"

"Mostly from the bureaucrats inside the terminal. Those customs guys will be looking for a bribe. Henri Cavet, one of our foreign nationals, is supposed to be at the airport to help get us through. I hope he's here."

Inside the terminal, they walk down an aisle with a four-foot railing blocking off the chaotic hundreds of locals waiting to greet the passengers.

"Monsieur Coppi!" they hear a man shout from behind the frenzied crowd.

James walks up to the railing. He can't see the man. "Henri?" he shouts into the mob.

The smallish mustached man forces his way through the crowd. "Oui, bienvenue. Did you have a pleasant trip?"

"Yes, the flight was fine," he says. "How do I proceed?"

Henri points to the front. "Use the customs booth on the far right; that man has been handled. I will meet you at the other side, there's a plane waiting for us at the back of this building."

James and Max walk up to the customs booth on the right. The customs agent is arguing with one of the passengers. The agent calls over a security guard and the unruly passenger is whisked to the side. James and Max walk up and hand the agent their passports. The attendant turns to where Henri is standing and smiling. Henri winks and nods at the agent. Without saying a word the rep hands back the passports. When they get outside, there is a small prop plane waiting. It has started to rain.

"How far are we flying, Boss?" Max asks him.

"I don't know," he answers. "We need to get to the other side of Zaire. Around four to five hours, is my guess. We're travelling right back here after our meeting. There's a flight back to Brussels tonight."

"We're flying in that little plane?" Max says. "That plane is too small to carry all of us." Max looks up at the sky. "How can the pilot even see where he's going in this weather?"

"Max, shut up and get on the plane," James calls out. "We don't have time for all your shit."

After a little over five hours of turbulence through the clouds, a military encampment comes into view. Max's knuckles are bleeding from his fingernails digging in. James looks over and smiles.

"See, no problem."

Max gives him a sneer.

The pilot announces, "You may want to fasten your seat belts tighter. There's no runway and we're landing on a muddy open field."

"Oh, shit," Max lets out.

The moment the plane touches down, it slides sideways. James is whipped around in his seat when the pilot tries to correct the approach. Another twist and the plane comes to rest sideways in the field. The pilot turns. "That was really not as bad as I thought it would be."

Max turns to James. "I'd kill that motherfucker if we didn't need him to take us back."

James opens the door, and once outside, he's met by a soldier draped in a black poncho that is dripping wet.

"Mister Coppi," he says in a thick South African twang. "I'm Sergeant Krosky." He hands James a poncho. "You may want to put this raingear on before coming outside. It's pouring."

The sergeant looks over at Max. "I'm sorry, I don't have another—I didn't know there'd be two of you."

James turns to Max. "Why don't you wait here in the plane?" He smiles. "You know, since you love the pilot so much. The meeting shouldn't take long—I should be back by the time they've finished refueling."

James hops off the plane.

"Right this way, sir." The sergeant leads him to a waiting jeep.

After slipping and sliding through the mud with the jeep, they end up at the military encampment. The driver points to a large tent surrounded by an eight-foot wall of pyramid-style staggered sandbags. "The Colonel is right inside."

Inside, another soldier points to the back of the tent. "He's right over there, sir."

To his right, a soldier is sitting at a table manning what appears to be communication gear. Other soldiers are behind makeshift desks built out of empty artillery boxes.

Ernie gives him that big Afrikaner smile when he gets there. "Hello, *boet*. With all this weather, I was beginning to get the sense that you weren't going to make it."

James walks over and removes his poncho, draping it carefully over the back of the chair. A puddle has already formed on the floor underneath. He looks at Ernie, who has a glass of wine in front of him.

He motions to the glass "Isn't it a little early?"

Ernie bellows out a laugh. "Never too early for a fine glass of wine. And this particular vintage is superb; it's from my own vineyard back home."

One of the soldiers walks over. "Can I get you something, sir?"

"Just a bottle of water, please." James takes a seat and turns to Ernie. "All right, let's get right to it. I want to fly back before the weather turns even worse. Fill me in on where we are."

Ernie begins giving James a report on how he and his troops had driven the rebels out of Zaire. Ernie is putting a positive spin on the performance of his unit emphasizing that the rebels were within a hundred miles from the capitol when his men got into the action.

Ernie smiles satisfactorily when he's finished. "James, we forced a division, three times our size, to retreat nearly six hundred miles in six months." He sits back in his chair and has a sip of wine. "That's one incredible feat!"

James isn't happy. "I don't understand, Ernie. Last week, you reported that you had the rebels on the run," he says. "'A complete rout' is how you phrased it. 'The rebels are in a disorganized retreat—it's just a matter of mopping up.' How the hell do more than ten thousand fighters slip away?"

"I know, James, but this damn weather," Ernie says, "it's almost impossible to move."

James's voice rises up a notch. "The fucking weather is also bad for the other side, you *domkop!*"

"Yes, you're right, James, but they don't have to move all these military vehicles."

He lets out an annoyed breath. "I'm really disappointed, Ernie—you read this situation all wrong. It wasn't a messy retreat—the rebels were withdrawing in an orderly manner. This rebel leader Benga completely outfoxed you."

"James, we can argue all day about what happened, but it'll lead us nowhere. The question is, what do we do now? Do we wait for the weather to clear and cross over the border? The rainy season will be over soon."

James answers in a calmer tone. "No, Washington won't stand for it if we escalate the war. And the truth is, we're not here to overthrow a government. We were hired by United Mining to protect the mines from the rebels that were looting. Stay tight in your position until I figure out what to do next. I've got to gage the political situation. Anyway, you're in a pretty good defensive position."

"Are you sure?" Ernie says. "James, you know that Benga will mount a counterattack. We're in a good spot right now, but that can change quickly."

He clears his throat. "We have no choice. Going into Rwanda will cause a major international incident, and the politicians back home would never stand for that."

Ernie lets out a breath. "James, you're not letting politicians run this campaign, are you? You, of all people, should know that won't work. Remember what happened in Vietnam?"

"No, Ernie, I'm not allowing the politicians to dictate the conduct of what we do here. I'll pull out before I let that happen. But I need to make sure I don't make more trouble for myself. Crossing into another country creates a serious situation."

James leans forward in his chair and lowers his voice. "To tell you the truth, Ernie, I don't know why the CIA is backing President Mobutu. The guy is a fucking crook. One of the most corrupt leaders in the world. But Mobutu is not our problem. Let's stick to the mission we're being paid to do—protect the mines."

He sits back up. "Anyway, this may be a good time to provide your men with a little rest. The men have been fighting for six months straight." James smiles slyly at Ernie. "Maybe you can share some of that fine wine you're hoarding with your men."

CHAPTER 4

A PHILLIPS SCREW

Three days later, James is back at his office for an early morning meeting. "Okay, guys, I guess Sam is running late. Let's not wait any longer. How is your audit into the Eisley collateral going?"

Charlie McGill, the head of the domestic security segment of Coppi Enterprises, leans forward. The big Irishman smiles. "You'll be happy to know that Ano verified the existence of the collateral in Texas. Everything that we were given to verify is accounted for. Next week, he'll validate the oil that is supposed to be in the tanker off the coast of New Jersey. After that, Ano will move on to verify the oil on the ship that's now moored in Boston Harbor."

James looks over at Ano Hiawalah, who is sporting a bright blue Hawaiian shirt. The burly Polynesian used to be his first sergeant when he served in Vietnam. Although Hiawalah is retired from the military and has been working for James as an investigator, James still refers to him fondly as Sarge.

"Is that true, Sarge? You're absolutely certain? All the collateral in Texas is there?"

"Yeah, James, I can guarantee it," Ano replies.

James sits back, lets out a breath, and smiles. "Whew, that's good news, Sarge. Really good news." James looks over at the two men. "I gotta tell you the truth, guys: I had my doubts. When the president called and asked us to get involved in this investigation, I became suspicious. *Why us?* I asked myself. *Why have our firm get involved in a simple collateral audit?* Any auditor of any descent accounting firm could have done the work and given the report to Eisley's banks."

James sits up again.

"The President and this guy, Phil Eisley, are personal friends. Those two guys go way back. Eisley is also a big campaign donor to the President. This fellow donated a large amount of money to the President's election campaign."

James looks over at Ano.

"Sarge, if you don't mind, let's go over what you got and how you did the examination. Not that I'm doubting you—I'm sure you did a good job—but I just want to be completely satisfied that you covered everything. I still have lingering doubts about this whole affair. Let's see if we can put my suspicions completely to rest."

Ano reaches down and lifts up a briefcase, pulling out a folder. "In this folder, there are photographs of every oil well that I verified as being owned by this fella Eisley. These pictures are of the oil wells that Eisley pledged as collateral to the banks." Ano hands James the file. "Take a look."

James begins looking through the packet and pulls out a few photographs. He takes one photo, pulls it close to his face, and begins closely examining the picture.

The door opens and Sam looks in. "James, are you busy? May I come in?"

James leaps to his feet and rushes over, giving her a kiss on the cheek. "Of course, honey, come in. I'm glad you made it. We were just discussing the work that the Sarge did in Texas." He pulls up a chair and places it behind the desk next to him. "Have a seat. You can give us your input."

"Tell me about the tankers," James says to Ano after he sits back down. "How are you verifying the oil on the ships?"

Sam lifts up the file that was on James's desk and begins perusing through the photographs.

"My plan is to first verify that the oil tanks actually exist," Ano says. "What I'll do is verify all of the serial numbers…." He pauses when he notices that James isn't paying attention, but is looking over at Sam.

"What do you think of the pictures?" James says to Sam.

"Uh? What?" Sam looks up from the file.

"I'm asking you about the photographs in the file," he clarifies. "You've been staring at the pictures intently since you got here. Is there anything wrong?"

"I was just wondering how you can tell one oil well from the other?" Sam responds. "All the wells look exactly the same to me."

"That's what I thought, too," Ano answers. "Especially when you consider the rigs are spread out all over Texas. It took all day to locate each one. We must have driven down hundreds of miles of dusty roads. I've never been around oil wells, and quite honestly, just as you observed, each structure looked exactly the same—I couldn't tell one well from the other."

Ano gets up from his chair and walks over to Sam. "So that I wouldn't get confused, I took photos of each rig. I took a picture of the well itself and another picture of the metal plate that's in the back of the oilrig. The metal plate contains the serial number of that particular rig. Let me show you." Ano reaches into the file and takes out one of the sets of photographs and shows it to Sam.

"See? The snapshots are stapled to each other. The front snap is of the rig. The back photo is of the plate with the serial number belonging to that particular well. There are forty-two pictures of oil wells, with forty-two plates and distinct serial numbers. All the serial numbers matched the list of rigs that I was given to verify." Ano goes back and takes his seat. Sam hands the file to James.

James begins perusing through the file again. He lifts up one of the photos and takes a closer look. James pulls the photograph apart from the others to get a better sight of the plate and serial number.

"So, what do you say, James?" Charlie asks James, who is still studying the picture intently. "Are you satisfied? I believe Ano did a good job, don't you? He verified all 42 rigs that were on the list. Are we done with this part of the examination?"

James looks up, puts down the photo, and frowns. "No, I'm sorry, guys. You're not done! I happen to agree with Sam. There's something fishy here." He looks over at Ano. "I'm afraid that you need to get back to Texas, Sarge, and reexamine all the wells. This job isn't finished."

Ano glances over at Sam. "What exactly is your concern, Mrs. Coppi?"

Sam turns to James and lifts up an eyebrow. "James, I didn't say there was anything wrong."

He looks over at her and shrugs. "You didn't? I could have sworn that you said something was wrong with the photographs." He looks back to Ano. "In any event, Sarge, you need to go back and take a new count. The examination that you did is unacceptable. This evidence is no good!"

"What's wrong with Ano's inspection?" Charlie gets louder. The rosy cheeks appear to get a brighter red. "Mr. Hiawalah personally visited forty-two wells and took pictures of each one. Ano reconciled the serial numbers with the list that he was given to verify. On that list are the wells that the owner provided to the banks as collateral for the loan that he took. All of the pledged rigs are accounted for, as you can see by the photographs that Ano took." Charlie looks over at Ano. "In my opinion, Ano did a great job. There's nothing wrong with his inspection. There's no need for him to go back and recheck the wells."

James looks over at him and says calmly, "All right, Charlie, then please explain to me why the owner of the wells can't afford to pay the loans he owes to the bank? With the price of oil at record highs, how come this guy can't pay his bills on time?"

"We weren't asked to look over the guy's financials." Charlie sits forward in his chair. "The banks asked us to verify the existence of the wells and the oil that's in the tankers sitting off the coasts of Hoboken and Boston. In Texas, Ano did exactly that. We weren't asked to look over his books to verify why the guy has no money."

James shakes his head. "Charlie, this man owes the banks three hundred and fifty million dollars. If we screw up this examination, the banks will come after us. We can't afford to take a hit like that."

"But I didn't screw up the audit." Ano gets louder and also sits forward in his chair—he points to the folder. "I verified each well and took pictures of each structure as evidence for my verification. There's no way the banks can hold us accountable if the guy defaults."

"All right, guys, let's try this in a different way." He hands out a photograph to each of the men in the room. "All of you take a closer look at the pictures. Now, you prove to me—how are these photos evidence that the forty-two wells exist?"

"Isn't it obvious?" Charlie speaks up after looking at the picture. He shows the photo to James and points. "There's the rig." He turns the photograph around. "And here's the picture of the plate with the well's serial number. It's right there in front of you, in black and white."

He looks at each of the men. "So, no one sees anything wrong with the photographs? Am I the only one?"

The men take another look at the photographs. Sam picks up a photo from the desk and begins examining.

"I'm sorry, James," Ano lets out, placing the picture back on the desk in front of James. "I just don't see anything wrong."

"Look at the plate with the serial number more carefully, Sarge." James hands the photograph back to Ano. "Take a real close look. What type of screws are holding up the plate?"

Ano and Charlie look down at the picture. "Phillips," Ano calls out, and looks up at James.

"Exactly my point!" He looks over at the two men and smiles. "Phillips. That's the problem."

"I'm still not getting it." Ano scratches his head and looks at the photograph one more time. "What difference can it possibly make that a Phillip screw is holding up the plate? Why is that type of screw a problem?"

James points to the photo. "Sarge, it makes no difference what type of screw is holding up the plate. That's not the point. It's that you're able to recognize the screw—that's important. These oil wells have been in use for years. Besides the oil and muck, they are exposed to the harsh Texas weather. The screw heads should be so loaded up with grime and dirt that you shouldn't be able to distinguish what type of screw is holding up the plate.

"However, right here, in these pictures," he lifts up the photograph and points, "as clear as day, you can immediately tell that it's a Phillip screw head. How is that possible?" He shakes his head. "Sarge, you've been had. These men pulled a fast one on you. They drove you around in circles and showed you the same wells, over and over again.

"The men simply switched the plate with a plate containing different serial numbers as you were riding around from what you thought was one rig to another." He leans forward. "There's fraud going on here, Sarge, I'm certain. We need to recount the wells. This time, I'm coming with you."

After the men leave, Sam says. "You know, if you're right we're going to be in quite a pickle."

James smile wryly. "You're not telling me anything that I don't already know. Are you ready to make the calls to the Secretaries on that Bolivian affair?"

"Let me go pee first," she says.

"Go ahead. I'll get the other men."

"Okay, guys, what's our plan?" James says to Vernon and Rodney when they're sitting across his desk. "The call will happen soon."

Sam comes out of the bathroom and sits next to James.

"James, we need assurances that we're not heading for any political or legal trouble by taking on this assignment," Vernon brings forth. "This war in South America has no legs with Americans. It's not a popular cause. I'm not even sure that most Americans could identify Bolivia on the map. If something goes wrong, the politicians will bail on the mission immediately and will look for someone to blame."

"Who's the biggest problem for us?" James asks. "Who is most against this cause?"

"Senator Hartley, from Massachusetts," Vernon replies. "He's the one most against America's involvement. You know this fella Hartley, James. I believe the Senator and his wife were guests at your ranch a few months back."

"Yes, Sam and the Senator's wife, Abigail, really hit it off." James looks at Rodney. "What about it, Rodney? Isn't Senator Hartley right? Why is the US getting involved? What does the US care who runs things in Bolivia?"

"It's the Argentinians and the Chileans that are putting pressure on the US," Rodney replies. "Those countries are saying that Castro is supporting the Federales and the dictator Pedro Dominguez Echeverria, who is their leader. Castro having a base of operations right on Chile's and Argentina's border is making everyone nervous."

"Okay, let me see if I get the picture." James spreads his hands out wide. He looks at his left hand. "On one side, we have Castro and this dictator Echeverria." He looks at his right hand. "On the other side, there's the Guerreros. Who's heading the Guerreros?"

"Juan Martinez Gaytan. He's a businessman," Rodney lets him know. "Right now, Gaytan is based in Santiago, Chile—the man isn't allowed back in Bolivia."

"A businessman?" James calls out. "What the fuck does a businessman know about guerilla warfare?"

"Gaytan doesn't know anything about fighting," Rodney says. "Gaytan has teamed up with a rebel group headed by Jose Rivera. Gaytan is the middleman who'll be handling our transactions that's to shield us from any problems. We won't have any contacts with Rivera or the rebels. Everything goes through Gaytan and his companies."

"Does Rivera and his rebels have a chance?" James asks. "From what I read in the reports, this rebel group doesn't sound well-organized. Can they really go up against someone like Castro? Vernon might be right—this thing will blow up, and they'll be looking for somebody to scapegoat."

James's phone buzzer goes off. "James, I've got the office of Secretary Zeist on the line."

"All right, Kathy, put him through."

"Hello, James," the caller answers. "It's Secretary Zeist. I have you on speaker, and with me is Secretary of State Reichwald."

"Good morning, gentlemen. I'm putting you men on speaker, also. My trusted advisers Rodney Davis and Vernon Dixon are here."

"Good morning, everyone," Zeist says. "James, General Farnwell mentioned that you had some misgivings about the operation with the Bolivians, and that you wanted to speak to me and Secretary Reichwald about those concerns."

"I'm troubled about the legality of the mission. General Farnwell wouldn't give us anything in writing stating that the US government is backing this operation."

"James, this is Secretary Reichwald. The US hasn't given you anything in writing because we're not officially involved in the operation. We're simply acting as advisers. The agreement will be between one of your companies and the firm of a Bolivian businessman. What leads you to believe that you're doing anything illegal?"

"Oh, I don't know—maybe because someone may take offense that a bunch of Americans are partaking in overthrowing a foreign government?" James says. "Someone in our government might just think that's just not a nice thing to do. A somebody like a certain senator from Massachusetts."

"James, you're not involved in any overthrow," Reichwald says. "Your company will be supplying goods and services to a company owned by businessman Juan Martinez Gaytan. A company based in Santiago, Chile, I might add, not Bolivia. What Señor Gaytan does with the merchandise after he receives the goods is his business."

"What about the legislation that's being discussed?" James presses. "The decree forbidding the sale of any arms to the rebels."

"There's no such bill that is being debated," Reichwald brings forward. "There's an amendment to a defense appropriation bill that's being offered, but the amendment hasn't been approved yet. That amendment only states that no taxpayer dollars are to be used in supplying arms to the rebels. This has nothing to do with your operation. There are no taxpayer dollars involved at all."

"All right, gentlemen, let me cut to the chase. Are you approving this operation? Yes or no?"

"Yes, we are!" Zeist answers.

"And if something goes wrong, I have your assurances that I won't be hung out to dry?"

"Of course, James, you have our full support. Anything else?"

James looks over at his men, who shake their heads. "No, that's it, gentlemen. We look forward to working with you."

"Thank you, James. Have a nice day," Zeist says, and hangs up.

"Well, Vernon, do you feel better?" James asks.

"I'll feel better when this project is over," Vernon replies. "There's something here that's just not sitting well with me. In any event, we got the secretaries to at least verbally approve the assignment, so I guess we can move forward."

"What about you, Rodney? Do you think we should move forward?"

"Frankly, James, we have no choice," Rodney signals. "A new administration came into power, and we need to stay on their good side. Remember all the other government work that our company procures? We don't want to start our relationship with the new people by turning down their first request."

James lets out a breath. "All right, Rodney, you and Ian will handle this assignment. No need for me and Vernon to be involved in the day-to-day stuff. The less Vernon and I know, the better. If something does happen, they'll be looking to question the heads of the company. Vernon and I can't answer to what we don't know."

"OK, James, will do," Rodney answers. "Anything else?"

"No, that's it for now."

Sam stands up after the men leave. "I guess you've decided to go into the business of overthrowing governments now."

CHAPTER 5

NO ONE IS WORKING ON THE RAILROAD

Two days later, James is on his private 727, staring out the window. Ano walks over and takes a seat across from him.

"What's got you so preoccupied?" Ano asks. "Are you going over in your head the upcoming meeting we have with Greenwald?"

James turns to him. "No, I was drifting back to Vietnam."

"What about 'Nam?"

"Sarge, do you remember when we were at Con Thien, Camp C-2? There was this nice little house, just a couple of clicks southeast of the camp. It wasn't your usual Vietnamese hooch. It was nicely built, with stucco walls. It had a long, quaint path to the highway. Do you remember the house?"

"Vaguely. What about the house?"

James sits up. "There used to be two young kids living in the house. A boy and a girl. The boy was a teenager, sixteen or seventeen maybe? The girl was a few years younger, a schoolgirl.

I'd watch those kids play in front of the place or go off to school and work."

He leans forward. "It always got me wondering. What the heck is a normal family doing in the middle of this mess? Weren't the people afraid of the incoming rocket or mortar fire that would hit our camp? How could this family sleep through those attacks? How could those youngsters appear so normal in the middle of all of that insanity?"

"You can drive yourself crazy thinking about 'Nam." Ano remarks. "By the way, speaking of 'Nam, do you remember Mendoza? He was in the mortar platoon."

James turns to Ano. "Who?"

"Mendoza. He was one of the three guys that turned against you in the Camby trial. He was a witness for the State."

"Yeah, I know who he is. What about Mendoza?"

"He's dead!"

James sits up. "No, shit! What happened? How did he die?"

"Somebody shot Mendoza dead while he was walking to work. His job was in a really bad area of Los Angeles." Ano looks over at James. "We're taking up a collection for him. He had a wife and two kids. You probably don't give a shit, since he ratted you out."

James shakes his head. "No, Sarge, that's not true. I feel really bad about the news. I have no ill will toward the three soldiers that turned on me. It wasn't their fault. Our government turned the screws on those poor saps and they had nowhere to go." James pauses for a moment. "It's all these fuckin' politicians and government bureaucrats. Whenever they don't get their way, these so called good guys turn on you. These assholes always justify what they're doing because of a higher cause. Vietnam was a perfect example of that shit. All that those poor people in 'Nam wanted was their own government, but some politicians in Washington couldn't accept that."

James looks out the window and turns back to Ano. "Over fifty thousand young men killed, and for what? For absolutely nothing! Even now, more vets are dying. You know why?"

When Ano does not answer, James continues. "Because they sprayed us with chemicals. Agent Orange! Those fuckers in Washington said it wasn't harmful to humans."

James lets out a hollow laugh. "Can you believe that shit? A chemical can wipe out a jungle and turn the place into a wasteland, but it doesn't hurt a soldier? What a crock!"

James's voice gets a little louder. "What about the fact that we signed a treaty agreeing not to use chemical weapons during war? What about that?"

James sits back in his seat and shrugs. "No, Sarge, you can't trust politicians or bureaucrats. They're capable of anything, including murder. All because of their supposed higher causes."

"Here's your coffee, Mr. Hiawalah." Mary interrupts the conversation and places the cup down in front of him. The stewardess turns to James. "Are you sure I can't get you anything, Mr. Coppi?"

"No, I'm good, Mary, thank you." After Mary leaves, he turns back to Ano. "Put me down for two grand for Mendoza."

"OK, sure."

"How about that house I was telling you about? Do you remember the place?"

"Not really, James. I was Top Sergeant back then—busy with all of the affairs of the company. I didn't have time to freeload like you." The big Polynesian laughs heartily at his last statement.

"Freeloader? Me?" James fires back. "You never worked so hard—I can't remember you ever going on operations. You were too busy hiding in your hooch, away from the action."

"Do you think about Vietnam a lot?" Ano asks. "It's been a while since you got out. What's it been?"

"A little over twelve years—I got out in '69. I don't think about 'Nam much. Just lately. This house and the family who lived there just keeps popping into my head, for some reason."

Ano changes the subject. "Why are we making a stop in Santa Fe? I thought we were heading straight to Texas to verify the oil wells."

"Greenwald called yesterday and said we were having some union problems," James replies, staring out the window of the jet once again. James pauses for a moment. "I need to get a fix on what's going on at the railroad. We need the unions to give us concessions on their wages and benefits. Without those concessions, we'll never turn a profit."

"What made you buy the railroad?"

James turns back to Ano. "I see the rail business as a great opportunity. Not for passenger travel, but for carrying freight. What with the oil prices going up, overland trucking is becoming very expensive. The rails are much more cost efficient. I just need to find a way to get the unions to cooperate.

"Congress is working legislation on getting rid of all these regulations affecting the rail industry. If they do get rid of these restrictions, the railway business is going to boom. When Greenwald offered to sell me a piece of the business, I couldn't turn it down."

Ano takes a sip of his coffee. "You and this guy Greenwald go back a way, don't you?"

A faraway look comes over James as he thinks back for an answer. "Yeah, Henry Greenwald gave me my first case, and he helped me get started when I first came back from 'Nam. If it weren't for Greenwald having faith in me way back then, I wouldn't be where I am today. I owe all my success to Greenwald."

"No, I don't agree with you, Coppi." Ano shakes his head. "Greenwald isn't the reason for your success. This fellow Greenwald may have given you a boost, but you'd-a made it no matter what. You have a great business head on your shoulders."

Ano takes a sip of his coffee. "Even when you were serving under me in Vietnam, you still made more money than anyone in the brigade." Ano sits back in his seat. "No sir, there's nothing that could have stopped you. Even if you'd never met Greenwald. You were destined for success."

"How do you like working for our new executive, Vernon Dixon?" James asks Ano. "How are things around the office when I'm not around?"

Ano smiles. "Less stressful, that's for sure."

"What are you saying? That I stress you out?"

Ano barks out a laugh. "You? No." he laughs again. "You're a pussycat. A real pushover, no problem at all." Then Ano gets serious. "Believe me, the office is much happier when you're not there."

"Well, after that last remark, I'm coming into the office more often," James says. "It sounds like you guys are having a little too good of a time—I wonder if any work is getting done when I'm not there."

Ano waves his hand dismissively. "The work is getting done—you don't have to worry."

"Oh, yeah, if everybody is so busy, then why is there less stress when I'm not around?"

Ano turns to him. "Oh, come on, James, you can't figure this one out?"

"No, not really. I don't know? That's why I'm asking?"

"You're very intimidating, James. People fear you. When you call someone into the office, they're terrified of facing you. All of your people know they have to be fully prepared when you call. You'll immediately recognize any misstep. You have a knack of seeing things that aren't as obvious to the common man."

"And, with Vernon, they don't feel like that?" James lifts his brow. "Honestly, I don't understand the fear. It's not like I punish anyone just for making a mistake."

"It has nothing to do with punishment," Ano tries to explain. "It's a person's pride. Your employees don't want to disappoint you. Vernon is more of an organization man. Policies, procedures, rules, and so on. Vernon believes in holding departments accountable, not just individuals. It's a lot less stressful on the person when they're not being singled out for accountability."

James stares out the window in a dismissive gesture.

"Don't worry! The company is doing just fine," Ano finishes. "Vernon is doing a good job."

· · · · · · · ● · · · · · · · · ·

"So, what do you have for me, Henry?" James asks the slender, silver-haired gentleman when he and Ano are sitting across from Greenwald's massive oak desk. "What's so important that you need me personally involved?"

"James, we're having big problems," Henry answers. "Believe me, I wouldn't be asking you to get directly involved if it wasn't serious. As you know, this railroad has lost money for three years in a row. This year is the end of our union contract. We have asked the union to agree to a ten percent cut in pay and give back some of their benefits, just like you and I discussed when you bought the business from me." Henry sighs. "I've already laid off twenty percent of our management staff and cut the remaining non-union employees' salaries ten percent. We can't cut any more from the indirect people. Any further cost reductions must come from the union personnel."

Henry fixes himself in his chair and lets out a groan. "The unions are playing hardball with us, James. There's a work slowdown. Nothing seems to be getting done on time. The union is putting the squeeze on us. James, if we don't get the concessions from the union, the railroad is in big trouble. All the great plans that you had on turning the business around are in jeopardy."

Henry throws up his hands. "After thirty years, I've lost total control of the business. The managers say it's the union that's the problem. The union says it's management. Everybody is pointing the finger at the other guy—I have no idea on who is telling the damn truth. We've got nowhere to turn; we can't trust anyone. We can't raise the railroad's freight rates any further. Our customers just won't stand for the increase. James, you need to find out what's going on at the railroad. I don't have a clue."

"What happened to the cooperation that the unions promised six months ago?" James asks. "We had that big meeting. That's why I went out and started buying those other rail lines that were in financial trouble and incorporating the routes into our company. The unions promised that they would give us their full support when we made those purchases."

Henry shakes his head. "That's the problem with these damn union people: you can't trust anything they say. They talk out of both sides of their mouth. They promise us cost savings and then go back and tell their people something else."

"All right, Henry, I get the picture. Let me get to work and find out what's going on," James gets up. "Where do you suggest I should start?"

Henry gets up and walks to the door. "Come on, let's get together with our managers. You met these guys before; it's time you got to know them better. You can begin by interviewing the supervisors and looking over their job sheets. See if you can make out what's going on."

* * * * * * * * ● ● ● ● ● ● ● ● ●

James and Ano are sitting in a small office set aside for them at the railroad's headquarters. There are mounds of files stacked on their desks. Papers are strewn loosely in front of the two men.

"So, James, can you make anything out of this mess?" Ano scratches his head. "We've been here for two days. What the hell do all these files mean? Have you been able to find anything worthwhile in these documents? I'm ashamed to say, I can't make heads or tails of the sheets."

James pushes back the papers. "No, Sarge, you're right: there's nothing in these papers that tell us anything about the difficulties at the railroad. We've basically wasted two days."

James stretches his arms and yawns. He rubs the back of his neck. "We already know that the company is being run inefficiently. We need to find out why. The answer is not in the files; it's out in the field where the men are working. You and I need to get out of the office and get to where the action is happening."

"What do you suggest?"

He picks up a file. "There's a railroad gang of forty men laying track in a stretch of an area just outside of Bernalillo. Let's go out to the site this morning and see for ourselves just what the fuck is going on. That's the only way of getting to the bottom of this problem."

An hour later, James drives up in his car and parks behind some shrubs. The railroad workers are about a mile down the road. It's a spot where he can observe the men while they are working, without being noticed. He reaches into the back seat of the car and pulls out a pair of binoculars.

"Come on," he says to Ano as he gets out of the car and walks over to an opening in the shrubs, kneeling down to have a look.

Ano kneels alongside. "What do you see?"

James puts the binoculars to his eyes. "There are the men." James hands Ano the glasses. "Here, look for yourself."

"Yeah, I see them," Ano remarks as he's looking though the specs. After a few moments, he adds: "they're all sitting around, doing nothing." Ano gives the binoculars back to James and scratches his head. "I guess Greenwald is right: there is a union slowdown."

James has another look through the lenses. "Let's wait a while and see what the men do. Maybe they're just on a break."

"How long are you planning to wait?" Ano asks about an hour later as he is looking through the binoculars. "The men are still doing nothing but bullshitting. The hardest work that they've done this morning is lighting up a smoke and taking a piss. Nobody has lifted a finger the whole time we've been here. Those men don't even make an attempt to look busy. What a bunch of goldbrickers. They're really giving you and old man Greenwald a screwing over."

"This doesn't make any sense." James shakes his head and takes the binoculars to have another look. "Those men haven't done any work all morning. They don't seem to give a shit at all about their job. I've seen enough." James walks back to the car.

"Come on, let's go!" he hollers to Ano. "Get in the car."

"Now what?" Ano asks when he gets back in the car.

"You and I are driving over there to have a talk with the men." James starts up the car. "We're asking those lazy bastards why aren't they working," he adds tersely as he drives off.

"Are you fucking crazy?" Ano scowls. "There's some forty men out there. That crew won't take kindly to us for spying and turning them in for sitting on their ass. This whole situation can get really ugly."

"I'm paying those men for a day's work," an angry, red-faced James spits out. "I mean to find out why they're not keeping their end of the bargain. The only way to find out is to ask the men directly." He turns to Ano. "I'm getting to the bottom of this crap."

"James, you've gone crazy," Ano fires back. "There's forty of them and two of us. When we confront that crew, they're likely to kick our fucking asses. That's what'll happen when we get there."

James stomps on the brakes. "Do you want out? If so—you can get out right now!"

Ano stares at James, but doesn't answer.

"Good!" James remarks. "Nothing will happen, trust me."

The gandy dancers are still sitting on their butts when James's car pulls up. James gets out and walks toward the men. Ano is following behind. "Who's in charge here?" James barks.

"I am," a bulky middle–aged man hollers back. He gets up and walks over to James. Two of the other trackmen get up and follow behind. "What do you need?"

"Hi," James smiles warmly. "I'm James Coppi. Maybe you've heard of me. I'm the new guy that just went partners with Mr. Greenwald." James offers his hand to the man to shake.

The man looks down at James's hand and—after a pause—he reaches over. "I'm Frank Buchanan. I'm the foreman." He shakes James's hand. "What can I do for you?"

"I'll get right to the point, Frank. Mister Greenwald sent me out here to find out why you men aren't working." James clears his throat. "I've been observing your crew for nearly two hours, and no one has lifted a finger the entire time."

James pauses and smiles again. "Now, I know that you are all honest, hard-working men. My father was also a union man. I'm sure that you believe, as my dad believed, that if you're paid a day's pay, you give your employer an honest day's work. I'm positive that you wouldn't take advantage of me and old man Greenwald. So, I just had to come out here and ask you—why are you not working? There just has to be a good explanation."

"There is a good explanation," the burly foreman growls.

James stretches out his arms. "Okay, I'm listening. What is it?"

"We were sent out here to replace old, worn-out track with new one." Buchanan points to the tracks "Now, take a look around the area, Mister. How can we replace the old track? Do you see any new tracks?"

James has a look around and scratches his head. "I don't understand. Where's the new track? I don't see anything."

"Exactly my point." Buchanan smiles wryly. "Where the fuck is the new track? Do you see any replacement tracks? Surely, you don't want us to remove the old track without replacing it with new track. Somebody in management fucked up. They sent a gang out here to do the work, but they forgot to send the material that we need to do our jobs. The new tracks never arrived. This is the third time in six months that this has happened."

Buchanan scowls at James. "If you and Old Man Greenwald want to find out why you're losing money, just look to your managers. Stop blaming us hard-working stiffs. I'm just like your old man, Mister; you pay me an honest wage for the day, and I'll give you an honest day's work. I'm not looking for a free ride. I'm certainly not trying to screw you and Old Man Greenwald. I've worked for the railroad for twenty-seven years, and I'm thankful for my job."

On the car ride back to Santa Fe, Ano asks James, "How'd you know? How did you know that there was more to the story?"

James looks over at the burly Polynesian and smiles. "Well, I guess it's just like you said on the plane coming over, Sarge: I have a knack of seeing the obvious that isn't visible to everyone.

"Sarge, do me a favor: you grab a flight out of Santa Fe and go on to Texas without me. You don't need me to inspect the oil wells." James reaches down in his briefcase and pulls out an inkpad and stamp.

"What's that?" Ano asks.

James hands him the merchandise. "It's a stamp and an inkpad. I was going to put my mark on each oil well when Eisley's people weren't looking. If I'm right, and Eisley's men are driving around in a circle, at some point we'd hit upon an oil well with the mark that I made. Since I'm not coming, you'll have to do the marking. Just make sure that no one sees you putting on the spot. Stamp the rig where it's not clearly visible. You and I will meet up again in New York when we go and check the oil on the barge."

CHAPTER 6

OIL, VINEGAR, AND COCKROACHES

A no leans forward, looking through the windshield, trying to find the trailer. He's moving slowly in the torrential rain, which is hitting the glass sideways. Although the wipers are at full speed, they aren't doing any good and can't keep up with the monsoon of water hitting the glass.

A quarter mile farther down the road, a gray aluminum trailer parked in the middle of Nowhere, Texas comes into view. There are two blue Ford pickups parked in front.

The rain continues as he stops the car—water is still coming down in sheets. Ano shakes his head and shudders. *What a fucking day I picked to go looking at oil wells.*

He's wearing his rain gear and long boots. After he jumps out of the car, his feet sink into a foot of sloshy mud. Looking down at his boots, he shakes his head and carefully makes his way through the slippery muck to the trailer.

When inside, he unties the hood of his poncho and knocks it back off his head, wiping his brow with the back of his hand. Four men are sitting around a table, looking as if they're doing absolutely nothing. Ano rubs the wetness off his face.

"I can't believe you're back," one of the men calls out. "What the fuck happened? Why are you back?"

"It can't be helped, Freddie," Ano replies, "I mixed up the damn serial numbers—I need to check all the wells again. Believe me, I'm just as pissed as you are."

Freddie looks out the window. "You picked one beautiful fuckin' day to do this job. How the hell are you taking pictures in this weather?"

Another of the men sitting next to Freddie calls out, "It's fucking pouring. You'll be lucky if the truck doesn't get stuck in the mud. You guys may never get back."

"Well, in that case, we'd better hurry and get started," Ano suggests. "We've got a long day ahead of us."

"Yeah, well, don't think for one minute that I'm getting out of my truck to help you," Freddie lets him know. "You're doing this all by yourself—I'm just driving." Freddie stands up and reaches for his rain jacket on the hanger. "Come on, let's go. I'd like to get done before sundown. There's no way we can do this in the dark."

"Hold up a sec, Freddie," Ano says when they are outside. "I've got to get my camera out of the trunk."

"Okay, we're good to go," he tells Freddie after hopping into the truck.

A half hour later, they arrive at the first rig. The rain has let up, but the mud is still a foot deep. Ano grabs his case with the camera and slops his way to the well. Freddie, true to his word, stays inside the truck, sitting on his ass.

Ano walks to the back of the edifice where the plate with the serial number is located. He peers over at the truck. Freddie isn't paying attention.

Reaching into the bag, he pulls out a stamp and pad. Quickly, he stamps the well in an area where it's not clearly visible and is protected from the rain. He takes the camera out of the case and snaps a picture of the plate and the mark he just made. Once again, Ano looks at the truck to make sure that Freddie isn't watching. Satisfied that Freddie didn't notice a thing, he puts away his gear and splashes his way back to the truck.

"Look at the fucking mess you're making in my truck," Freddie yells out, pointing to the floor. "It'll take me a week to clean the mud out."

Ano smiles. "I'll pay for the car wash. Send me the bill."

"Don't worry, I will." Freddie turns on the car and the windshield wipers, as the rain has started up again. "You better get a move on, or we'll never get done."

It's at the eighth well that Ano notices the mark that he previously made, proving James was right. Freddie is driving him around in a big circle. In all, when the day is done, Ano can only vouch for eighteen of the forty-two wells that were supposed to be here. Freddie drives him back to the trailer. The other three men that were there this morning are still sitting in the same position.

"Well, did you have fun flopping around in the mud?" one of the men asks when he walks in. "I hope you did your job right, this time. I'd hate to see you make another trip back."

"Yeah, I did," Ano tells the man. "I'm sorry you had to run out in that rain."

"Me, no... I was right here in the trailer all day, nice and dry. You're the asshole that schlepped through that sludge."

"Yeah, well, if I was trying to pull something on someone, I'd learned to clean the mud off my boots." Ano grins, and points to the man's muddy boots. "Tell your boss that the asshole counted the wells right, this time. Eighteen wells." Ano turns to the man and grins. "I didn't count the wells where you went out and switched the plates. You got all wet for nothing." Ano smiles broadly. "Guess who's the asshole?"

• • • • • • • • ● • • • • • • • •

Two days later, James and Ano are on the tugboat, headed for the tanker moored twenty miles offshore from Hoboken, New Jersey. The other tanker is anchored off the coast of Boston, and they will be examining that freighter when they are done here.

James is out of sorts. He's concluded that there is a problem with the inventory. Earlier, Ano gave him the results of what he discovered in Texas. James now knows for certain that this fellow Eisley committed fraud, and at the very least, some of the collateral is missing. Today's exercise will be further proof of the scam.

The banks will be stuck with the loss if Eisley can't pay. What's really worrying him is the political fallout. This scandal will reach the White House and go right up to the president. It will be a mess, and James and his company will be knee-deep in the shit.

Although it's a beautiful, sunny autumn day, the ocean is rough and the water is full of whitecaps. Waves are hitting the top of the boat. Despite the rough seas, James is atop, getting fresh air, as his stomach is queasy. The last thing he needs is sea sickness. The mist from the waves hits him in the face and feels good.

James fastens the hood of his poncho a little tighter. So much water is striking him that the water from the hood of the poncho drips down his face and he can taste the salt on his lips. Ano and the rest of the party are inside, comfortable and dry. They are gorging on egg and bacon sandwiches.

Peering through the dampness, he notices the oil barge coming into view. One of the crew members comes alongside as the boat begins to slow. The crew is readying to pull the tug next to the big rig. *This won't be easy*, he thinks. The boat is bouncing up and down violently in the rough sea.

Someone from the deck of the trawler tosses down a line, and it's retrieved by the deck hand. Another crew member makes an appearance next to James. Yet another line is tossed from the big ship and recovered by the new deck hand. Carefully, the tug is pulled closer to the side of the ship and is moored alongside. There is a metal ladder hanging down on the side of the tanker.

"Be careful climbing up the ladder, sir," one of the crew warns. "The steps are wet and slippery. Make sure you hold onto the rail with both hands."

James turns to look for Ano, who is standing behind him. Ano is wearing a backpack with the equipment that they will need once they get on board.

"You ready?" James asks him.

"Yeah, let's go."

When a wave rises the boat to its proper height, James steps onto the ladder and scurries up the steps. The stairs are not as slippery as he had anticipated. One of the three men waiting for him on board the ship gives him a hand to the deck. Another of the men walks up and grabs his arm, helping him on board.

"You must be James," the man voices. "I'm Ari Stefalos. I work for Mr. Eisley. Welcome aboard."

James shakes the man's hand. "Thank you!"

"This is Captain Vramis." Stefalos motions to the grey-bearded man standing alongside.

"It's nice to meet you, Captain." James extends his hand to shake.

"Let's get inside and discus the game plan," Stefalos suggests.

Inside the cabin, Stefalos asks, "How do you want to proceed?"

"How is the oil stored?" James asks.

"The merchandise is in tanks. Each tank compartment holds 5,800 gallons," Stefalos explains.

"How many tanks are on the ship?"

"This ship has ten. Each tank is split into three independent compartments."

"Um," James scratches his chin, "that means we need to take thirty samples."

"James, I only brought twenty bottles," Ano reveals.

"Twenty should be more than enough," Stefalos replies. "You're not testing all the tanks, are you?" Stefalos turns to James. "Just select the containers at random." Stefalos lets out a belly laugh. "You don't really need any testing. Just have a look. It's pure 100 percent Texas crude. Best oil on the market."

James sits there, pondering for a moment. "No, we better examine all the tanks. We'll have to come back tomorrow and finish the job. When we're done collecting, we'll send the samples to the lab for verification that it's indeed pure Texas crude." James smiles at Ari. "No offense, Ari, but I have a job to do. I'm playing it strictly by the book. No shortcuts."

"No offense taken, James," Ari smiles. "You do whatever you feel is necessary. We've got nothing to hide. Come on, let's get started. I'd like to get done early—I have an appointment in New York later this afternoon."

Captain Vramis leads them out on deck where the tanks are stored. Ano hops on top of the first tank.

"What's the serial number?" James calls up.

"N69142M," Ano yells down. "We'll need bolt cutters to cut the seal."

James writes the tank seal nomenclature in his pad. He hands Ano a jar and turns to the captain. "Do you have something to cut the seal?"

"Get me the bolt cutter," Vramis shouts to one of the crew.

When the man comes back with the cutter, Vramis hands it to Ano, who snaps the seal. Ano dips the ladle into the tank, scooping out a jarful of oil and handing the full jar back to James. James places a sticker with the tank's serial on the container.

Ari takes the jar before James closes the lid. "You don't need a lab to tell you this is pure oil. Just have a look." Ari lifts the bottle into the sky. "Crystal clear, pure Texas crude."

James lifts his hand up dismissively. "I'm sorry, Ari, but I have a job to do. My eyesight isn't suitable enough to assure the banks that this is pure Texas crude. I'll let the labs do their work, if you don't mind."

James checks off the seal number in his pad and hands the seal back to Ano to close the tank. Ano hops off and walks over to the next container, repeating the exercise. Nineteen containers later, Ano hops off the last one for the day. He brushes himself off.

"Well, that's it for today," James says. "We'll be back tomorrow to finish the job. Bright and early."

The men are on the tug back to shore early that afternoon. The rough sea has calmed. The ride back is much more pleasant. James's stomach is still a little queasy—he's still feeling the effects of the ride out, this morning.

"Make sure the samples are safely stowed in your room," James orders Ano. "You don't want the maid knocking them over. First thing tomorrow, pick up the other ten jars and we'll finish the job. Where do you want to have dinner tonight?"

"I'd love a nice, juicy New York steak," Ano smiles. "That ocean air made me hungry."

"Yeah, sure. There's a good steak place, Smith and Wollensky, not too far from the hotel."

• • • • • • • • ● • • • • • • • • •

That night, at the restaurant, the waiter walks over. "Are you ready to order?"

James looks over at Ano, who is busy reading the menu. "Do you know what you want?"

"There're so many steaks on the menu, I can't make up my mind," he remarks.

"Have the porterhouse," James suggests. "If you're hungry, that's the best."

"All right, you talked me into it." Ano turns to the waiter. "Medium rare, and I'll have a Bud with that."

"I'm sorry, sir, the porterhouse is for two. It weighs 44 ounces."

Ano looks pitifully at James, who laughs. "Don't tell me you can't eat that tiny steak by yourself?" James turns to the waiter. "I'll have the porterhouse also."

"Yes, sir." The waiter writes down his order on his pad and turns back to Ano. "The steak comes with creamed spinach and a baked potato. Is that okay with you?'

"Yeah, that'll be fine."

"How about a Caesar salad to start things off?" the waiter asks.

"Sure thing, I'll have the Caesar," Ano says.

"How about you, sir?" the waiter asks James.

"I'll have a regular salad, not the Caesar, please. Bring me the oil and vinegar. I'll stir the salad myself."

"Yes, sir. What will you have to drink?"

"Just mineral water for me, please."

The men are sitting quietly, waiting for their order.

"What's the matter, James?" Ano asks. "Why so quiet? You look preoccupied."

"I'm just thinking about the work we did today."

"What about today? Everything appeared to check out okay. The tanks were filled to the top."

James turns to Ano. "That's just it, Sarge. Today doesn't make any sense. If this guy Eisley is committing fraud, why are the tanks okay? Why go through all the trouble of fooling the banks on the oil wells?" James sits back in his seat. "There's something wrong here, Sarge, I just know it."

A few minutes later, the waiter brings over their salads. James is mixing the oil and vinegar into his lettuce. A bus boy comes over and pours him a glass of water. James stops and gazes at his salad.

"What's the matter? Are you okay?" Ano asks him, with a mouthful of Caesar. "Is something wrong with your salad?"

James ignores him. Instead, he moves the lettuce to the side. He lifts the bottle of olive oil and carefully pours a drop into the empty portion of his dish. He reaches over for the vinegar and pours a drop on top of the oil. The vinegar and oil form droplets on the plate.

James pulls his water glass close and pours a drop of oil into the water.

"What are you doing?" Ano asks. "Is that some sort of ritual? Is that a religious thing?"

James looks over at Ano. "Sarge, how many inches was the ladle that you used to scoop the oil?"

"I don't know; ten inches, I guess? Why do you ask?"

James doesn't answer—he lifts up the bottle of oil again, pouring a few more drops into the glass of water.

James turns to Ano. "When you go to the store to buy the jars, Sarge, pick up a hose."

"A hose? What kind of hose?"

James sits back in his seat and shrugs. "I don't know. Any kind, it doesn't matter. About a twenty-five-foot long hose should be more than enough."

"Why do you need a hose?"

"You'll see tomorrow," James smiles. "Enjoy the steak. The steaks in this place are as good as any steakhouse in Colorado."

As he's eating the salad, Ano looks up at James. "James, can I ask you a question? Why did you hire me? Why did you give me a job?"

"Why are you asking? Don't you like your job?"

"No, I like my job—I was just wondering, that's all. When I applied for the job, I had no experience investigating; I was in the Army for thirty years. Why did you take a chance on me?"

James thinks about the question for a moment. "Sarge, do you know what a punk is? You know, a New York City punk?"

"Some kind of bad young man," he replies.

"Yeah, maybe. But, more, some sort of worthless human being. No better than a cockroach. When I was young, I hung around the streets of New York. Even as a teenager, I stayed out all night. Drove my mother crazy with worry. And to live in the streets of New York, you had to learn the rules of survival."

James picks up his glass of mineral water and has a sip. "Never stick your head out too far. It's better to avoid a fight then to get into one. Much like a cockroach." James looks around the restaurant. "Sarge, what would you do if you saw a cockroach by your feet right now?"

Ano bellows out a laugh. "I'd stomp on the bug and get the fuck out of this place." Ano looks down at the floor. "But this place is clean; there're no roaches."

"That's what you think," James laughs. "Believe me, there're roaches here, but you can't see them. And you know why?" James doesn't wait for an answer. "Because roaches have learned that if they come out and stick their necks out, you stomp on them. That's why roaches have survived for hundreds of millions of years. And that's exactly how a street punk survives in this city. Always staying in the shadows and never sticking his neck out."

James lets out a sigh. "And that's the way I felt I was being treated when I was in the military. An unimportant, lowly draftee. Just another number on a dog tag. A number that started with the initials US, not RA, like the regular soldiers. A draftee wasn't good enough to be considered a regular soldier. Just another statistic to be analyzed by that war criminal McNamara. A number that was tabulated on McNamara's IBM computers."

James smiles warmly at Ano. "You were one of the lifers, Sarge, that actually treated me like a human being. Most of the other lifers treated me as expendable, just like the roaches.

"When you got out of the service and asked for a job, I remembered your kindness. It was my turn to reciprocate."

Ano says, with salad in his mouth, "What act of kindness? I seem to recall that we gave you two article fifteens and we busted you down a grade."

James smiles. "That's true, Sarge. But you didn't do anything that I didn't deserve—I broke the rules, and you had no choice. You were like the reluctant father that has a task to do when a child misbehaves. Sarge, you took no pleasure in meting out the punishment, unlike the other lifers."

The waiter comes by and places their steak orders on the table. James cuts a piece of the steak and is about to stick the morsel in his mouth when he looks over at Ano, who's not moving, staring at his meal. A broad smile forms on James's face.

"I was only kidding, earlier. There are no roaches in this place. Dig in."

• • • • • • • • • ⬤ • • • • • • • • •

James and Ano are sitting in Captain's Vramis's office the next day, preparing to take more samples. The sea is much calmer today, and James is not nauseous at all.

"What's with the hose?" Ari points to the hose wrapped around Ano's shoulder.

James looks over at the captain. "Captain Vramis, I don't mean to be rude, but can you leave us alone for a few minutes, please? There's a delicate matter that I'd like to discuss with Mr. Stefalos. It shouldn't take long."

"What's going on, James?" Ari bellows after the captain leaves. "What the hell are you up to?"

"I believe you already know, Stefalos," James replies sternly, and takes the hose from Ano, waving it in front of Ari. "You know exactly why I have this hose. The gig is up. Do you really need me to take more samples? This time, I'll sample from the bottom of the tanks. We both know what I'll find at the bottom."

Ari sits back in his seat and rubs his hands through his thick dark hair. "What are you going to do?"

"There's only one thing I can do, and that is to give the banks the bad news. My question for you is: Do you have a good lawyer? You'll need one. You and Eisley are going up for a long time." James smiles. "Maybe you can cut a deal with the feds when they come calling."

James turns to Ano. "Come on, Sarge, let's head back. No need to take any more samples, our work is done."

On the ride back to shore, Ano asks, "What's up, James? Are you filling me in? Why did we cut the inspection short?"

"The tanks are filled with mostly water. There's only a small amount of oil in each tank. Eisley is scamming the banks. Oil floats to the top of water. I tested that fact last night at the restaurant, when we had dinner. You remember when I was putting the drops of oil into the glass of water?"

James takes a breath. "The samples we scooped yesterday with the ladle were all from the top of the tanks—no more than ten inches down. Stefalos provided the ladle. It was a perfect length— Stefalos made sure that we didn't go too deep. All the samples we took yesterday will be Texas crude. No need to send those to the labs for testing."

James pauses for a second. "Today, I was planning on using the hose to suck the liquid from the middle and the bottom of the tanks. When Stefalos noticed the hose, he realized that I was on to him."

James sits back in his chair. "Crap," he utters. "This is some mess. This scandal will be all over the news. You know, Sarge, I'm becoming completely jaded about the world—I don't believe that there are any more honest people left on this good earth. Humans are no better than roaches."

· · · · · · · · ● ● · · · · · · · ·

Jack Dalrymple is headed for the Oval Office. The President himself called and asked him to come immediately. In the office, the President is behind his desk and the President's campaign manager, Drew Reese, is sitting on the sofa.

The President points to a chair. "Have a seat, Jack."

After sitting, the President says, "I just received a call from my buddy Phil Eisley. Phil said that this fellow Coppi is about to cause trouble." The President glares at Jack. "I thought you said Coppi is a reasonable man and could be trusted."

Jack shrugs. "I'm sorry, Mr. President, I'm in the dark. You'll have to fill me in on what Phil said."

"Phil said that Coppi's report will say that there is a shortage in Phil's collateral with the bank."

"I'm not sure what it is that you want me to do, sir?" Jack says. "I haven't seen the report."

"You need to pay a visit to this fellow Coppi," Drew yells out from the couch. "Impress upon Coppi the importance of his report. This news will be a huge problem for the President."

Jack turns to the man on the couch. "If the collateral isn't there, what do you expect Coppi to do; lie?"

"I spoke to Phil," the President says. "He says he just needs a little time to straighten this problem out. Just convince Coppi to delay issuing the report. Once Phil has his affairs together, no one will care what the report says."

"How much time does Phil need?"

"A year," the President says.

"A year?" Jack sits up. "I'm not sure that I can convince Coppi to a year's delay."

The President smiles. "I'm sure you can. Go have your talk with the man. Remind Coppi about how many government contracts his company gets. Maybe we can find a way to increase those procurements to his firm."

After Jack leaves, the President turns to Drew. "What else can we do to persuade Mr. Coppi that it's in his best interest to play ball?"

"I'll have a talk with the IRS commissioner," Drew answers. "Maybe I can persuade him to have a look at Mr. Coppi's financial affairs. If there's one thing that strikes fear in any person, it's an IRS audit. And I'm quite certain that you don't achieve Coppi's immense wealth without playing a little fast and loose with the tax loopholes."

"OK, that's a good idea," the President says. "Anything else? What else can we do to keep Coppi quiet? This guy has to be stopped, or we're in big trouble! If the press starts digging into the history of my relationship with Eisley, who knows what they'll turn up—my whole presidency can be tied up with this affair."

CHAPTER 7

CARDIZ

James is down by one of the barns of his ranch the next morning after returning home from his audit of the oil on the ships. They are loading his two-year-olds onto the trailers. His ranch boss Jeff walks over.

"We're ready to load the young ones up, Boss," Jeff says to James. "Four thoroughbreds to Santa Anita and four to Belmont, just like you wanted. What made you decide on that strategy?"

"I just want to see where my race horses do best. Up to now, I've shipped them out without giving it much thought."

Cardiz comes out of the van. "That's it, Jeff, that's the last. The horses are ready to go."

"Hey, Cardiz, take a little walk with me," James says. "I want to speak to you."

After they get a little way from the barn, Cardiz asks, "What did you want to talk to me about?"

"Mendoza is dead!"

Cardiz stops with a stunned expression on his face.

"The Sarge told me that he was murdered near where he worked," James says.

Cardiz shakes his head. "Damn, that's too bad, I always liked the guy. Everybody in our platoon liked him. Do they know who killed him?"

"No, the Sarge didn't know more than that Mendoza was gunned down going to work."

They walk once more, and Cardiz turns to James. "You know, Mendoza would've never turned on you if the Feds didn't force him."

James stops. "I know. I have no hard feelings toward the guy. What's done is done!"

They start walking and Cardiz lets out a laugh. "You remember that time in Gio Linh?" Cardiz is laughing so hard, he can't continue the story.

James looks over at him. "What about Gio Linh?"

Cardiz is still laughing, and has to catch his breath to resume. "We'd been on operations for four days. The battleship *New Jersey* was offshore, providing artillery support. Everybody was dirty and miserable. It was lunch time and we were eating our c-rations. Mendoza opened up his box and nearly puked when he pulled out a can of ham and motherfuckers."

James lets out a laugh. "Yeah, those ham and lima beans were brutal to eat."

"And to make matters worse," Cardiz continues, "those were our last c-rations, so for Mendoza, it was either eat that shit or starve."

James smiles. "Yeah, I remember. That's when someone yelled out, 'I wonder what Popeye is eating right about now—I bet it's not spinach or c-rations. Popeye is sitting in his air-conditioned mess on the ship and having a nice, hot, juicy steak.'"

"That's right, that was me," Cardiz says. "I was the one that hollered." Cardiz looks over at James. "That's when you said to me, 'give me that fuckin' radio.' Do you remember?"

James bursts out laughing. "Yeah, I do."

Cardiz also laughs. When he collects himself, he restarts the story. "You got on the horn and called the battleship. 'A battalion of NVA has been spotted. If you move fast, we'll get them all.' You gave them the coordinates and yelled into the radio, 'Hurry, *didi mao*, get off your asses and fire for effect.'"

Cardiz is laughing so hard that snot is coming out of his nose. "The whole fuckin' field lights up as those 2,000-pound bombs from the New Jersey's 16-inch guns started exploding a thousand meters in front of us.

"The CO came running over. I thought he was going to have a shit fit. He screamed at you, 'Coppi, what the fuck are you doing?' You turned to him. 'I thought I saw some activity out there, sir.'

"The captain looked through his field glasses and shouts at you, 'There's nothing there.'

"You turned to him. 'I guess they're gone now.'

"The Old man yells up at you, 'Call in the ceasefire. Do you have any fuckin' idea how much those fuckin' bombs cost?'"

James smiles at Cardiz. "That was a good day."

Cardiz nods. "Yeah, it was a good day. And when those Navy boys called you and asked how they did, you wouldn't even give them any satisfaction."

James lets out a laugh. "Yeah, that's right, I said, 'You were too slow; the battalion of NVA got away.'"

Cardiz shakes his head. "Yeah, Coppi, that was really nasty. You spoiled Popeye's lunch and didn't even give him any credit."

They start walking back. After a pause, Cardiz turns to him. "That was a tough break for Mendoza. He survived all that shit in 'Nam, only to get himself killed right at home."

"Yeah, it was," James says. "I need to get back. You take care, Cardiz."

James is back in his study when Sam comes bursting in, dragging their son Michael. His smiling daughter, Molly, is following behind.

"Go ahead, tell your father what you said," Sam shouts.

"Stop it!" Michael wails, and buries his face against her leg.

James looks up. "You know, just because I'm working from home doesn't mean I'm not busy and that you can interrupt at any time."

"I'm sorry, James, but this is important," Sam says.

James stands up and walks around the desk, looking at Molly's smiling face. "What are you so happy about? You like seeing your brother in trouble?"

"No!" she answers.

James points to the door. "Wait outside."

He leans over to Sam and whispers in her ear, "What did he say?"

"Fucking son-of-a-bitch," she whispers.

"Oh!" James laughs.

"It's not funny!"

James wipes the smile off his face. "I know." He squats in front of his son. "Michael, look at me!"

"No!" Michael answers.

"Michael, where did you learn to say those words? Who said them?"

Without turning, Michael points at him.

Sam shakes her head. "I should've known."

James looks up and wrinkles his nose at her. He turns back to his son.

"When did I say that?"

Michael peeks out. "Outside, when you were with Jeff and the other guys."

"Unbelievable," Sam lets out.

James looks up. "Maybe you should wait outside with Molly."

"Oh no, I want to hear what you've got to say for yourself!"

James turns back to his son. "Michael, I want to say I'm sorry. It's because of me that you're in trouble."

Michael turns to him. James reaches into his pocket for his handkerchief and wipes the snot off Michael's nose.

He puts the hanky back in his pocket. "Earlier, I was outside helping the men fix the lean-tos that were damaged by the hailstorm last night. A plank fell on my foot, and, in pain, I yelled out something that I shouldn't have. You heard me say those words and thought it was okay to repeat them. So, in essence, it's my fault that you're in trouble. If I promise never to say those words again, will you forgive me?"

"Yes," Michael says softly.

"Good!" James points to Sam. "Now, Michael, you need to say that you're sorry to Mommy. You shouldn't have said those words to her. So, tell Mommy that you're sorry and that you'll never say those words ever again."

Michael looks up at Sam. "I'm sorry, Mommy."

"And?" James says.

Michael looks at James and furrows his brow. "What?"

"And you'll never say those words again."

Michael snaps his head up to his mom. "And I'll never say it again."

James stands up and rubs his hand through Michael's dark hair. "Good! You can leave."

Michael runs out of the room.

"What?" James lets out, looking over at Sam, who is gawking at him.

"That was really brilliant. Here I was ready to give you a lecture, but you were simply marvelous. You not only taught your son not to say those words, but you also showed him how to take responsibility."

James smiles slyly. "Yes, that *was* brilliant, wasn't it?" James points to the door. "Now, can you get the fuck out of my office so I can get some work done? I've got a meeting this afternoon at the office and I've got to get prepared."

• • • • • • • ● • • • • • • •

Later that afternoon, there's a knock at Sam's study and the butler looks in. "Excuse me, Mrs. Coppi. Jeff is out here and needs to speak to you—he said it's urgent."

Sam looks up. "Send him in, Mr. Billingsley."

Jeff walks in with hat in hand. "I'm sorry to interrupt you, ma'am, but Mr. Coppi isn't around—I thought you should know that Cardiz and Billy were shot."

"What?" Sam turns pale. "What happened? Are they all right?"

"I don't know, ma'am. I'm on my way to the hospital right now."

Sam jumps up. "Come on, let's go!"

At the hospital's ICU, Sam runs into Mattie, Cardiz's wife. "How's Cardiz doing?"

"I don't know," Mattie says with a tremor in her voice. "He's in surgery."

"What are the doctors saying? Did they tell you anything?"

"No, nothing." Tears begin flowing down her cheeks. "Oh, Sam, I'm so frightened."

Sam takes her in his arms and starts rubbing her back. "I know." She lifts up her chin. "What about Billy? Where's he?"

"I don't know. You should ask one of the nurses at the station over there."

"All right, I'll be right back." She releases Mattie and looks into her face. "Why don't you sit down?"

"I'm too nervous to sit."

She turns to Jeff. "You stay with her."

One of the nurses tells Sam that Billy is in Cubicle 6. When Sam gets into the room, Billy is sitting up. His arm is in a sling.

"Hi, Mrs. Coppi," Billy says.

"Are you okay?" Sam asks.

"I'm in pain but the doctors say I'll be okay—I took a bullet in the shoulder. Cardiz is in bad shape. He took two in the back."

"What happened? Who shot you?"

Billy shrugs. "I don't know, ma'am. We were at the lumberyard, carrying a load of plywood onto the truck. Some guy started shooting at us—I got hit first and went down. I must've passed out, because the next thing I knew, people were all around me."

Sam sits on the chair next to Billy. "Do you know why? Did you guys have an argument with somebody?"

"It's just like I told the police, we just went in and picked up the lumber. We didn't talk to anybody except for the clerk and the warehouse guy."

"What did the shooter look like?"

"I don't know, I never saw him coming. After I was hit, I dropped to the ground."

Sam stands up. "I'll have investigators from our office come and speak to you. Are you sure you'll be all right? What did the doctors say?"

"The doctors said I'll be fine. They removed the bullet."

"Okay, feel better." Sam walks back out to Mattie. She looks over at Jeff. "Billy is in Number 6, go look in on him."

Sam takes a hold of Mattie's arm. "Come on, sit. This may take a while." After she sits, she asks, "Do you know who's doing the surgery?"

"No. I haven't even seen the doctors."

Sam glances down the hall and notices two men in blue surgical attire coming his way.

"Here they come now," she says.

"Oh, God!" Mattie reaches for her hand.

"Mrs. Coppi," the doctor hails when he gets to them. "I didn't expect you here. I'm Dr. Falansky. I was at the gala when we dedicated the wing that you funded for the hospital."

"It's a pleasure to see you again, Doctor," she says, and points to Mattie. "This is Mrs. Cardiz. Please, she's anxious to learn about her husband."

"Yes, of course." The doctor turns to Mattie. "Your husband had two shells in him. Neither bullet hit any vital organs. We removed one and left the other. The reason we left one of the bullets in your husband is because it is lodged next to the spinal cord. We're concerned that removing the bullet at this time may cause more damage and put your husband's life at risk."

Dr. Falansky lets out a breath. "We'll further evaluate the need for surgery when we have another look in a few days, when the swelling goes down."

"Doctor, is my husband going to make it?" Mattie asks.

"Yes, there's nothing life-threatening."

"Can I see him?"

"In a few minutes. They're still cleaning him up. He's not awake yet. Someone will come and get you."

"Doc, can we take a little walk?" Sam says.

When they get farther down the hall away from earshot of Mattie: "All right, Doc, let me have it," Sam says. "What's the real scoop? You're talking about the spinal cord—that's serious stuff. Will Cardiz be paralyzed?"

"Mrs. Coppi, there's not much more that I can say at this time. There may be paralysis, and that may also be temporary. We just don't know yet. We need a little time to evaluate him. In my opinion, doing the surgery now would put Mr. Cardiz in greater danger and worsen his chances for recovery."

When Sam gets back to Mattie, she asks, "What did the doctor say?"

"The same thing that he told you."

Mattie scowls. "Come on, Sam, tell me the truth. Don't hold back—I need to know."

"Mattie, if there was anything else, I'd tell you, but there isn't. Come on, there's the nurse waving at us. Let's go see for ourselves."

Later that night, Sam is telling James about what happened.

"Will he be all right?" he asks.

Sam shrugs. "If it weren't for the bullet lodged by his spine, I'd say yes. But now, nobody knows. We'll have to wait and see. I've got Charlie involved in the investigation. We need to find out who did this and why."

"What about Cardiz's boys? With Mattie at the hospital, who's taking care of the boys?"

"I offered to take the boys home with me. The boys said they would rather sleep in the bunkhouse, so I had Jeff set them up. Mattie called her mother, and she's flying out tomorrow."

Sam frowns. "I feel so bad for that family."

"Yeah, me too. They're in for a rough ride."

CHAPTER 8

THE REQUEST

The next day, Miles is at the office giving Jen a tour of the facilities. As they are walking down the hall, they notice James coming the opposite way.

"Good morning," James says as he passes by quickly.

Jen turns as she sees James walk away. "Is that James?"

"In the flesh," Miles answers.

"Wow!" Jen lets out and smiles. "He's even better looking in person than the pictures I saw of him in the papers."

"Put those eyes back in their socket lady! And stop drooling."

Jen laughs and reaches for Miles. "You can't blame me, can you?"

"Yeah, well enjoy your visit to the office today. That's the last time you're coming in—at least not coming in when James is around."

Jen gives him a kiss on the cheek. "You're jealous, I love that."

"Come on, I'll show you my cramped cubicle." Miles points to the partition when they get there. "See what I mean?"

"Yes, I see," Jen says as she looks around. "It's right in the open. You have no privacy."

Just at that moment Charlie and Ano come dashing by.

"Is everybody always in a hurry around here?" Jen says.

Miles nods. "There always seems to be some sort of crisis. It always feels that something big is about to happen and the place will come crashing down."

Jen looks into his face. "What do you mean? Should we worry about your job?"

Miles smiles and gives her a kiss. "No! Stop being so insecure. Everyone tells me that this is business as usual at Coppi Enterprises, there is never a dull moment. There is always some sort of pending disaster that needs to be managed."

"How many disasters have you handled?" she asks.

"Not many. To tell you the truth Jen, I've hardly met with James at all. Except for the brief cursory hello's like this morning we've hardly spoken."

Jen smiles at him slyly. "Why don't you invite him over for dinner one night?" Her smile gets wider. "You know, so you can get to know your boss better."

Miles gives her a side glance. "Suddenly my reticent wife has become sociable?"

Jen laughs. "It would certainly cause me anxiety entertaining your boss but I'd set aside my fear and make that sacrifice for you." Jen smiles broadly. "You know—because of your job."

"Yeah, well if James ever comes over for dinner, I'm not leaving him alone with you, not even for a minute!"

Inside his office, James is meeting with Charlie and Ano. He looks over at Charlie. "What did you find out about the shooting yesterday?"

"Not much," Charlie answers. "No one saw anything. All I've got is that the bullets were fired from a .32-caliber revolver. A Colt 1903. Other than that, nothing."

James's brow goes up "A Colt 1903? Wasn't that a military pistol?"

"Yeah, but the weapon wasn't very popular and wasn't used by the military all that much."

James shrugs. "How would someone get a hold of such a weapon? It's not likely to be sold by gun dealers."

Charlie shakes his head. "I don't know."

"All right, stay on top of this investigation. Put someone on the case." James pauses for a moment. "Put Frank Gurney on it. Tell him to hunt down the pistol. There couldn't have been that many sold. The gun may lead us to the shooter."

"All right, will do," Charlie says. "How about the oil and this guy Eisley? What did you and Ano uncover?"

James fills Charlie in on what they found.

After James is done, Charlie lets out a whistle. "Wow, you exposed quite a mess."

"Yeah, we're knee deep in shit!"

James's phone speaker goes off. "James, I'm sorry to interrupt, but Rodney is out here," Kathy says. "He says he needs to speak to you right away."

"Okay, Kathy, send him in."

Rodney, walks in. "I'm sorry to barge in on your meeting, James, but I received a call from Jack Dalrymple. Dalrymple's call may have something to do with what you guys are discussing."

"Who is Jack Dalrymple?" James asks. "The name sounds familiar."

"Jack is an adviser to the President," Rodney says. "You and Samantha met him when you were in Washington for the President's inauguration a few months back. Dalrymple asked me to set up an appointment with you for tomorrow afternoon. He said that it's an urgent matter.

"When I pressed Dalrymple for more information, he stated that he couldn't talk about the subject on the phone. Dalrymple did say it has something to do with an investigation that our company is doing. Other than that, he wouldn't go any further. I told him that I'd check with you and get back to him."

James gives Charlie a wry smile. "That was quick—I guess this thing will be getting very interesting, very fast."

"Why do you say that?" Rodney asks.

"This oilman, Eisley, is a personal friend of the President. And remember, it was the President who asked me to take on the case. I'm pretty sure the President suspected something, otherwise, he wouldn't have asked me."

James sits back in his seat and shakes his head. "Damn it! I should've read the situation when the President called and asked us to do the work. Why did he want our company to do a job that any accountant could've done? Now we're caught in the middle of the mess."

"What will you do?" Rodney asks. "Drop the case?"

James's voice gets louder. "How can we drop the case? The banks know we're auditing the collateral. What will the bankers say if we suddenly pulled out?" He shakes his head. "No, we're screwed! We need to move forward, no matter the consequences. Unless any of you guys have a better idea?"

The men sit there silently.

James smiles. "Just as I thought." He looks over at Rodney. "Call Dalrymple and tell him that I'll see him tomorrow. Might as well hear what he's got to say, although I have a pretty good idea what he wants."

• • • • • • • ● • • • • • • •

James looks over at the crew-cut blonde sitting across his desk the next afternoon. James knows the type: clean cut, white, Anglo-Saxon. Jack is a poster boy for the party in the White House.

Dalrymple looks around the room and back at James. "I'm sorry that I didn't make myself understood, James, but this meeting needs to be in private."

"Jack, I trust both Vernon and Rodney. You can count on their discretion."

"Yes, I'm sure that both men can be very discreet; but nevertheless, I prefer that just you and I talk."

James looks over at his men. "Fellows, do you mind?"

"No, of course not," Vernon says, and the men get up to leave.

"Okay, Jack, go ahead. What's on your mind?"

"James, you just completed an examination of Phil Eisley. I'd like to know the result of that investigation."

James smiles shrewdly. "Come on, Jack, cut the crap. You know exactly what we uncovered. I'm quite sure this fellow Eisley already let you know. Frankly, I believe the President must've suspected a scam from the beginning. What I don't understand is why he called on me to do the investigation? The President must've known that I'd unearth the fraud."

Dalrymple sits forward in his chair. "Not true, James. The President believed that Eisley was clean. He thought that's what your investigation would've concluded. The President wanted to let the public know that a man of your impeccable reputation found nothing wrong. The President wanted everyone to know that the entire probe into Eisley was done cleanly and above-board."

James smiles slyly. "All right. If that's the President's motive, why are you here? My work is finished. A report will be out shortly. The report will state that Eisley conducted a massive fraudulent scheme to obtain bank loans and other financing."

Jack leans forward in his chair and looks over at the door—he turns back to James. "The President would like a favor."

"What favor?"

Jack gives James a sly glance. "Come on, James. You're a smart boy; you know what the President wants."

"Jack, if what I'm supposing you're proposing is correct, I suggest that you get out of my office. And right quickly, because I'm getting ready to kick you out on your ass!"

Jack raises his hand. "Give me a few more minutes. Let me finish."

James stands up. "Jack, this conversation is over—I didn't get my impeccable reputation that you alluded to earlier by being underhanded. It's best if this discussion goes no further." James points to the door. "You really need to leave right now. I'd hate to throw you out."

Jack points to James's chair and smiles. "Please, sit down. Just listen to my proposal. Just a little more of your time."

James purses his lips, shakes his head, and sits.

Jack smiles once more. "As you know, James, your firm gets a lot of government business. I'm here to let you know that if you can see your way to helping us out, we can increase that business."

James gets loud. "I'm not fudging my investigation! I don't give a fuck if I lose all the government contracts. I'm not lying for anyone, not even the President."

"We're not asking you to lie—just delay your report. Eisley told the President that he can come up with the money to pay the banks. The man just needs time to raise the capital. After Eisley pays off the loans, you can issue the report. No need to make any alterations to your findings. Once the loans are paid off, no one will care what the report says."

"How much time do you need?"

"A year."

James rises up in his chair. "A year! Are you fucking kidding me? There's no way I can delay this report a year." James sits forward in his chair and lowers his voice. "Jack, you guys are being had. This guy Eisley is a con man. He'll never come up with the dough—he's just stalling. The guy is desperate. Tell the President that the best course of action is to come up with a strategy to distance himself from Eisley."

James sits back in his chair and rubs his chin. "I'll tell you what I'll do. I'll delay the report a month—that won't make any difference to the banks. That'll give you guys a little time to get your act together. Beyond that, there's not much else that I can do."

Jack stands up. "Okay, if that's how you feel, I'll report what your proposing back to the President. But I've got to warn you that he'll be very disappointed."

James stands up. "Well, that's the best that I can offer. One month, and then I hand in the findings to the banks."

After Dalrymple leaves, there's a knock and Vernon looks in. "James, are you done? Can Rodney and I come in?"

"Yeah, come in, guys."

"Rodney and I were wondering how the meeting went."

James forces out a laugh. "You really don't want to know."

"Will there be a problem?" Rodney asks. "Will this affect the company's government contracts?

"There'll be problems unfortunately but it won't affect our business. The US needs us just as much as we need them." James lets out a sigh. "The dispute is personal. I'll let you know if I need you guys. For now, it's best if I keep everything to myself."

• • • • • • •• ⬤ •• • • • • • •

The next Saturday morning, James is in the dining room having breakfast with his three children. He looks up and notices Sam walking in.

"What happened to you?" James calls over to her. "It's almost ten. You're missing out on the pancake breakfast that we planned."

"My dad called." She sits next to James. "Daddy is very worried. Yesterday he got a surprise visit from two people that work for the IRS."

James's eyes widen. "The IRS came unannounced?"

"Yeah, it was a complete shock to him. The men started asking about contributions to the church. In particular, they were extremely inquisitive about our donations to the church."

Mrs. Billingsley, the cook, walks in. "Would you like something to eat, ma'am?"

Sam turns to her. "Yes. I'll have a fruit bowl."

"Mommy, it's a pancake breakfast, not fruit," her son Michael calls out.

Sam smiles at him. "I can't have the fruit?"

"No!" Molly chimes in. "Pancakes."

Sam turns to Mrs. Billingsley. "I'll have the pancakes, but please put some fruit on top." She turns to her children. "Are you guys happy, now?"

"Yes!" they answer in unison.

Sam turns to James. "Where were we?"

"We were discussing your dad and the IRS agents," James answers. "Did they just show up?"

"Yes, that's what Daddy said."

James gets up.

"Where are you going?"

"I'm calling your father—I want to know exactly what the IRS said."

James comes back ten minutes later and takes a seat.

"What did my father say?" Sam asks.

"Not much. He's still not sure why they showed." James looks over at his children. "If you guys are done, go get into your riding gear so we can get going."

"Daddy, can I wear a cowboy hat instead of a helmet?" Michael asks.

"No, put on the helmet."

Michael lets out a moan. "Jeff and all the other guys have cowboy hats."

"They're older, and they're cowboys. Now stop complaining and get going."

After the children leave, Sam asks, "So what about this IRS stuff and my dad?"

James picks up his coffee and takes a sip. "Your dad said that the IRS guys were looking over our contributions that we made to his ministry. There was a check for a hundred grand made to the church signed by you that the auditors were questioning?"

"Why?" she asks. "What's so important about that contribution?"

"The money to cover that check was drawn from one of our accounts in the Cayman Islands."

She looks over. "Oh. And I gather the IRS doesn't know about that account? What's going on James? Why does the IRS have sudden interest in our activities?"

James tells her about Jack Dalrymple's visit earlier in the week.

Sam picks a strawberry and takes a bite. "So, you believe this is the White House's way of pressuring you to submit?"

"Yeah, I do."

"What are you going to do?"

James shrugs. "Nothing that I can do. We're caught in a no-win situation. If I don't issue the report, we're in trouble with the banks—I release the report, and we piss off the President."

"That doesn't answer my question. What are you going to do?"

Just then, Molly and Michael walk in, dressed in their riding clothes.

James looks over and smiles. "Wow, look at you guys. You look like real grown-up equestrian riders." He gets up and kisses Sam. "I better get going."

Sam tucks at his arm. "You didn't answer me. What are you doing about the report on the President?"

James smiles. "You already know what I'm going to do! I'll send Jack, my head of finance, down to Lubbock to help your dad with the audit. Don't write anymore large checks until this clears up."

CHAPTER 9

AN INVITATION AND AN OFFICE

Miles, not Jack, got the assignment to go to Lubbock and help Reverend Powers, Sam's father, with the IRS problem. Miles had worked at a top tax accounting firm in Boston and Jack believed he had more experience with the IRS. Miles's wife, Jen, always gets nervous when Miles has to travel for work, especially now that they just moved to Colorado and she doesn't yet know any of her neighbors. Miles makes sure to call her every chance he gets.

After work that night, Miles called Jennifer from his hotel. Jen tells him about an invitation that she received.

"When did you get the invite?" Miles asked.

"Today, Mrs. Coppi's secretary called me. She said that Mrs. Coppi was having a tea tomorrow afternoon at her ranch for all the spouses of the executives." There's a slight pause. "Miles, I don't want to go. You know these affairs make me very nervous. Please, can I back out of this request?"

"I think you should go. It's important; everyone will be there."

"Please, Miles? I'm already working myself into a panicky state."

"All right, call the secretary back. Give her the excuse that you couldn't get a babysitter on such short notice."

"Thank you! I'll call right now."

A few moments later, Jennifer calls Miles back. "Mrs. Coppi just called. She insisted that I come and wouldn't take no for an answer."

"Did you explain to her about your babysitting problem?"

"Yes, I did. Mrs. Coppi said that I could bring Liz with me. She has a son, Christopher, about the same age, and Kathy was bringing her daughter Marlene. The house staff will be watching the children."

"Oh. What are you going to do?"

Jennifer let's out a breath. "What can I do? I'm stuck. I'll have to go."

"All right, you can tell me all about the affair tomorrow night when I get home."

"That's if I don't have a nervous breakdown before then," she says.

At the tea, Jen is having to use all her strength to fight off the anxiety attack. Forty women are at the affair, and she finds a quiet corner away from the group. No one seems interested in seeking Jen out, and that's just fine with her. The two mimosas that she's downed have really helped calm her nerves. Jen has not seen her daughter since she arrived, and she's too nervous to ask about her. She gets up to get another drink when she notices Mrs. Coppi coming toward her. *Oh crap*, she thinks.

Sam reaches over and grabs both of Jen's hands. She smiles. "You don't look like you're enjoying yourself."

Jen smiles back nervously. "I'm sorry, I'm just very shy. These affairs panic me."

Sam laughs. "You sound like my James."

Jen's brow furrows. "Mr. Coppi is shy? Miles says he is so confident and forceful."

Sam laughs some more. "At work, he's in his environment. At socials, James is like a fish out of water, completely out of his element." She takes Jen's hand and pulls her. "Come on, let's you and me escape to the patio. We can talk out there by ourselves." When they're sitting outside, she asks, "How are you adjusting to Colorado Springs?"

"We're just getting accustomed to the town," Jen answers. "It'll take me a while to acclimate. As you can see, I'm not exactly the outgoing, sociable type. One of the reasons Miles took this job is because of all the travelling he had to do in his previous place. I hated staying home alone. Miles even took a significant pay cut to come here."

"So, Miles was willing to take a step back in his career to make you happy? I wish James was a little more like your husband. He travels so much."

Jen notices that this conversation was bothering her. "Mrs. Coppi, you shouldn't blame him. I'm sure it must be hard on Mr. Coppi, too—you know, with all the responsibilities that he has."

Sam frowns. "That's why we hired people like your husband. To take over some of James's responsibilities. I've got to find a way to get James to let go. And, please, no more 'Mrs. Coppi'. Call me Sam."

Just then, the back door opens and Kathy comes out. "I looked in on the children and they're all having fun with your maid, Maria." She sits down next to Sam and Jen.

"How does your husband like his job?' Sam asks Jen.

"He loves his work. Miles's only complaint is that his cubicle is too small."

Sam looks over at Kathy. "Why doesn't Miles have his own office? He's a controller."

Kathy shrugs. "To tell you the truth, I didn't know anything about it. I thought Jack, his boss, was handling Miles's office accommodation."

"Make sure you correct it right away," Sam says. "In fact, call the office right now and have someone move Miles's stuff right away."

• • • • • • • • ● ● • • • • • • • •

The IRS agents were done with their preliminary work auditing Reverend Powers. The examiners would be working on another assignment and were temporarily ceasing their activities with the Reverend. The hundred-grand contribution to the church came up again with the auditors. This contribution if not handled properly might end up being a big problem for the Coppis. The auditors were demanding more information on that Coppi account in the Cayman. The IRS men were also questioning whether there were other overseas accounts of the Coppis.

That night, Miles flies back from Lubbock, and decides to stop in his office to drop off files before going home.

When he gets to his cubicle, there's nothing there. The place has been completely cleaned out. For a moment, the thought runs through his head that he's been fired. Miles looks around for someone on the floor. Because it is late, there's no one around—he walks out and heads for the office of his boss. He knocks on the door and looks in.

"Jack, have you got a minute?'

Jack looks up from his desk. "Yeah, sure, Miles; come in."

Jack does not sound like a man who is about to fire one of his workers. "Do you know what happened to my stuff? I went to my cubicle, and the place is empty."

"They moved everything to your new office. Right down the hall, three doors to the right. Your name is on the door."

Miles gives him a smile and a sigh of relief that he's not being canned. "Thank you for the office."

Jack shrugs. "Don't thank me. Kathy called earlier today and arranged for your office move, and she didn't bother to discuss the matter with me."

Jack looks over at Miles. "What about the IRS? Do we have a problem?"

Miles nods. "Yes, I'm afraid so." He tells Jack what the IRS was digging into.

Jack sits back in his chair. "Wow! That is a problem." Jack sits forward in his chair and lowers his voice. "You know the Coppis have a lot of money overseas. The IRS begins digging, who knows what they'll uncover? Do you have a solution?"

"I'm working on a plan," Miles says. "My approach maybe a little dastardly so I don't want to discuss with anyone until I have it all worked out in my head."

Jack laughs. "In that case don't mention the scheme to me at all! If this IRS audit blows up, people are going to jail."

"I hope James understands the trouble that he's in," says Miles.

"If I know James, he fully appreciates the threat."

That night, when he gets home, Miles tells Jen about his new office.

"I know," she says. "I was there when Sam told Kathy to get you an office."

His eyes widen. "Sam?"

Jen laughs. "Yes, Mrs. Coppi insisted that I call her Sam. And when I told her that you were complaining that your cubicle was cramped, she ordered Kathy to get you an office right away."

Jen proceeds to tell Miles the conversation that she had with Sam. How Sam invited Jen to join the women's volunteer group in Colorado Springs. They have a luncheon every month to discuss ways to raise money for needy causes.

"I'll have to give the group five or six hours a week, so we'll need to find a babysitter for Liz," she says as she walks away. She turns back to Miles. "Oh, and by the way, Kathy is introducing me to other women that have children of about the same age as Liz. You know, this way Liz can have some friends."

Jen smiles at Miles. "Sam and Kathy are just regular gals, and there were a lot of laughs. They were reminiscing about some of their crazy escapades back in high school and how they always got into trouble together. They made me feel so comfortable."

Miles looks over at her. "What happened to that shy, timid lady from Massachusetts?"

Jen smiles broadly. "Those two ladies convinced me to leave that meek lady back in New England. This is Colorado! A brand new start for us, I'm so looking forward to our future here." She walks away again, but before leaving the room, she turns back. "Oh, and one last thing: there is no way that Kathy, Sam's lifelong friend, is having an affair with James. That's just filthy office gossip, and if you ever hear those rumors again, you need to forcibly straighten that person out!"

CHAPTER 10

THE BAD DUDE

James gets out of his limo the following Monday and looks up at his massive office building. He still has moments of disbelief when he sees the place. The entire building was his vision. The architects tried to make changes, but James was having none of that.

The structure has three distinct frontages. Two sides of the building are a combination of pink stucco walls and glass. The middle is all glass. The building is six stories and takes up an entire city block. The top of the building features three large letters, S C J, the initials of Sam and James Coppi.

"Are you okay?" Max, his bodyguard, asks.

James nods and smiles. "Yeah, I'm fine—I was just thinking about something."

Up at his office, James is getting a report. "What did you dig up on Eisley?"

"It's just as you suspected, James. Eisley is one bad dude. The rumor is that he owes a lot of money. He lost his shirt in a real estate development deal in Galveston. The whole project went bust when mortgage interest rates hit thirteen percent."

James forces out a laugh. "Yeah, I know that feeling. I'm having the same problem with my developments."

"How are you surviving?" Charlie asks.

"We cut way back on the venture. We're only building homes if we have a solid contract. Nothing is being built on spec." He looks over at Charlie. "So, how is Eisley surviving?"

"Eisley owns a company that's in the process of building an oil pipeline from Midland to Houston. The company had a public offering two months ago on the New York Stock Exchange. He stands to make a lot of money on the pipeline."

James gives him a wry smile. "If I were Eisley, I wouldn't be in a hurry to spend that money. It's a nightmare getting regulatory approval for pipelines."

"Eisley already has federal approval. And, with his connections, I don't think local support will be much of an issue."

James's eyes widen. "How the hell did he get the feds to go along so quickly?" James looks over at Charlie, who gives him a knowing stare. "Never mind, I know. He's got politicians in his pocket."

James clears his throat. "What about the President? What can you tell me about that relationship with Eisley?"

"Only that he and Eisley go way back, and the two are very close." Charlie sits forward in his chair and looks at the door, lowering his voice. "James there's a rumor that the two were involved in a murder."

"Murder?" James sits up.

"Yeah, murder. It happened twenty years ago, when the President was first running for Congress. Apparently, the DA uncovered something on the young, would-be Congressman, and was planning on charging him. The DA was found dead with a bullet in his head, and the charges were never filed."

James's speaker goes off. "James, I have Phil Eisley on the line," Kathy says. "Do you want to take the call?"

James looks up at Charlie. "Speak of the Devil." He looks over at the phone. "Put him through, Kathy. What can I do for you, Mr. Eisley?"

"James, I was hoping that you can give me a little time tomorrow," the loud voice says. "I can be at your place around ten."

James frowns. "Phil, I've got to warn you...a meeting is just a waste of time. There's nothing that you may say that will change anything."

"Oh, come on, James. Give me a half-hour. That's all I'm asking."

"All right, I'll see you tomorrow." James looks over at Charlie after he hangs up. "Any advice?"

Charlie smiles wryly. "Yeah. Be very, very, careful."

• • • • • • • • ● ● ● • • • • • • •

Sam is in James' office the next day, and they're waiting for Phil Eisley to show up.

"I don't know why you insisted that I be here," she says. "I don't know anything about this fella."

"You can be a big help and get a read on this guy," James says. "As I told you, we're knee-deep in a political quagmire, and the whole mess can blow up in our face."

Kathy walks in with the big Texan wearing a ten-gallon hat, who smiles over at James and extends his hand. "It's a pleasure to finally meet you, Jimbo."

James reaches for the hand to shake it. "It's a pleasure, Phil."

Still holding onto James's hand, the big man continues to smile. "It feels like I already know you, Jimmy."

James pulls away and points to Sam. "This is my wife, Samantha."

The Texan tips his hat. "It's a pleasure, ma'am." He turns to James. "I'd rather speak to you alone."

"Sam is not only my wife, but also my confidant in business affairs," James replies. "Especially on matters as touchy and important as this one. Her advice is critical for me. I insist that she be here."

Eisley hesitates for a moment. "All right. If you insist."

James points to a chair. "Have a seat, Phil."

Eisley takes off his hat and places it on the chair next to him. He reaches into his pocket and pulls out a cigar, looking over at James. "Do you mind?"

James pushes an ashtray toward the man. "Not at all."

"Would you like one?"

James shrugs. "I don't smoke."

The man lights up the cigar, taking a few puffs to get it started. He blows smoke up into the air. Takes another drag and places the lit cigar in the ashtray, blowing another puff of smoke into the air.

"Thanks for agreeing to meet with me, Jimmy."

Sam stands up. "I'm sorry, James, I can't take this guy anymore." She leans over. "Mr. Eisley, if you want anything to get done with my husband, I suggest you cut the crap. There's no need for this bravado act you're putting on. My husband likes to be called James, not Jimmy or Jimbo, and if you did any homework, you'd know that already—I suggest you stop trying to bully him."

Phil shrugs. "James or Jimmy, what's the difference? It's the same damn name."

Sam looks at him. "Just get to the point. Tell James what you want. You called for this meeting." Sam turns to James. "You're on your own." She storms out.

"That's one tough gal you got there."

"Just tell me why you called for this meeting, Phil."

"All right, I will. Jimmy...er...I mean, James...as you may have realized by now, your investigation into me accidentally knocked over a hornet's nest." The Texan looks slyly at James. "Crazy thing about those little critters, the hornets—you never know who they'll bite when they're stirred up and feel threatened."

James furrows his brow. "Are you threatening me?"

Phil puts up his hands in a dismissive manner. "No, of course not! I've done a little checking on you, and everyone tells me that you can't be intimidated. I'm just painting a picture of the pickle that we're in."

"All right, Phil, get to the point. What do you want?"

"Tomorrow, I'll be visiting the four banks that hold notes on my oil business. Those are the banks that hired you to investigate the collateral for my loans. I'll be offering the banks the stock that I hold in my new pipeline business as additional collateral for the loans. In turn, I'll ask the banks to forego the audit that you're doing."

James shrugs. "What's this have to do with me?"

Phil picks up the cigar and takes a puff. "Well, if the banks don't want the audit any longer, there's no need for you to issue a report." Phil smiles craftily at James. "Wouldn't you agree?"

"As long as the banks provide in writing that they're withdrawing their request, I would agree."

Phil smiles. "Good. I knew you'd be a man that I could reason with."

"The banks will still pay me for the work."

Phil's smile gets wider. "Of course. I'll personally guarantee that you get paid." Phil takes another drag from his cigar and exhales the smoke up into the air. "Now, James, I need you to assure me that you won't do anything with that information that you uncovered. That's troubling stuff, and a lesser man might be tempted to use it, at some point."

"Once I get the withdrawal letters from the banks, the matter is concluded," James says. "There'll be no further mention of my findings."

Phil stands up and smiles. "Good; that's really good to hear. I'll let the President know of your cooperation. I'm sure he'll be very appreciative."

James gives him a smile. "Speaking of appreciative, you need to contact the President and tell him to call off the IRS audit into my father-in-law's church."

"I don't know of any IRS audit."

"It doesn't matter if you know; just relay the message to the President. He'll know what to do."

"I'll see what I can do."

James points to him. "That IRS audit is a deal-breaker, Phil. It needs to get called off, or we have no deal."

"I gotcha!"

Sam comes walking into the office after Phil has left. "It'll take a week to get rid of that cigar smell," she says.

"Even longer to get rid of the other stench," James says. "I'll work from home for a while. Thanks a lot for bailing on me."

"How did things work out? Anything bad?"

James smiles. "No, pretty good, actually. We may be able to come out of this affair unscathed."

Sam smiles at him slyly. "I guess it was a good thing that you had me at the meeting to put that guy in his place!"

James rolls his eyes. "Yeah, it's a good thing you were here for those ten seconds."

CHAPTER 11

SENATOR HARTLEY

There's a knock at James's door after Eisley leaves, and Vernon peeks in. "Have you got a minute?" he asks.

"Yeah, come in," James says.

"Well, they passed the Hartley amendment," Vernon says after sitting down. "It was added to a defense appropriations bill."

"What does the bill say?" Sam asks.

"It says that no U.S. taxpayer funds may be used to purchase arms for the Guerreros or any other group in the overthrow of the government of Bolivia. The amendment specifically targets Bolivia."

"Did the amendment mention the Guerreros?" James asks.

"No I believe it is more general in nature. But Bolivia was in the amendment."

"And it is taxpayer dollars that the law bars? Dollars for the purchase of arms for the purpose of overthrowing the government? That's the exact legislation?"

"Now that you ask, I'm not absolutely sure. But I believe that's what it says: no taxpayer dollars for the purchase of arms. Medicine, food, and other humanitarian aid is exempt."

"Do me a favor and have our legal people read the legislation," James says. "If that's what the provision reads, it sounds like pretty much what we expected. What does Rodney have to say?"

"I haven't spoken to Rodney yet—his door is closed. He's in a meeting with Ian and Miles."

"Ian is here in the States?"

"Yes."

James stands up. "I'll be right back. I've got to speak to Ian."

"Samantha, while James is out, may I speak to you about something important? I could really use your help."

"Sure, Vernon, what is it?"

"Our railroad company is getting ready to close on the purchase of the Kansas-Texas line. Six months ago, we bought the Denver and Rio Grande Railroad."

She shrugs. "All right, what do you need from me?"

"Do you know how many of these lines James intends on acquiring?"

Sam forces out a laugh. "If I know James, as many as he can get his hands on."

Vernon lets out a breath. "That's the problem, Samantha. We're piling up a lot of debt to acquire these lines, and the bondholders are getting very nervous."

"Did you speak to James about this subject? What did James have to say?"

"Oh, James just shrugged me off. He said, 'Because of the Staggers Act, we now have the opportunity to snap up the smaller railroads that are clogging up the routes and slowing us down. And when we finish acquiring the lines, we'll be able to significantly improve our logistical performance.'"

"What do you need from me?"

Vernon leans forward. "I need you to help me convince James to curb his buying of these railroad lines. James refuses to quantify the number. James believes these purchases are great buys and that he needs to move quickly to snap up all that he can. The Staggers Rail Act passed in 1980 deregulated the business. We can now set our own freight rates. No more regulatory oversite of our industry and procuring rate approvals. James is of the mind that if we don't snap these lines up right away, others will.

"And besides, James said, 'the small railroad lines are being sold for a fraction of what they're really worth. We're consolidating these routes with our current operations. Pretty soon, we'll be able to handle all the freight in the south and Midwest, from the Mississippi to the Pacific Ocean.'"

Sam raises her shoulders. "Vern, I'm not sure that we should stop buying the rail lines. I seem to recall we've had this discussion before, at our strategy meeting. The most important element of logistics is speed. Cost is a secondary concern. Our railroad can move the freight cheaper than overland trucking, but can't compete when it comes to speed.

Sam pauses for a moment. "We're not the only ones trying to buy these small lines. Other large railroads are doing the same thing. It's our prediction that there'll be a tremendous consolidation. When the dust settles, there'll be no more than five or six railroads in the country. It'll either get bigger and more efficient, or fall by the wayside.

Sam smiles. "Vernon, we have no choice. We must buy the routes."

Vernon frowns. "Yes, I know, but we're piling up a lot of debt and making creditors nervous."

Sam gets a little louder. "So, what do you want us to do? Stop buying? I just finished telling you that we have no choice. If we stop, we're out of business—our competitors will buy the railroads right from under us. We might as well sell out right now and get out of the business. We won't be able to survive."

"I've got a suggestion," Vernon says. "Something that'll accomplish what we're trying to do and also make the creditors happy. How would you feel if we did an IPO of the railroad business?"

Sam's eyes widen. "You want to take the railroad public?"

"Yes, Samantha, I do. An initial public offering could bring in a large chunk of much-needed capital, which could be used to buy all the railroads that become available."

Sam shakes her head. "I don't know, Vern. James has always said that going public can be a big headache. There're all these regulatory reporting requirements with the SEC. And, besides, I don't know if Henry Greenwald will go along with the idea. Don't forget, Henry still owns twenty percent."

"Please give me the authority to look into the IPO for us, Samantha. We don't have to decide until we have all the facts. I'll call our contacts at the investment firm Drexel. See what Drexel thinks of the IPO. If Drexel feels it's a good idea and they come up with a proposal that's acceptable, we'll present it to Henry. If either you, James, or Henry don't like what Drexel comes up with, we don't do the deal."

"All right, go ahead. It can't hurt to hear what Drexel has to say."

$$\bullet \bullet \bullet \bullet \bullet \bullet \bullet \bullet \bullet \bullet \bullet \bullet \bullet \bullet \bullet \bullet \bullet \bullet$$

While Vernon is speaking to Sam, James knocks on Rodney's door and lets himself in. "What are you scalawags up to?" He looks over at Ian. "What brought you in from London?"

"Hi, James," Ian says. "I thought you wanted to stay out of the day to day stuff regarding Bolivia?"

James gives him a shrewd look. "You're right, I don't want to get involved. Let's go over a hypothetical. Remember, guys, it's a hypothetical.

"Let's say that this fellow Gaytan, who supports the rebels, wants to get a deuce-and-a-half truck to the rebels in Bolivia. The truck is needed for humanitarian purposes, of course. It will be used to transport food and supplies to the people—nothing military, like transporting troops. How would Gaytan go about doing that?"

"Well, speaking, hypothetically, of course," Ian smiles slyly, "since the deuce-and-a-half will be used to transport just food and supplies to feed the starving population, it will not be considered military equipment. One of Gaytan's companies in Chile would simply place a purchase order for the merchandise with one of our companies. Maybe our company based in India, for example."

"How would Gaytan's company do that?" James asks. "Through an international letter of credit? That would leave an easy trail to follow."

Miles jumps in. "No need to get the banks involved at this time. It's a simple commercial transaction. A purchase order would suffice. The matter could even be done verbally."

"I see." James scratches his head. "What next?"

"Our firm in India would scour the world to find a truck suitable for the job," Ian continues. "Maybe a supplier in Israel or South Africa. Our people would arrange for the purchase and shipment of the vehicle to Chile."

"How would our firm in India pay the supplier?"

"Our company wouldn't," Ian says. "The supplier would be paid directly from Gaytan through a bank located in Chile."

"How do we get paid? Where do we get our cut?"

"The shipper from South Africa would pay us our commission," Miles speaks up.

"Where is Gaytan's company getting the money to pay for the equipment?"

"We don't know. Colonel Chase is handling that part of the deal," Miles reveals.

James rubs his chin.

"What's the matter, James?" Rodney asks. "What's bothering you?"

"Colonel Chase is the weak link," James lets out. "That's where we can get burned. That's the spot where we lose control of the transaction."

"What's the difference, James?" Rodney yells. "It's not illegal to do business with the rebels in Bolivia. There's no law stopping us."

"There is now," James lets him know. "Congress just passed legislation barring the use of taxpayer money for the purpose of arming the rebels in Bolivia. Humanitarian aid is still allowed." James pauses for a moment. "Miles, you guys need to get with Chase. Get a better handle on how the money is moving. Make sure this guy Chase knows what he's doing.

"Chase has a military background, not financial or banking—I don't like leaving this part of the operation to an outsider. Especially an outsider that may not know what he's doing." James stands up and walks out of the office.

James heads back into his office. Sam went to lunch with Kathy, and his phone is ringing. "Mr. Coppi, this is Mattie. I have Senator Hartley's office on the line, and Kathy is out to lunch."

"What the fuck, already?" James says under his breath. "All right, Mattie, put him through."

"Hello," James says.

"Please hold for Senator Hartley," the caller says.

"Hello, James, long time no speak!" the senator yells out.

"Yes, Senator, it's been a while. How have you been? How's Abigail?"

"I'm fine, and so is Abby. Thanks for asking, James. How is that lovely wife of yours?"

"Sam is fine also." James is getting tired of the small talk—he's waiting for the bomb to drop. "What can I do for you, Senator?"

"James, the Senate just passed a piece of legislation that may affect your business. Due to our friendship, I wanted to fly out and personally speak to you about this particular piece of legislation. There is a provision in this law that may affect your business."

James is thinking *that was quick. He already knows about our involvement in Bolivia.* "Is there anything that you'd like to discuss now?"

"No, James, it's better that we do this in person. Can I come out tomorrow? Are you free? I can bring Abigail along. I'm sure she'd love to reconnect with Samantha."

"Tomorrow will be fine, Senator. You and your wife can stay at our guest house. Plan to spend the weekend."

"Well, thank you, James, that's very gracious of you. I'll see you tomorrow. We should be arriving around noon."

James gets right up and storms right over to Rodney's office, barging in without bothering to knock. "Hartley knows about our involvement in Bolivia."

"How do you know?" Rodney asks.

"I just got off the phone with him," James says. "He's flying out this weekend to discuss this new legislation with me. Why else would he be making the trip unless he knows? Who the fuck have you guys been blabbing to?"

"James, it's not us, I swear," Ian yells back. "It's got to be Chase or Farnwell or someone on their staff."

"What will you do about Hartley?" Rodney asks.

"I'm going to find out what Hartley has to say. What else can I do? Get to Chase and Farnwell and let them know about Hartley. Tell them to find the leak on their staff." James walks out, and in the hall, he runs into Sam and Kathy.

"How was your lunch?" he asks.

"Wonderful," Sam answers. "Are you ready to head home? Are you still busy?"

"No we can head out. I'm done. Is our driver downstairs?"

"Yes, I told Marvin that we might be right down."

"All right, let's get going. By the way, Senator Hartley and his wife Abigail will be our guests this weekend. Have Billingsley get the guest house ready."

Sam looks at James. "When was this decided? I'm really not in the mood to entertain anyone."

"I'm sorry to spring this on you at the last minute, but Hartley wants to meet with me on a business matter. The Hartleys are only staying one or two nights; it shouldn't be a big deal."

• • • • • • • • ● ● • • • • • • •

James is on his back porch, looking up at Cheyenne Mountain. He spent the morning with his children and is now taking a break. The mares and their foals are grazing in one of the large paddocks of his ranch. This is his favorite way of relaxation—just sitting on his patio and taking in this scene. Sam is over at the guest house, making sure everything is perfect for the Senator's visit later today.

He's deliberating this upcoming meeting with Hartley over in his head. The Bolivian project just started; he could easily back out now. Doing so would ruffle a few feathers with the new administration, but that might be a lot easier than fighting the Democrat-controlled Senate. The back door opens and Sam comes walking out.

"So, Inspector, was everything at the guest house to your satisfaction?" he teases.

Sam sits down next to him. "Yes, the place is perfect. By the way, I forgot to tell you. Roy Emerson, the director at the hospital, called yesterday. In his own quiet, polite way, he reminded me that we still haven't sent in the $75,000 check for the pledge that we made."

"This Emerson guy is a real pain in the ass," James says tersely. "The money isn't due for another two months. Still, I better send the check. Emerson will keep calling and harping on me until he gets the money. This guy has a real nerve busting our chops when you consider all the money we've donated to that hospital. We built an entire wing and loaded the place with the newest medical equipment. Next year, I'm putting a condition on my pledge that if he calls me at any time before the contribution is due, the pledge is off. That hospital better give us the royal treatment when the baby is born."

Sam laughs. "You're in a good mood."

"I'm sorry, it's this Hartley guy. This weekend will be a real bust."

"What's going on? Why does Hartley upset you so much?"

"It's not just Hartley. We're caught in the middle of a political tug of war. The new administration asked us to work on an operation, and the other side doesn't want the mission to go forward. Either way, we'll come out the losers. Hartley is here to try to get me to pull back and join his side."

Sam looks over at him. "What are you going to do?"

"What the fuck can I do?"

Sam lifts her left brow. "Is that language necessary? Since when do you use that language at home?"

"I'm sorry! I'm just frustrated, that's all."

"So what will you do?"

"Sam, we took on the project. Once we take something on, we need to see it through. I'll listen to Hartley and see what he has to say. But if Hartley wants me to pull back, he'll have to give me a really good reason. Not just some political baloney. I'm not getting in the middle."

• • • • • • • • ● • • • • • • • •

Sam walks into the parlor where Senator Hartley and his wife Abigail are chatting with James.

"How was the ride?" Sam asks.

"It was wonderful," Abigail answers. "I wish you could've come with us."

"I wish I could've come, too," Sam says. "Because of my pregnancy, I haven't been on a horse in months." She takes a seat next to James.

"I just love your guest house. It reminds me of back home," Abigail says. "What made you come up with that style? I would think that a Cape Cod would be the last theme you would hit upon out West."

"James and I spent a couple days in Nantucket a few years ago and I just fell in love with the homes," Sam says. "When I first decided to build the guest house, I had a little hesitation about building a Cape. I thought a Cape would look out of place on the ranch. James convinced me. He said, 'What difference does it make, as long as you like the look?'"

"Well, it works," Abigail smiles. "The guest house fits right in on this property."

"This entire spread is absolutely beautiful," Hartley remarks. "And it's huge. How many acres is this estate?"

"About 11,000," James answers. "We just added another property that abutted the ranch. They tell me that my land is almost as big as the island of Manhattan."

"Magnificent, simply magnificent," Hartley says.

"May I get you something to drink?" Sam asks.

"Not right now, Samantha," the Senator answers. "I'd like to chat with James for a bit. Maybe you ladies would like to step out onto the veranda. This is government stuff."

"Senator, if what we're to discuss has to do with business, then Sam needs to be here," James lets him know. "Sam is an equal partner and I trust her implicitly in any matters."

"All right, James, if that is your wish." Hartley turns to his wife. "Abby, dear: unfortunately, what I'll be discussing with the Coppis may be considered confidential."

Abigail stands up. "No need to say anymore. I'll just mosey on outside and enjoy the beautiful day."

After she leaves, Hartley sits forward in his seat. "James, as I mentioned to you on the phone yesterday, legislation was just passed that may affect some of your business dealings."

"How so, Senator?"

Hartley raises his voice a bit. "James, can we just not play coy? You and I both know what I'm trying to get at. You are providing assistance to rebels in Bolivia. This legislation forbids the use of American taxpayer money toward that cause. I'm here to request that you to stop giving the rebels aid. The main reason your company was hired for this operation is because you would know how to get around this particular piece of legislation. I need you to stop what you're doing."

James clears his throat. "Senator, as you are already aware, my companies get involved in many international affairs, some of which are for the US government. We, as a general rule, don't take political sides—we just follow legitimate orders. What you're asking is for me to choose a side, and I won't do that."

"It's not about picking a political side, James, it's about doing the right thing. This new administration has embarked on perilous adventurous affairs around the world. These adventures will cost peoples' lives. The administration needs to be stopped."

"With all due respect, Senator, that last statement from you is making exactly my point. This new administration of the opposing party is embarking on what they consider sound foreign policy; and you of the opposition will make sure they're not successful. It sounds like politics to me. And as I said, I don't get involved in politics."

"James, I came here with all good intentions. You are a friend, and I was hoping that you'd listen to reason. I can just as easily go in another direction. We can haul you and your companies in front of our committee and get to the bottom of what you're up to. Not in just this affair, but all of your other foreign dealings."

"Are you threatening me?"

Sam has been sitting quietly, but she is now getting concerned. The conversation is beginning to spin out of control. She needs to come up with something, and soon.

"You know, James, you and your wife sit here in Colorado enjoying your luxurious lifestyle. You don't care, or give a damn, about these poor people in Bolivia and those poor people in the other countries where you conduct business. The peoples' wretched existence doesn't matter to you at all. All you see is an opportunity to make money."

Sam looks over at James and sees the vein popping on his left temple. She knows exactly what is about to come, and needs to act quickly.

"How dare you!" Sam yells out.

The senator is startled, and turns to her. "Pardon?"

"How dare you! How dare you come into my house disguised as a friend. We open our home to you, and you insult us in this manner. My husband has more compassion in his little finger than you have in your entire body. You begrudge us our lifestyle. A life that was achieved by hard work and sweat.

"Do you know what James and I had when we started out? Five hundred dollars. And do you want to know why we had only five hundred dollars? Because James gave every last penny that he had in savings to a widow of a friend that was killed in Vietnam. So don't you dare lecture my husband about charity and compassion.

"While we're at it, let's discuss about your wealth and how you got there." Sam shakes her head up and down. "Oh yes, Senator, I know all about you. Isn't your wife Abigail on the board of that company that is building that oil pipeline? What is the name of that firm? Oh yes, Regis Petroleum."

She points to the back patio door. "What is your wife's salary for attending four meetings a year? I believe it's one hundred thousand dollars. Your wife must be really good at her job to earn that kind of money for four days' work. And how about the permits that the oil company needed to build the pipeline? Wasn't it convenient, how fast the company was able to get those permits?

"And I wonder what will happen to those poor families that live along the pipeline's route? There are a lot of homes between Midland and Houston. I'm sure that those families' welfare was taken into account before approving the legislation to build.

"Oh, and what happened when that oil company went public? Rumor has it that some of the government officials and a certain senator from Massachusetts had advance knowledge that the company was to be listed on the stock market. The rumor was pretty specific: it said that the senator made five million dollars.

"Maybe that senator will donate the money that he earned from the deal to help those poor people who are being evicted to make room for the pipeline? After all, he cares about the little people!"

James cuts in. "Sam…"

Sam looks over at James and points to the senator. "I want these hypocrites out of my house! Right now!"

"Sam…" James tries to speak

Sam points her finger at the back door and sneers over at the senator. "Get your wife and get out!"

"Sam…" James tries again.

"I said that I want them out!" Sam hollers.

The Senator jumps up, walks to the door and gets his wife, and they hurry out of the house.

After the couple leaves, James turns to Sam and tries to say something.

"Don't you say a word!" she orders. "Someone had to speak up and put that man in his place. You just sat there."

Sam stands up, walks over, rubs her hand through James's jet black hair, leans over, gives him a kiss, and strolls away.

James shakes his head and smiles. He gets up and follows her out. "Where did you get all that background information on the Hartleys?"

Sam turns around and smiles slyly. "It was good, wasn't it?"

"Very impressive. Where did you get it?"

"I have my sources," she smiles shrewdly.

"No, really, where did you get the info?"

"I called Charlie after you told me that the Senator was coming. He gave me the report."

"So fast? I could never get Charlie to move that quickly—maybe I should stay home and you go to work from now on."

James thinks for a moment. "It's curious, the connection between Hartley and Eisley. We may be able to use that association to our advantage."

CHAPTER 12

AN AMBUSH

Richard Faulk, Section Chief of the Criminal Division for the Justice Department in Denver is walking down the hall for a meeting with his boss, US Attorney, Barney Folroy. Richard was called yesterday and told to drop everything that he was working on and come right away. His boss, Barney, a political appointee and an incompetent boob, has a habit of doing that to him. As soon as someone from Washington calls, Barney immediately freaks out. Richard heaves a sigh before walking into Barney's office. *That's the nature of this job, if you want to get ahead, you've got to play the political game.*

Richard knocks and opens the door. "You wanted to see me, Barney?"

Barney looks up from his desk. "Yes, come in Richard." After Richard takes a seat. "How was the Coppi party?"

Richard shrugs. "It was ok."

Richard doesn't want to tell Barney that he got shit-faced drunk and made a complete fool of himself. Still the night turned out pretty good. Because he was too drunk to drive, that beautiful blonde offered him a lift home. That ride led to two more dates with that beauty.

"The Coppis are what I want to speak to you about," Barney says. "I received a call from Washington. They want us to investigate the Coppis."

"Investigate the Coppis, why? That family is clean. A pillar of the community."

"So what are you saying, Richard? Do you not want the assignment?"

Richard shakes his head. "No, I'm not saying that. I was just wondering what led to this decision?"

Barney looks at the door and turns to Richard leaning forward. "Richard, this assignment came directly from Washington. I cannot impress upon you enough the importance of this mission. You've been stuck at your current position for seven years. You bring down the Coppis, I can assure you a straight path to a promotion. Maybe even the running of your own office." Barney sits back. "Can I count on you to give this task your undivided attention or do I need to look for someone else?"

"You can rely on me! How do you want me to proceed?"

Barney smiles. "Good! There are two FBI agents on their way over. They will assist you in the investigation. We need to get someone inside the Coppi organization on our side. Someone who can get all of the Coppi's dirty laundry exposed, and I have just the right person in mind, Miles Cornish."

"Who is he?"

"He's the Coppis' new controller. We have uncovered some disturbing material on his background. We can use that information to put pressure on Mr. Cornish to cooperate and assist with our investigation. Even better, I hear he's writing a book on the Coppis. Cornish's notes will be very useful in our probe."

Barney stands up. "That's it for now, when the FBI agents get here we'll discuss a plan of action. We'll also make arrangements to pay Mr. Cornish a visit."

Richard stands up and Barney has a final say. "You don't get promotions by not giving Washington what they want. I'm quite sure that the Coppis didn't get to their status by being completely clean. Do you read me?"

"Loud and clear," Richard answers.

• • • • • • • • ● ● • • • • • • • • •

Sam is accompanying James to the airport three days later. "I don't know why you have to go back to Africa," she says. "Why can't you send someone else?"

"Because this is really important," he says. "The warlord, Benga, contacted Ernie and wants to talk. Benga wants to work out a truce. If we can come to a resolution with Benga on a ceasefire, it would save a lot of lives." He leans over and gives her a kiss. "I won't be long, just a couple of days."

"You know I can't sleep when you go on these journeys."

He smiles. "There's nothing dangerous about the trip. A quick meeting and I'm flying right back."

Sam frowns. "You have no idea on how much of a toll these quick meetings have on me. And why are you going without your bodyguard?"

"Max had some personal affairs to handle, and besides, I don't need a bodyguard. As I said, it's in and out, a really quick meeting."

The next day, James is once again landing in an open field next to the military encampment. The flight this time was less eventful; the rain had let up and the trip was almost comfortable. He was met at the plane by the same sergeant as on his last trip. Immediately, he was escorted to the main tent where Ernie was waiting.

"You arrived just in time," Ernie says. "Benga and his entourage will be here in about an hour. How do you want to work the negotiations?"

"Let's have Benga start the conversation and see what he has to say. I've got some ideas, but I'd rather not make any proposals until I hear what the other side is offering." He has a look around. "How are things around here? Has there been any action?"

"No everything has been quiet. We're hunkered down, just as you ordered."

James nearly jumps out of his chair as explosions vibrate through the tent. "What the fuck?" he yells out.

Gary runs into the tent. "We're under attack." Gary runs right back out.

Ernie leaps from his chair and reaches behind him for his flak jacket.

James turns to Ernie. "Give me a rifle."

"What the fuck do you think you're going to do with a gun?" Ernie barks. "You get under my desk!" Ernie looks over at two soldiers. "You two, stand guard over Mr. Coppi. Make sure nothing happens to him."

Ernie looks over at James, who has not moved. He smiles. "Come on, James, let us handle this problem. You'd only be in the way." James walks over to the other side and crawls under the desk.

"Stay tight, I'll be right back," Ernie says.

Cowering under the desk is not sitting well with him. He remembers the days sitting in a bunker in Vietnam while being shelled. Those were always the tensest moments, just waiting, unable to fight back. He would much rather have a rifle in his hand and joining the fight. At least with the gun, he would have some measure of controlling the situation.

The explosions appear to stop. Small arms fire still rings out. He crawls from under his desk and stands up.

"Sir, the orders were for you to stay under the desk," one of the soldiers says. "The situation is still unstable."

James dusts himself off. "If that's so, hand me a rifle. I'm not kneeling under the desk."

The soldiers look at one another. After a moment, one shrugs, walks over to the rack, and picks out a rifle.

As he's handing it to James, he says, "Do you know how to use the weapon?"

James smiles. "Yes, and the rifle would work a lot better if you also gave me a magazine clip."

James loads the clip into the gun and heads out of the tent. One of the soldiers runs up and grabs his arm.

"Sir, you should stay in the tent."

James removes the hand and continues out of the tent.

The two soldiers who were supposed to keep an eye on him look at each other.

"What should we do?" one says to the other.

"I'll go with Mr. Coppi. You find the Colonel and let him know what's happening."

James looks around the area when he gets outside. About three hundred meters to his right he notices six soldiers firing their guns behind a barricade of sandbags. As he is making his way toward the men to join the fight, someone rams into him and knocks him down. His rifle flies out of his hand and lands across the path. James looks up and a raider swings a machete down at his face. He manages to turn and the blow misses the target. The assailant readies the machete for another blow. Two shots ring out freezing the attacker in mid action. The lifeless man falls face down to the ground still gripping the blade.

The soldier who was guarding him in the tent runs over and points his rifle at the body. After assuring himself that the man is dead he turns to James. "Are you sure you wouldn't rather stay inside the tent."

James walks over, picks up his gun. "Thanks for the help."

He proceeds to the wall and joins the men. After checking his rifle, he rises up on the wall and fires a burst at where he perceives is the enemy. A soldier next to him smiles. "I believe they've retreated, sir. There's no one there."

A few moments later, Ernie crawls next to him. "I guess you decided not to listen."

"I didn't like the view from under the table. Besides, I wasn't feeling good about these men risking their lives while I hid."

"My man told me you had a close call."

James smiles. "I had it under control."

"You know you were the target of this raid? The rebels get rid of you and the whole project comes to an end and all my men lose their jobs. My men know that, and believe me, they like their jobs." Ernie tucks at James's arm. "None of the men want you out here. Their job is to make sure you don't get hurt. All the men would be really upset and consider themselves failures if something happened to you."

James smiles wryly. "Yeah, I get the picture. How bad was it?"

"We lost two men. Another two-dozen wounded, some seriously. We captured ten of their men. Gary is interrogating the prisoners as we speak." Ernie looks at him. "You're not letting those bastards get away with this, are you?"

"No, of course not. I'm contacting Ian as soon as I get back. I'll call you in a few days and let you know what I have in mind."

"Why don't you just let my unit continue on to Rwanda? In a few months, we'll have the entire rebel force mopped up."

James shakes his head. "No, the international situation hasn't changed since the last time I was here. No country will condone white South African forces raiding another African country. Any retaliation that I devise has to be swift and decisive. And, more importantly, without much fanfare."

Gary comes walking up with one of the prisoners.

"Who's that?" Ernie asks.

"He's one of the men we captured," Gary answers.

"What's so special about him?" Ernie says.

"He's Cuban!"

"Cuban!" Both James and Ernie yell out at the same time.

"Yes," Gary lets out. "Cuban. They're in Rwanda, helping the rebels."

Ernie looks over at James.

James smiles. "Don't worry, we'll hit the Cubans along with Benga's forces. No mercy, no matter what their nationalities. Swift and decisive," James says. "Listen, Ernie, I'd like to thank your men for today, they really came through. Is it safe to call an assembly and round up the entire brigade?"

"Sure, James. Give me a half-hour to get the unit in formation."

James walks up the stairs of a stand where speakers have been installed. The unit is in parade rest of columns of fours. Ernie walks up to a microphone.

"If I could have your attention for a few minutes, Mr. Coppi, the commander of this outfit, would like to say a few words."

James walks up to the mike. "I'd like to thank you for the bravery you showed today in repelling this sneak attack. Without your valor and swift call to action, I wouldn't be here speaking to you."

He clears his throat. "I'd like to express my condolences for the two men from your unit that perished. Let me assure you that those lives will not go unavenged."

With that, a big roar goes up from the cadre.

"Once again, thank you."

When he's finished and is walking away, Ernie comes up, grabs his hand, and takes him back to the microphone.

Ernie gets on the mike. "I just want all of you men to know that Mr. Coppi was not hiding in the safety of a bunker. He was right among the men, rifle in hand, fighting off the attack."

Once again, another roar goes up from the unit.

• • • • • • • • ● • • • • • • • •

Two days later, Sam is just getting to the office when she passes the cafeteria where three women are standing in a group. She stops when she hears James's name. She walks into the room.

"What about James?" she asks the women.

"What?" one of the startled ladies says.

"You were talking about James? I'd like to know what you were saying about him."

"We weren't talking about Mr. Coppi, Mrs. Coppi." Another of the ladies says. "You must have misheard what we were saying."

"I know what I heard." Her voice rises. "Now, you can either tell me what you were talking about, concerning James, or we can have this conversation at personnel. Believe me, you won't like that talk."

The three women look at each other. After a moment, one speaks up. "We were just saying wasn't it wonderful that Mr. Coppi wasn't hurt in that skirmish in Africa."

Sam turns pale. "What skirmish?"

"I'm sorry, Mrs. Coppi," the woman says anxiously. "I've already said too much. Please, you should speak to Mr. Dixon."

"Please get Vernon and have him report to James's office immediately." She storms out of the cafeteria and hurries down the hall. She points at Kathy when she gets to her desk. "You! Get in the office!"

She walks into the office and sits behind the desk. Kathy comes in and sits across the way.

"I thought you were my friend," Sam says.

"I'm so sorry, Sam. I just found out a little while ago."

"Is he all right?"

"Yes, he's fine."

"Where is he? I'd like to speak to him."

"You can't, James just boarded a plane in Brussels. He'll call when he arrives in New York."

There's a knock at the door and Vernon looks in. "You wanted to see me."

"Yes, come in and take a seat." After he sits, she says. "I'd like to know why everyone at this company knows that my husband was in a shootout but me?"

"I'm sorry, Samantha. James called last night and gave me specific instructions not to tell you. Since I knew he was ok, I thought that it would be best if James told you himself, when he got home."

She points her finger at Vernon. "In the future, you are never to follow those types of orders. You call me!"

"Understood."

"Now, tell me what happened," she says in a calmer voice.

"I really don't know most of the details. James was to meet with the rebels to discuss a ceasefire, but the rebels decided on an ambush."

"What about Gary and Ernie?"

"Gary and Ernie are fine; our casualties were light."

Sam shakes her head. "So, there were casualties and some of our guys were killed."

Vernon grimaces. "I'm afraid so."

• • • • • • • • ● • • • • • • • •

The next night, Sam and James are in their bedroom. Sam has been shouting for the last half hour.

"Can you please keep your voice down?" James says for about the tenth time. "Everybody in the house can hear you."

"I don't care!" she yells. "I was so upset that I nearly gave birth when I heard the news."

He walks up to her, pushes back a lock of her strawberry blonde hair that's fallen on her face and gives her a hug, rubbing her back. "I know, but I'm ok—I was never in any danger. Ernie had two men guarding me."

"Are you going back there?"

"I don't plan to." He releases her. "I can handle everything from here."

Sam looks into his face. "James, can you make love to me tonight?"

He pulls back. "Please," she says. "Will you make love to me?"

"Yes, of course."

"How are we doing this?" she asks, and motions to her prenatal belly.

James smiles. "Let's put our heads together and figure something out."

Sam is holding onto the headboard as James is pounding her from behind. "Just a little longer," she says.

James grabs a tighter hold of her hips and increases his pace. Sam lets out a moan as she reaches her climax. A few moments later, James gives a final thrust, and she feels his member beating inside her as it deposits its fluid. Sam turns her head and reaches for him, pulling his face to her. She gives him a kiss.

"That was wonderful. I don't know why I was so afraid to have sex."

James pulls out. "That has to be a new world record," he says. "What's it, now—seven weeks before the baby is due?"

"Yeah, well, I'll be paying a price for this escapade for the rest of the night," she says. "The baby woke up and is kicking away."

James gives her a kiss. "It was worth it, don't you agree?"

He hops off the bed. "I've got to make a call."

CHAPTER 13

STRIKE AND COUNTERSTRIKE

James walks to his study and dials Ian.

A groggy Ian answers the call. "What's up, James? Anything wrong? It's three in the morning here in London."

"Yeah, I know. I'm sorry, but I need you to get busy right away. We need three transport planes for Ernie in Zaire. We're planning a raid on the rebels in Rwanda. The planes will be transporting a company of commandos. About two hundred and fifty men is my guess. Call Ernie to coordinate—he'll tell you what else he needs."

"Okay, will do. Anything else?"

"Yeah, call Rodney at the office. Tell him to get in touch with Kayumba Buresa— he's in Rwanda, and on our payroll. We need a full layout of where the rebels are located. Buresa will be able to get us the information."

"Who is Buresa?" Ian asks.

"He's a Rwandan Tutsi restaurant owner, but also works for us. The rebels are backed by the other tribe in Rwanda the Hutus. The Tutsi hate the Hutus that are in power. We can use the Tutsi to help us in this raid. Rodney will know how to get in touch with him. Buresa will be able to locate the rebel camp. Call Rodney right away. I believe he's still in the office, but if not, reach him at home."

Twenty minutes later, James gets a call from Rodney.

"James, I just spoke to Ian and he told me what you have in mind. Are you sure this is a good idea? This is a serious escalation of the conflict. It has grave international implications."

"Yeah, Rodney, I'm aware."

He hears Rodney letting out a breath. "James, the whole world will come down on you. Africa is a touchy subject. Especially since the men under your command are white South Africans. I can assure you that no country will be pleased. Our company will be out there taking the flak all by ourselves."

"Rodney, I'm aware of the possible ramifications. I've taken that into my calculation. Get me the report of where the rebels are located. I don't want the men landing in an empty field. Have our man Buresa get a complete layout of the rebel base. Hurry up and get Ian the information. I'd like to make the attack this week, if possible."

Rodney is not letting go. "What changed your mind? I thought you were hunkered down?"

"There's a Cuban presence, and they killed two of our men—we can't let them get away with that. We need to deliver a strong message to the Cubans and the rebels that any attack on us will result in severe consequences right back at them."

"All right, James, it's your call, I hope you know what you're doing and are ready for the consequences."

Five days later, Vernon is walking down the hall toward James's office. He looks at his watch. It's after ten pm. James's bodyguards, Max and Regis, are sitting on each side of the door to his office.

"I'd like to speak to James," he says to Max. "Can you let him know that I'm out here?"

"I'm sorry, Mr. Dixon, but Mr. Coppi left explicit orders not to be disturbed."

Vernon walks away and bumps into Kathy in the hall. "Kathy, what's going on? Why is everyone working so late? And why wasn't I told anything about it? Why the hush-hush?"

"I'm sorry, Vernon. James gave the instructions," she says.

Vernon walks off, knocks on Rodney's door, and looks in. "Have you got a minute?"

"Yes, come in."

"Do you know what's up?" Vernon says when he's in the office. "What's James up to?"

"There is an operation overseas. Our facilities specialist was setting up communication gear in James's office earlier today."

"Do you know about the action?"

"It's in Zaire."

Vernon looks into Rodney's face. "What is it?"

Rodney smiles shrewdly. "I better not say, and you really don't want to know. Let me put it this way. When James locks himself in the office, something big is about to happen. If you really want to know, check the newspapers tomorrow."

• • • • • • • • ● ● • • • • • • •

In his office, James gets on the phone to Ernie. "Good morning, Ernie."

"Good morning, James."

"What's happening? Why can't I hear anything on my field radio? I thought the troops were moving in?"

Ernie bellows out a laugh. "Calm down, *boet*. The operation hasn't started yet. The units are observing radio silence until they arrive at the landing zone."

"How come you're in such a good mood this morning?" James asks.

James hears another laugh. "I'm always in a good mood at the start of a battle. Why are you so uptight? The plan is a good one."

James lets out a breath. "I hope you're right. This plan goes wrong, we've all had it."

"If you feel that way, why did you order the attack?"

"I'm beginning to wonder about that, myself."

"How sure are you that we're just hitting Cubans and rebels?" Ernie asks. "I hope it's not a Rwandan military base."

"I'm not 100 percent certain, but the report Rodney gave me from our man Buresa seems reliable."

The radio comes on. "Thor has landed," James hears.

"Did you hear that?" Ernie asks. "Our men are on the ground."

"Yeah, I heard. Was that Gary, who called himself Thor?"

Ernie bellows out another laugh. "Yeah, he's Scandinavian."

"How long will they take to unload?"

"Shouldn't be long," Ernie says. "There're only four armored personnel carriers."

"Why no tanks?"

"The tanks would be too heavy. The C-130s had to make an assault landing onto an open field. The extra weight would have been a problem. Anyway, the unit has plenty of firepower. In addition to the four APCs, the men have mortars, grenade, and rocket launchers."

The radio comes on again. "Giddy up!"

"What's that?" James asks.

"They're on the move," Ernie answers. "Five trucks carrying forty men each, and four APCs, each loaded with a squad."

"Where did they get the trucks?"

"They arrived three days ago, disguised as medical transports. They're the ones that created the landing zone for the C-130s."

"How far are they from the rebel camp?"

"About 12 kilometers," Ernie replies. "They should be at the camp in about 35 minutes. The unit is moving slowly and deliberately. We don't want any of the vehicles to get into a wreck and screw up the mission."

Thirty-five minutes, later the radio blares. "Snooze."

"What's that mean?" James asks.

"The men are on the perimeter of the rebel base," Ernie answers. "Gary is waiting for the secret word from all the squads that they're in position."

"What's the word?"

Ernie laughs. "Swift and Decisive."

"Very funny!"

"Let's go, move out." James hears Gary's voice on the radio after the platoons have reported that they are in position.

In the background, explosions and small arms fire can be heard. Machine guns appear to be firing nonstop. The attacking party is no longer on radio silence, and James hears Gary barking orders. There is constant chatter from the platoon leaders reporting back to Gary. It sounds like total chaos, but James knows better. He had been in similar battles in Vietnam. That is the sound of a disciplined military operation.

These soldiers are seasoned mercenaries and know their jobs exactly. The men are all consummate military professionals. All the platoon leaders know what has to be done. The commanders bark their orders to the squad leaders who, in turn, encourage their men. If a soldier is confused, it is the head of the team that he turns to for direction.

If the squad leader is not around, that combatant will turn to his fellow troop members. No one will freeze up in their assignment. Every man in the unit knows that if he doesn't do his job and kill the enemy, he can cost lives of his comrades and himself. It is kill or be killed.

Twenty minutes later, Gary is on the radio. "Cease fire! Let's head home. Slowly, an orderly withdrawal. Report back when you are in position."

An hour later, a final radio communication. "Thor is in the sky. Coming back to Valhalla."

"That's it, James, it's over," Ernie says. "I'll get you a report on the damage and the casualties as soon as I debrief the men."

"When will that be?"

"In about two hours."

"All right, I'll be here. Let's hope everyone is safe."

James walks out of his office. "Kathy, you can leave now."

Kathy reaches for her pocketbook. "Will you need me later today?"

James smiles. "Probably not. Go home and get some sleep. If anything changes, I'll give you a call. Thanks for your help."

"Oh, by the way," she says before leaving. "Both Rodney and Vernon are still here."

"Okay, thanks," he says, and turns to his two bodyguards. "Why don't you guys head over to the cafeteria and put on a pot of coffee? I could use a cup."

James walks down to Vernon's office and lets himself in. Vernon is sleeping on the couch. Rodney is sleeping in a chair.

"Wouldn't you guys have been more comfortable sleeping at home?" he calls out.

The fellows wake up. Rodney stands up and rubs his neck.

"How did it go?" he asks.

"It went well. I'll get a report after the debriefing."

"I hope you're ready for the political fallout," Rodney says.

"What fallout?" Vernon asks.

James smiles. "Nothing that you should be worried about, Vern. Go home, guys, and get some rest. Thanks for hanging around."

• • • • • • • • ● ● • • • • • • •

The next morning, Rodney knocks at James's office door and peeks in.

"Did you hear the news? It's all over the television," he says.

"What news; about our raid?"

"No." Rodney walks into the office. "Anwar Sadat was assassinated."

"No shit? What happened?"

"Some Jihadist opened fired during a military parade in Cairo."

James shakes his head. "Wow, that's really going to destabilize the region." He looks over at Rodney. "Do we have any personnel in Egypt?"

"No, I don't think so."

"Good." James smiles wryly. "You know, Rodney, in a way, the Sadat assassination may be good news for us. Everyone will be focused on Egypt, so no one will care what happened in Rwanda."

"Yes, I guess you might be right." Rodney takes a seat. "How did our operation go? Did you get a debrief?"

"Yeah, everything went exactly as planned—caught both the rebels and the Cubans completely by surprise. They were not expecting an attack by us—Gary said that the camp wasn't even being guarded when he went in. We had only four wounded, and none of the injuries were life threatening. On the other hand, the rebels and Cubans had nearly five hundred casualties. We not only taught them a lesson, but also dealt them a serious setback."

James stands up and stretches. "I'm beat. I'm heading home. Rodney, on another matter, do me a favor and check with your sources in Washington. Find out if there's a government investigation into me and Sam."

Rodney looks at the door, lowering his voice. "You think that the FBI is investigating you guys?"

"Maybe. See what you can find out. This Senator Hartley is being a real pain, and I need to know what he's up to."

"All right, I'll make a few calls."

CHAPTER 14

KATHY'S MAN

Two days later, Kathy stands up from her desk as she sees James coming down the hall at the office.

"Good morning, James," Kathy says when he gets to her. "Coffee?"

"Good morning, Kathy. Yes, coffee, please."

A few minutes later, she walks into his office and places the cup in front of him, taking a seat across from his desk.

James takes a sip and looks up at her. "You look nice."

Kathy smiles. "Thank you. What have you got for me? Anything important?"

"No, I've got nothing. Do you have anything for me? Does anyone need to speak to me?"

"Not yet," Kathy answers. "James, since there's not much happening at the office, do you mind if I take a long lunch today?"

"No, I guess it's okay. What's up? Why do you need the extra time?"

"I've got a lunch date."

James takes a long look at Kathy, and after a moment a smile forms on his face. "You met someone? Who's the lucky guy?"

"How do you know it's a guy?" she laughs.

"Because it's written all over your face. And you're dressed especially nice. That blonde hair looks like it's just been to a beauty parlor. And if that weren't enough, you're wearing your favorite perfume. So, come on, spill it out! Who's the guy?"

"You know the guy, James. His name is Richard Faulk."

James creases his brow. "Richard Faulk? You say that I know him? The name doesn't sound familiar."

"I met Richard at a party that you and Sam gave a while ago at the ranch. He's an assistant district attorney for the DOJ. Richard was a guest at your party. Well he wasn't actually the one invited—his boss, Barney Folroy, was the invitee. When his boss couldn't make the affair, Richard took his place."

"Oh, now I remember the man." James frowns. "An annoying guy who wouldn't leave me alone. How did you end up hooking up with an irritating guy like him?"

"When I was leaving that night, Richard was outside your house, waiting for a cab that hadn't shown. He said that he had too much to drink and didn't want to drive home. So, I offered him a lift. One thing led to another on the ride, and he asked me if I'd go out with him. Anyway, I've been out with him a couple of times, and Richard seems nice."

"Well, I hope that when I meet him again, he's a lot less bothersome."

Kathy nods. "I'm sure he will be; he just had too much to drink that night. So, will it be all right if I take a long lunch?"

James waves his hand. "Go ahead, enjoy your lunch. Give the man my regards. Have Sam's secretary Helen take your place while you're out, just in case something pops up unexpectedly."

Kathy buzzes James after lunch. "James, I'm back!"

"Come into my office."

"Have a seat," James says after Kathy walks in.

"So, how was the lunch?" He gives her a big smile.

Kathy shrugs. "It was okay."

"Uh-oh!"

"What do you mean, uh-oh?" Kathy's voice gets a little louder.

"I'm guessing that the date didn't go well, that's all."

"No, the lunch went just fine—I just don't like you sticking your nose where it doesn't belong. Do you have anything for me, workwise?"

"No, we're good."

Later that afternoon, Kathy knocks at James's door and lets herself in. "James, it's four-thirty. Do you mind if I leave a little early? There's nothing happening."

James looks up and laughs. "Nice job you have—long lunches and half days. Go ahead, go home. I'll get by." Just before she closes the door, he adds, "Kathy, I'm sorry. When I asked you about your lunch, earlier, I didn't mean to pry."

"It's all right, James, forget it." Kathy closes the door. A moment later, she walks back in and takes a seat across from James. "You were right! The lunch didn't go well."

"What happened?"

Kathy pauses. "I don't know if I'm making too much of this, but Richard had three drinks at lunch. Don't you think that's a little much? I suspect he may have a drinking problem. This is the third time I've been out with him, and each time he seems to drink just a little too much."

"Does he get drunk?"

"No, but three drinks over lunch? Isn't that a lot? And remember, James, the guy was plastered when I gave him a lift home from your party."

"Why don't you talk to him about his drinking? See what he says."

Kathy shakes her head. "I don't know; how do you ask such a question? I barely know the guy. I've only been out with him three times. Maybe I should just ditch him?"

"Well, I think you should speak to him and see what he says. Give him a chance to explain himself. Remember, Kathy: I had a drug problem when Sam met me, but we worked it out. Have a conversation with the guy about the drinking. There's something that you must like about the man, otherwise you wouldn't have agreed to go out with him. Have a talk, and if you're not satisfied with his answers, then you can ditch him. Don't be so quick to pull the plug."

"All right, James I'll do that. Thanks for your advice." Kathy stands up. "I'm sorry I snapped at you earlier—I guess you just caught me off guard. It's really disarming how well you know me."

James laughs. "Why wouldn't we know each other? Look at all the time that we spend together. Good night, Kathy."

A group of the company's executives are walking down the hall as Kathy heads for the elevator.

"Good night, Kathy," the men hail as they pass.

Kathy looks over at the men, she runs up to one and grabs his arm. "Rodney, what's up?"

"James wants to meet with us."

"When was this decided? This meeting wasn't on the calendar."

Rodney shrugs. "I don't know why the meeting wasn't on your calendar. James called earlier and asked us to come to his office."

Kathy walks with the men to James's office. "James, I didn't know about this meeting. Do you need me to stick around?"

James looks over and smiles. "No, Kathy, we'll be fine. Go home."

"I really don't mind."

"Well, if you insist, get your pad and take some notes."

"All right, let's get started," he says after Kathy comes back. "Rodney, what were you able to uncover?"

"You were right, James. There's an investigation."

"Are you sure? How good is the source that gave you the news?"

"My source is reliable."

"What else were you able to find out? What's this investigation about?"

Rodney looks over at the other people in the room and turns back to James. "Maybe we should discuss this in private?"

"No, Rodney, that's why we're having this meeting. To get everybody's input."

Rodney clears his throat. "The bureau is investigating you and your wife Samantha. They're looking at both your personal and business affairs." Rodney leans forward. "James, this situation is about to get ugly. My source tells me that they're looking to obtain warrants to search your property and maybe even our companies. The Feds are just lining up their game plan. The Feds can make your life and ours at the company a living hell."

"Damn it!" James yells out, and sits back in his seat. "These fuckers will never let us live in peace. It's always personal. They can't separate work from people's personal lives. Who's doing it? Who's behind this investigation?"

"John Meany. He's a deputy to the attorney general," Rodney says.

"Why would this guy Meany go after James and Samantha?" Charlie asks Rodney. "What's he got against them?"

Rodney waves. "I don't know—I just know that he's the guy behind the investigation in Washington. On a local level, they've assigned the matter to Barney Folroy, who turned over the case to one of his assistants, Richard Faulk."

"Who?" Kathy lifts her head up from her pad.

"Barney Folroy!" Rodney answers.

"No, the other guy. Who did you say is doing the investigation?"

"Richard Faulk!"

James looks over at Kathy and shakes his head no. He turns back to Rodney. "Who's behind the investigation? It has to be Hartley, don't you agree?"

Rodney nods. "Yeah, that makes sense. He's the most logical choice."

"How does Hartley have that kind of pull with the Justice Department?" James brings out. "He's of the opposing political party. Why is the Attorney General helping him?"

"James, I really don't know," Rodney answers.

James turns to Kathy. "Do me a favor. Get the Secretary of State on the phone for me." He turns back to Rodney. "Who's the Attorney General?"

"Edward Massey."

"James, Secretary Reichwald is on the line," Kathy buzzes in.

"Good evening, Mr. Secretary," James hails.

"Good evening, James. What can I do for you? Your assistant said it's urgent. She yanked me out of an important meeting."

"Yes, Mr. Secretary, it's serious. I need to know why your Justice Department is investigating me and my wife. What are you guys up to?"

"James, I don't know anything about any investigation."

"Well, do me a favor and get in touch with Ed Massey. Find out what's going on. Have Massey give me a call."

"All right, James, I'll call him right away."

James begins tapping his pen on the desk after he hangs up.

"Are you okay?" Rodney asks.

"Yeah, I'm good." James gets up. "I'll be right back." He walks out of his office and walks over to Kathy's desk.

"It's quite a coincidence, don't you agree, that Faulk, the man you're dating, is on this investigation?"

"I'm having a talk with him as soon as I get home tonight."

"Don't do it over the phone. Speak to him in person."

"All right, will do. Do you still need me for this meeting?"

"No, I'll be all right. Call me after you speak to Faulk." James walks back into the office.

The phone rings and James answers. "Hello."

"Ed Massey for James Coppi, please."

"This is James, Ed."

"Good evening, James. Secretary Reichwald spoke to me of a difficulty that you're having with my department."

"Yes, Ed, it's a huge problem. Why are you investigating my wife and me?"

"James, believe me, I didn't order the investigation. It's one of the Deputy AGs. The man is a leftover from the previous administration—I haven't had the time to find a replacement for him yet."

"Can you quash this case?"

"Unfortunately, James, I can't stop the probe without a lot of political fallout. All I can do is keep an eye on Meany and make sure that investigation doesn't spin out of control. Once I have a replacement on board, we may find a way to close the inquiry."

James purses his lips. "It's my understanding that they may be looking to obtain search warrants. Can you at least stop your men from doing that? At least have a serious talk with this deputy of yours. Let him know that you're looking over his shoulder, so he doesn't run roughshod on me."

"Yes, I can do that."

"Lousy fucking politicians," James utters after he hangs up the phone. "All right, I think we're done here."

James goes out to Kathy's desk and looks through her Rolodex cards after the men leave. He pulls out the number of the Colorado Springs sheriff and heads back to his office to make the call.

"This is James Coppi. May I speak to Sheriff Wilde, please?"

"Hello, James, how've you been?" the sheriff asks when he's on the line.

"I'm fine, Sheriff. Listen, can you stop by the ranch sometime tomorrow? I need to speak to you about a matter."

"Sure, James. Does around three work for you?"

"Yes, Sheriff. I'll see you tomorrow."

• • • • • • • • ● ● • • • • • • • •

Kathy gets right on the phone when she gets home and calls Richard Faulk. She asks Richard to stop over. An hour later, Richard is sitting on the couch in Kathy's living room with Kathy across the way.

"What did you want to speak to me about?" He asks.

"Are you dating me so that you can get dirt on James and Sam for your investigation?"

Richard sits up. "What? What makes you say that?"

"So, are you saying that you're not investigating them?"

"Kathy, you know I can't talk about any investigations by me."

"Well, you need to tell me something, Richard, because I'm getting ready to throw you the fuck out of here."

Richard pauses for a moment. "Well, since you already know about the investigation, I can tell you that I just got the assignment. At lunch, I was trying to tell you that, because of the possible conflict, I won't be able to see you until this case was over.

"Even after three drinks, I couldn't find a way to broach the subject with you. But you must believe me, I would never use you to get to James or Sam."

Kathy stares fixedly into his face. "What are you going to do?"

Richard shrugs. "What do you mean?"

"About the investigation? Are you continuing with the case?"

"Yes, of course. I have to. This is my assignment. What else can I do?"

"You can turn it down."

Richard leans forward. "Kathy, think about what you're asking of me. This is my career. If I turn down this assignment, I might as well leave the Justice Department."

"These are my best friends that you're investigating. I've known Sam since I was a toddler. We grew up together in Lorenzo."

Richard raises his shoulders. "I know that, Kathy, but there's nothing that I can do about it now."

"Can't, or won't?"

"Both! Kathy, this order came directly from Washington. This is a big deal. It can make my career."

There's a period of silence.

"Well?" Richard breaks the quiet.

"I guess if that's how you feel, you'll have to leave," she says.

"Is that it, then? Are we through?"

"Yes!"

"Just like that?"

Kathy's voice goes up. "These are my closest friends. You go after them, you might as well go after me."

"I'm sorry you feel that way." Richard stands up. "All right, I guess that's it." Richard begins to walk out.

"Richard," Kathy calls out.

Richard turns around. "Yes!"

"A warning! You go after Sam, and James will destroy you. James will never allow Sam to get hurt. That so-called career of yours that you're striving to achieve will be over before it even gets started. You might want to take that into consideration before moving forward with this investigation."

"Thanks for the warning. Goodbye, Kathy!"

CHAPTER 15

A PIECE OF ADVICE

Two days later, James flies down to Houston and is sitting outside Eisley's office, waiting to be called in. The investigation into him and Sam has him worried. Hartley is out for blood, and he needs to be stopped. It's an all-out war, and James has to fight dirty.

The secretary looks up at him. "Mr. Eisley will see you now."

"Thank you," he says, and walks into the office.

The big man points to a chair. "I hope you make it fast, Coppi. I've got a really busy schedule today."

James takes a seat. "This shouldn't take long. Thanks for taking the time to see me on such short notice."

"What's this all about?"

"I need a favor."

"A favor?" Eisley gets louder. "You must have some pair of balls, coming in here and asking for a favor. You were about to ruin me."

James smiles. "Yeah, but I didn't, did I?"

"That's because I had to give the banks the stock I have in my company as collateral. Your audit became moot after that." Eisley pauses. "Anyway, we had a deal. The banks withdraw the audit, and you don't issue the report. That was our agreement. Are you backing out of the deal? Because, James, in Texas, we don't back out of an understanding. When a man gives his word, he keeps it!"

James smiles broadly. "Phil, I'm not from Texas. My wife is, but I'm not—I was born in Italy, and among Italians, when a man does you a favor, the other man owes him one. That's understood. You don't ask for a favor if you don't want to keep that bargain. I'm here today to collect on that debt."

Eisley's lips tighten, and he spits out, "You are a no-good motherfucker, you know that? I've got a good mind to throw you out of the fucking office."

James smiles. "Yeah, no, that wouldn't be a good move on your part. Not if you don't want the results of my investigation into your oil wells to leak out. Are you going to listen to my proposition?"

Eisley sits there, glaring at James. Finally, he barks, "What do you want?"

"You have Senator Hartley in your pocket. His wife is on your board of directors. I'm also pretty sure that Hartley made a substantial amount of money on the IPO when your company went public." James leans forward and rests his hands on Eisley's desk. "What I want, Phil, what I need, is documentation on all the transactions that you did with Hartley, his wife, and any other of Hartley's family. I want all the Hartley dealings with you—every last one."

"What will you do with this information when you have it?"

"Give it to the district attorney."

Eisley nearly comes out of his seat. "Are you fucking crazy? Do you want me to get locked up?"

James sits back in his chair. "No, Phil, nothing is happening to anyone. If this is played right, that information that you give me will never see the light of day. It'll be buried."

"What if it doesn't get buried?"

"Phil, you really have no choice. Either you hand over those documents, or I make the report on your oil companies public."

"Isn't there another way? Maybe I can talk to Hartley. Get him to back off."

"No, I don't want Hartley to know what I'm doing. That weasel will try to find a way to worm out of his predicament. And, by the way, don't think for one second that Hartley wouldn't turn on you, too."

Eisley rubs his chin. "What do you need?"

"As I said, Phil, all the documents concerning Hartley and his family that passed through you and your companies. Every last one."

"When do you need it by?"

James stands up. "Two weeks."

Eisley stands up. "You know, James, let me offer you a piece of advice. You're messing with some very dangerous and powerful people. I'd be very careful and watch my back, if I were you."

James smiles at Eisley. "Thanks for the advice but I already know how dangerous and malicious these people are." He looks into Eisley's face. "So, can I expect everything in two weeks?"

Eisley nods. "Yes! What choice do I have? You got me over a barrel. How sure are you that the DA won't do anything with the information?"

James stands up. "Absolutely sure. There's no upside for the DA to pursue this case." James looks intently into Eisley's face. "All the transactions, Phil. Every last one. Don't leave anything out, or the deal is off. You got that?"

"Yeah, yeah, I got it."

After James leaves, Phil gets on the phone. "We have a problem," he says when he gets the man on the line. "This fellow Coppi is making more demands."

"What kind of demands?" The man says.

Phil fills the man in on the conversation he just concluded with James.

"Will this be a problem for you?" the man asks.

"Maybe," Phil answers. "But we really don't have much choice, do we, Mr. President?"

"I guess everyone was wrong when they said Coppi could be dealt with," the President says.

"What do you want me to do about this latest problem?" Phil asks.

"Continue to cooperate with Coppi for the time being, and try to stall him as long as possible. I'll see if I can come up with an idea on how to take care of him."

• • • • • • • • • ● • • • • • • • • • •

Billingsley greets James at the door when he gets home from Houston that night, telling him that Ernie Bauer called and wants a call back.

James is in the study when he has Ernie on the phone.

"What's up, Ernie? What's so urgent?" James says.

"The warlord Benga reached out to us," Ernie says. "He asked to sit down with us again. He says we can work out all of our differences and come up with an accommodation suitable to both parties."

"Yeah, right. Another meeting. What does Benga take us for, a bunch of fools?"

"Benga said that he'd meet us anywhere, and he suggested Kinshasa—I don't think we should dismiss the offer. His side took quite a beating. Benga may be serious this time. We can pick a site that has full security."

James quiets for a moment. "Well, if we could come to an agreement with Benga, that would certainly make our life easier. I've got nothing against Benga and his forces as long as he leaves us and the mines alone." He lets out a breath. "Work out the details of the meeting and get back to me."

Sam comes walking into the study. "What happened to you? You got home and didn't even come to say hello."

James gets up and walks over, giving her a kiss. "I'm sorry—I had an urgent call from Ernie Bauer."

"Everything all right?"

"Yes, he was just giving me an update."

Sam gives him a stern stare. "You're not going to Africa again, are you?"

"No, I don't have any current plans for any trips. You're stuck having me around." James stretches and yawns. "It's late and I'm beat, I can't wait to hit the sack, it's been a long day."

CHAPTER 16

THE WATER BROKE

James is in a deep sleep for about an hour when Sam gives him a shove. "James, wake up. My water broke."

"That means nothing, honey. Go back to sleep," he says somnolently.

Sam shoves him harder and yells, "James, wake up! My water broke and the bed is all wet!"

James jumps up and leaps out of bed, running to Sam's side. "When did that happen?"

"I don't know." Sam sits up. "It's the wetness that woke me. Can you help me up? I'd like to get to the bathroom."

"Shouldn't we get going to the hospital?" James helps Sam to her feet.

"Let me clean up a little. Get me some clothes."

"Forget the clothes, just put on a robe. It's three o'clock in the morning; no one will see you."

"No, I need to clean up and take off these wet clothes."

James walks her into the bathroom and pulls out towels from the closet.

"What are you doing with the towels?" she asks.

"To put down in the car seat for the ride to the hospital. I'll be right back—I'll get your robe." James leaves the bedroom and knocks on Billingsley's door.

A few moments later, the butler peaks out. "Billingsley, call Dr. Donovan and tell him that Sam and I are on our way to the hospital."

"Is it time?" Billingsley asks.

James smiles. "Yes, Billingsley, it's time. The baby is coming. Please call the doctor." James runs back in the bedroom and fetches Sam's robe. He knocks on the bathroom door. "Are you ready?"

"Yes," Sam answers. "Please give me a hand."

James walks in and places the robe around Sam's shoulders. "Are you having contractions?"

"I had a small one just now."

"We better start out."

James looks over at Sam on the drive to the hospital. "How are you holding out?"

"I'm doing okay."

"Any more contractions?"

"Yes, but they're still far apart."

James parks the car in front of the emergency room door. "I'll run in and bring you a wheelchair."

"That's not necessary," she says. "I can walk."

"Stay here and wait." James opens the car door. "It'll only take a minute." He runs into the hospital, coming out with a wheelchair a few moments later. "Let me help you out." James opens the door and helps Sam into the chair. "Are you comfortable?"

"Yes, I'm good."

· · · · · · · ● · · · · · · ·

Four hours later, the nurse is wiping Sam's face with a moist towel.

"You're becoming quite good at this, Samantha," Dr. Donovan says.

"Yeah, well, this is it for me," Sam answers. "This baby is the last."

Dr. Donovan smiles. "No, I don't believe so, Samantha. I've got you down for five."

"No way, doc. It's not happening." She looks around the room. "Where's my husband?"

The doctor looks around. "I don't know—the last time I saw James, he had the baby in his arms."

"I'll go outside and find him," the nurse says.

A few moments later, James comes back into the room, smiling broadly and with the baby in his arms.

"There's James and Deborah," Dr. Donovan says.

James gives Sam a side glance. "Deborah?"

Sam smiles and lips, "Please?"

James leans over and gives her a kiss. "Deborah is just fine, it's a wonderful name. You do know they'll call her Debbie?"

"They'll call her what I allow them to call her," she says. "May I hold her, please?"

James carefully hands her the child.

"What's that black and blue mark on your arm?" Sam asks as she takes the baby.

"That's from you squeezing me when you were in labor." James turns his arm to the other side. "And those are the claw marks from your nails."

Sam lets out a laugh. "I'm sorry!"

James waves his hand and gives Sam another kiss. "Don't worry; it's nothing compared with what you went through."

"You should feed the baby," Dr. Donovan tells Sam.

James looks up. "Isn't the breastfeeding too soon?"

"No, the sooner the better," the doctor says. "For both baby and mother."

"Sam, I'm getting a cup of coffee," James says. "Would you like something?"

"No," she replies, taking one of her breasts out of the hospital gown.

Except for Sam with baby Deborah in her arms, the room is empty when James comes back with his coffee. James reaches into his pocket and takes out a jewelry box.

"Here." He hands the box to Sam.

"What's this?"

"It's a present from me and Deborah. Open it!"

"Take the baby." She hands Deborah to James. Sam opens the box and takes out a string of white pearls. Her eyes moisten and she looks up at James. "They're magnificent. Thank you."

James leans over, giving her a kiss and placing the baby in her face. "No, thank you for my present—she's absolutely beautiful."

• • • • • • • • ● • • • • • • • • •

The ranch is a mad scene the following week. Sam's family is visiting to have a look at the new baby, and the place is about to burst. In addition to Sam's parents, her two brothers and two sisters are staying at the ranch, and with them are fourteen of their children. To make matters worse, some of the higher-ranking employees of the company are at the ranch for an emergency meeting. The home gets so noisy that James moves the business meeting from his study to the patio.

James is coming back inside from the backyard when he grabs ahold of his daughter Molly, who is running down the hall with two of her cousins.

"Molly, that's enough!" he shouts. "Stop running through the house. Take your cousins out front and play out there."

James walks into the parlor where Sam is breastfeeding little Deborah with a blanket over the baby.

James looks at Sam's siblings, sitting in the parlor. "Can some of you get off your behinds and get control of your children? They're running roughshod through the place." James shakes his head. "Eleven thousand acres, and they have to play in the house."

A few of the mothers stand up and leave the room.

"Are you almost done?" James asks Sam. "We're waiting for you to wrap up the meeting."

"A few more minutes," Sam replies.

"Why do you need Samantha?" Mrs. Powers asks. "Why can't you finish the meeting, James?"

"Because this is an important meeting," James tells her. "And I may need her advice. Sam is my partner in business as well as at home."

"James, while you're waiting for Sam, can you give us a few minutes of your time?" Reverend Powers asks. "My son Michael has a topic he'd like to discuss with you."

James takes a seat and looks over at Michael. "What's up?"

Michael clears his throat and leans forward in his seat. "James, as you may know, I'm very involved in the Dallas, Fort Worth community. As well as having my own church, I'm also on several committees promoting Christian causes."

James smiles dryly. "Michael, I'm well aware of the work you're doing. Sam and I pay for a lot of that work. I've got the feeling that you're about to hit us up for some more freaking dough."

"James, your mouth!" Sam calls out.

James looks over at Sam and creases his brow. "What? What did I say? Since when is 'freaking' a bad word?"

"James, you're quite right, I am asking you for money," Michael continues. "But it's for a real worthy cause, I can assure you."

"Michael, do you have any idea how many worthy causes Sam and I donate to? And don't forget how much we contribute to you and your father's ministries every year."

"Yes, James, I'm well aware of your philanthropic efforts," Michael says. "And, believe me, I'm extremely grateful for what you and my sister do for us. But this is really important; can you hear me out?"

James looks over at Sam. "Do you know anything about this?"

"This is the first that I'm hearing about it."

James looks back at Michael. "Okay, let me hear your proposal."

"Texas Christian University is looking for an endowment for a project that they'd like to do. When this venture is complete, the trustees of the university believe that the undertaking will put the school on the national map."

"What's the project?" James asks.

"The university would like to build the James and Samantha Coppi Sports Complex. The place will be beautiful. It includes an indoor arena for their basketball and volleyball games. A state-of-the-art workout gym. New lockers for the athletes."

"How much will this cost?"

"Eight million dollars."

"Eight million!" James nearly comes out of his chair. "Are you freaking kidding me?" He looks over at Sam. "Yes, and I did say freaking! Believe me, you don't want to know the other words running through my head right now."

"James, you wouldn't have to come up with the entire eight million," Michael clarifies. "The university will float a bond issue covering most of the amount that's needed to build the place. The school simply needs a donor to pledge and guarantee the payments on the bond and cover the remainder."

"Oh, it's that simple." James smirks at Michael. "Thanks for clarifying. I didn't know that. In that case, sign me up for a couple of these projects."

"James, there's no need for sarcasm," Sam warns him.

James looks over at her. "Do you have any idea what your brother is proposing? Have you any clue of what we'll be shelling out? Interest rates on borrowed money is ten percent. Just the money to pay the interest will be around eight hundred thousand a year."

"James, the interest rate won't be ten percent," Michael explains. "The university will issue a tax-free bond. What with the tax credits and accelerated depreciation, I'm led to believe that the true interest is closer to three percent."

"That's still two hundred and forty grand a year," James argues. "And that doesn't even include the payment on the principal due on the loan. What happens if the university can't pay? Sam and I will be stuck with the bill." James sits back in his chair. "I'll pass!"

"May I ask why?" Reverend Powers gets into the discussion. "You've done this before. The James and Samantha Coppi Medical Research Center at Texas Tech, for one."

James turns to his father-in-law and, in a more temperate voice, says, "Yes, you're right, Sir. And I must remind you, that was also done at your suggestion. Sam and I have also built a medical wing at the hospital here in Colorado Springs. Those are worthy causes, but what you're proposing now is different."

James takes a breath to collect himself. "This new proposition is just a sports center to make a bunch of jocks and their fans happy. I'm not dishing out this kind of dough for people to entertain themselves."

James looks over at Sam. "How come you're not getting into this? Are you for this idea?"

Sam smiles. "No, I've nothing to say. You're making the point quite nicely." Sam turns to her brother. "I'm sorry, Michael, but I agree with James. This is not something that James and I should be contributing our money to. There are far more worthy causes in need of our resources."

Sam closes up her blouse when the baby is done feeding and gets up. "Let me hand the baby to Gilda and we'll go out for our meeting."

As they're heading out of the parlor, Billingsley stops him. "Mr. Coppi, your mother is in the foyer. She said that she'd like a word with you."

Sam and James head for the foyer. "Hello, Mom," he says. "Billingsley said you wanted to speak to me?"

Mother Coppi looks over at Sam. "Hello, Samantha." She walks over and gives the baby a kiss. "*La bambina e' bella*, just like her mother." Mamma turns to James. "Giacomo," she says, referring to James by the Italian translation of his name. "Father Mazzola wants to know when are you putting in the new roof at the church that you promised to do?"

James shakes his head and looks over at Sam. "This never ends." He turns back to his mother. "Mom, I told you, I'll send Tomaso over with a crew as soon as they have some time. The men are busy working on my real estate development. Or do you want the men to stop in the middle of what they're doing and rush over to the church?

"Tell Father Mazz that I'll have Tomaso give him a call." He gives his mom a kiss. "I've got to get back, there're people waiting for me." James turns to Sam. "I'll see you outside as soon as you have the baby situated. Please don't be long."

• • • • • • • • ● ● ● • • • • •

"I'm sorry, guys," James says when he's out in the courtyard. "My in-laws are visiting, and this place is completely crazy trying to keep up with everybody. Sam is on her way, so we should be finishing up shortly." He pauses when the back door opens. "In fact, here she is right now."

The men stand when Sam comes out. "Please, gentlemen, stay seated. Make yourselves comfortable."

"How's baby Deborah doing?" Vernon asks.

"Little Deborah is doing just fine, thank you, Vern." Sam turns to the rest of the men. "And thank all of you for the flowers, balloons, and well wishes."

"Okay, Vern, now that we're all here, let's get started," James says. "What's this last item that you wanted to discuss? What's so urgent?"

"Our company has been invited to appear in front of the Senate Intelligence Committee to testify about our dealings in South America."

"Already," James remarks. "That Hartley doesn't waste any time. When are we supposed to testify?"

"In three weeks," Maxwell says.

"It's an invitation, not a subpoena?" James asks.

"It's an invitation," Maxwell answers.

James shrugs. "What if we refuse? Maxwell, you're the company's legal counsel. What if we don't want to testify? Force their hand. What can the committee do about our refusal?"

"I'm pretty sure that they'll issue a subpoena if we refuse," Maxwell lets him know.

"So, who cares?" James says. "Let the committee issue a subpoena. Why make it easy on them?"

"James, you really don't want to appear in front of this committee as an adversary," Rodney brings forward. "Right now, the Republicans on the committee are on our side. Some of the Democrats, too. Only this fellow Hartley is pressing the point.

"If we become uncooperative, we'll piss off a lot of the other senators. It's better if you show up voluntarily and provide the appearance that you're fully accommodating."

"Maxwell, are they requesting that James show, or the company?" Sam asks.

"What's the difference?" Maxwell remarks. "I'm quite sure they expect James to be there. After all, he's in charge."

"Why can't Vernon go?" Sam questions. "Vernon is the president and runs the day-to-day operations."

Maxwell looks over at Vernon and back to Sam. "I guess Vernon could attend."

Vernon looks over at James. "James, I don't believe that me appearing is a good idea. I've never been in front of a Congressional committee—I have no experience in these types of affairs. You, on the other hand, have been on in front of these committees dozens of times."

James smiles. "No, I agree with Sam. You should go, Vern. Besides, how will you ever get experience if you don't start attending these inquiries?"

"But I don't know anything about what's happening in South America. How will I be able to answer any of their questions?"

Sam looks over at Vernon. "That's very simple. You'll just answer that you don't know anything."

"All right, that's settled," James says. "Vernon, you'll attend the hearing. Contact Raymond Marr, our attorney in Washington. Marr will prep you on what you can expect." James looks over at Maxwell. "Contact the Senate committee and tell them we need more time—another three weeks. That'll give Vernon more time to get ready."

He looks around at the men. "Is there anything else?" When no one answers, he stands up. "Good. Sam and I need to get back to our guests."

When they get back inside, he gives Sam a kiss. "Thank you. That was absolutely brilliant, suggesting that Vernon attend the meeting instead of me."

"Don't be so happy. I'm sure Hartley will call you back when he realizes that Vernon knows nothing."

James lets out a laugh. "I'm sure Hartley will. I'd love to be there to see his face when Vernon shows up instead of me. Anyway, it'll take a while for Hartley to get his act together and call me back. I'll at least have the summer off. Which, by the way, I want to speak to you about." He stops her. "I want to spend the summer at our chateau in France. We haven't been there in two years."

"Oh, James, do we have to? It's just too much for me, what with the baby and all."

"Please, can we go?" James puts on his sorry face. "I have to get away from all these leeches asking for money. Please? I really need this vacation."

Sam walks up to James and gives him a kiss. "All right, we'll go."

CHAPTER 17

THE RAPTOR

The next morning, Sam walks into James's study and sees he's at his desk, speaking to Billingsley.

"What are you guys doing?" she asks.

"We're planning our trip to France," James answers.

"Do you need me? I was heading over to the guest house to say goodbye to Michael and his family."

"Not right now, maybe later."

Sam is walking towards the guesthouse when she notices her brother Michael coming out.

A smile forms on his face. "I thought you were letting me leave without saying goodbye."

Sam smiles widely. "Now, you know I'd never do that, little brother."

"Do you have some time?" he asks. "Walk with me a bit. Your place was so crowded, I hardly got to talk to you."

Sam gives him a sly grin. "You're not trying to hit me up again for the donation on that sports complex, are you?"

Michael laughs. "No, I'm done with that. Quite frankly, I wasn't too keen on that idea, either. I'm with you and James—there are far more worthy projects in need." Michael offers her a side glance. "Which, by the way, I'll be calling soon to discuss."

Sam forces out a laugh. "I'm glad that we're leaving for France."

As they walk, Michael looks out at the rows of paddocks with horses munching peacefully on the Colorado grass. "This is one beautiful place you have here. This ranch is absolutely magnificent—I just love the Southwestern theme for the barns. Pink stucco walls, red tiled roofs, and emerald-green window shutters. Those colors work beautifully in Colorado, it's perfect."

"James designed most of the landscape. I did our home and the guesthouse."

Michael has another look around. There are ranch hands working out in the field. "Well, you guys did a marvelous job."

Michael stops walking and looks at Sam. His tone is serious. "You know, Sam, I'm so proud of you. So proud of all that you've accomplished."

"James is responsible for all of it."

"No, I don't agree." They begin walking once more. "James doesn't do much without involving you. I saw yesterday that he wouldn't finish up the business meeting unless you were there. You guys make a good team. Everything you've achieved, you've done together. Both of you deserve the credit."

Michael stops once more. "I remember the day you left home. It was six months after you graduated high school—the day you had that massive fight with Daddy. You took off from Lorenzo for Colorado Springs with eighty-seven dollars in your pocket—I was so worried about you.

"And, of course, I was really dejected. My big sister, leaving." He gives her a smile. "Who would protect me from the bullies in school?"

Sam smiles back. "I guess you did all right; you made it."

"That's because I told everyone that you were only leaving temporarily, and you were coming back."

They lean on a fence looking out at one of the paddocks. Michael points to the sky. "Is that a falcon?"

Sam looks up. "Yes, I believe it's a peregrine."

"Did you see that?" Michael yells out. "The falcon nosedived about a hundred yards and plucked that bird right out of the sky!" Michael shakes his head. "That was truly amazing!"

"If you like falconry, the next time you come out here you should stay at the Broadmoor, they have a program that you can go falconry. The hotel has peregrine's that have been tamed."

They walk a bit without saying anything and eventually Michael turns to her. "How are you getting along with James?"

When she doesn't answer, Michael asks. "What's the matter, sis? Is anything wrong?"

"It's these dangerous expeditions James takes," she says and looks at Michael. "I don't know why he keeps going on these trips. We have good people working for us; he doesn't have to go. He keeps putting himself at risk. It's as if he doesn't care what happens to him. James has a family and four children; doesn't he ever think of us?"

"Did you speak to him about your concerns?" Michael asks.

"Yes, I have, but he always poo poos my fears." She looks away toward the paddocks for a moment. "Michael, can I tell you a story? Maybe you can make sense of James."

"All right, go ahead."

"James didn't have to go in the Army. He had a college deferment. He gave up his deferment to get drafted. When he was in the Army, James had a soft job driving a colonel around, but he kept getting into trouble. Eventually the Army got fed up with his antics and shipped him off to Vietnam."

"So you believe he was purposefully trying to go to a war?" Michael says.

"Yes, that's exactly what I believe!" She shrugs. "And I still think he's constantly seeking out these dangers. That's what I don't understand. Why does James do that? He has a loving family."

"Sis, some men are just built that way. These men have to have a challenge, like race car drivers and mountain climbers. The men feed on that adrenaline rush when facing danger. James may be one of those types of guys."

Michael turns her to him. "That doesn't mean James doesn't love you or the family, it's just in his personality. That's what makes him so successful in the business world: the ability to assess the risk, and he's not afraid to take a chance. He's like that raptor we just saw soaring through the skies searching for prey to feed his family. And just like that falcon, at the end of the hunt, he always returns to his nest."

Michael takes Sam's hand. "Sis, you always get down on yourself after you have a baby. Stop worrying; this feeling will pass, just like it always does."

"Come on, let's head back, I want to help your wife pack," she says. When they get a few steps, she looks over at Michael. "I promise you this, Michael: that bird is getting his wings clipped. I'm not putting up with anymore of James's adventures. It's time he comes back down to the ground."

CHAPTER 18

AT THE FOOT OF THE ALPS

Five weeks later, Vernon and Maxwell are walking into attorney Raymond Marr's office in Washington DC. It's the day before Vernon is scheduled to speak in front of the Senate Intelligence Committee. Marr will spend the day advising Vernon on what to expect and prepping him for his testimony.

The big man, Marr, comes from behind his desk and approaches the men when they walk in. With a huge smile on his face, he extends his hand. "Maxwell, it's so nice to see you again."

After shaking Maxwell's hand, Raymond turns to Vernon and extends his hand. "You must be Mr. Dixon." He shakes Vernon's hand. "It's a pleasure to meet you." Raymond points to a man sitting on the couch. "This is Ted Gibbs; he'll be assisting us in this affair."

"Gentlemen, it's a pleasure." Ted waves to the men.

Raymond points to the chairs. "Please, have a seat. Can I get you guys anything? A cup of coffee?"

"No, we're good," Vernon answers, and takes a seat.

Raymond walks to the other side of the desk and takes a chair. He looks over at Maxwell.

"So, what's this all about?" Raymond asks. "James told me this Senator Hartley is being a pain in the ass." Raymond looks over at Vernon. "Which means that this won't be your typical committee meeting—you're in for a bit of a rough going. Bring me up to speed. This affair has to do with Bolivia?"

"It's a little more than Bolivia," Maxwell explains. "Hartley wants to hand the new administration a black eye right off the bat. He wants to handcuff their foreign policy and make the administration look inept. We're caught in the middle of a political tug of war. The new guys in power are looking for our help, and the old guard wants us to back off."

Raymond scratches his chin. "I see." He quiets for a moment. "All right, what are you guys doing in Bolivia? It's my understanding that you're assisting rebels."

"Not directly," Vernon answers.

"What does that mean, 'Not directly'? Just what is your involvement?"

Vernon clears his throat. "Our dealing is with a company headquartered in Chile. Our business deals are strictly with that firm."

"Okay, I get the picture. Now, who asked you to get involved? Who set this up?"

"A Colonel Chase and retired General Farnwell. We also spoke to the Secretaries of Defense and State, and both of those gentlemen assured us that we had their support."

"What are you expected to supply this Chilean company?

"Anything that they ask for."

"Including arms?

Vernon smiles. "Anything they ask for!"

"How much have you supplied so far?"

"I don't know. The project is being handled by one of our overseas companies. James gave orders that only the people directly involved in the undertaking know the details."

"What about the money?" Ted calls out from the couch. "How do you get paid?"

"Through the Chilean enterprise."

Raymond shakes his head. "I'm sure the Chileans are doing the actual payments, but where are the Chileans getting the funds to pay you?"

Vernon shrugs. "I don't know. Colonel Chase is in charge of that part of the deal. We've been led to believe that the funds are not coming from the United States, and it's not taxpayer money."

Raymond looks over at his associate. "What do you think, Ted?"

"James was right when he spoke to us last week. This Colonel Chase could be a problem." Ted looks over at Vernon. "Not to worry, Chase won't be a problem for you tomorrow. In fact, I don't believe you'll have any problems at all in front of the committee. Just follow our instructions and you'll do just fine. Are you ready to get started, or do you need a short break?"

"I'm ready," Vernon answers. "Let's get started."

At ten to nine that night, Raymond stands up and stretches. "Well, that's it, guys. We're done." Raymond smiles at Vernon. "I'm sorry we worked you through lunch and dinner, but I wanted to make sure we covered everything."

"It's quite all right," Vernon replies. "Is there anything that I need to do between now and tomorrow?"

"Just look over your notes that you took today and get a good night's rest." Raymond smiles warmly. "And don't worry, you'll do just fine. Make sure you're at the Senate chambers by 9:30. The hearing is scheduled to start at ten, but they never begin on time. Still, we can't be the ones that are late and holding up the proceedings."

· · · · · · · · ● ● ● ● ● ● ● ● ● · · · · ·

The next morning, Vernon and Raymond are sitting outside the committee room, waiting to be called into the hearing. Three men wearing olive green drab military uniforms walk up to Vernon.

"You work for Mr. Coppi, don't you, señor?" one of the men says.

Vernon looks at the man. "Why do you ask?"

The man smiles slyly. "I'm Presidente Echeverria, I have a *mensaje* for your boss, Señor Coppi. *Buen yungue no teme el martillo.* A good anvil does not fear the hammer."

Vernon looks over at Raymond as the men walk away. "What was that all about?"

Raymond gives him a wry grin. "I'm not sure, but I believe he just threatened James." Raymond stands up. "Come on, they're calling us in."

Vernon has just finished being sworn in for the hearing, and just sat down.

"Where's James Coppi?" Senator Hartley asks immediately. "Didn't Mr. Coppi believe that this was an important enough matter to attend personally?"

"Mr. Coppi is in Europe on an extended and much-needed vacation," Raymond, who is sitting to the right of Vernon, replies. "Mr. Dixon is the company's president and is well qualified to answer any of your questions."

"No; I'm sorry, Mr. Marr, I don't agree with you," Hartley's voice is brusque. "I know how Mr. Coppi runs his operation. Nothing happens without his say-so. Mr. Coppi should've been here today."

"Well, Senator, we'll just have to leave it that we disagree," Raymond rebuts. "I'm quite sure that this committee will be satisfied with Mr. Dixon."

"Can we move on?" one of the senators from the opposing party cuts in. "Hartley, if you wanted Coppi in person, you should've made your request clearer. Now, Mr. Dixon is here, and Mr. Coppi is not. I'm quite sure that Mr. Dixon can answer our questions. Let's get this meeting going; we have other business matters to attend to."

Hartley turns to Dixon. "Mr. Dixon, are you aware of a piece of legislation that was recently passed? Legislation forbidding the use of taxpayer money for the purpose of arming rebels who are trying to overthrow the legitimate government in Bolivia."

"Yes, I'm aware of the legislation."

"And you, and all of your firms that are under your control, are in compliance with this bill. Even your overseas operations."

"Yes, I believe so."

"What business does your company have in Bolivia?"

"Senator, I'm not aware of any business that we have in Bolivia."

"None, whatsoever?"

Vernon pours himself a glass of water from the pitcher sitting in front of him. "None that I'm aware of," he says, after taking a sip.

"How about Bolivian nationals, including those that may be domiciled outside of Bolivia? Individuals domiciled in other countries in South America."

"Senator, we do business with many other companies in South America, but I wouldn't know the nationalities of the principals of those firms. Nor would I know the nationalities of their employees. It's possible that some are of Bolivian descent."

The questioning continues in this manner for several hours. Hartley and his Democratic cohorts question Vernon vigorously and try to press him into revealing something that they can use.

Attorney Marr continues to interject and object to most of the line of questioning.

On the rare occasion that Vernon does say something, he supplies nothing useful. The refrain of "I don't know" is used continuously by Vernon throughout the hearing. As the proceedings are about to close, Hartley takes over the microphone.

"Mr. Dixon, I'm extremely disappointed in your performance at this hearing today. You're either unprepared, incompetent, or evasive. Possibly all three. You said that you're here to cooperate and answer our questions, but you provided nothing useful at all."

Raymond speaks up again. "Senator, that's an awfully unfair characterization. Mr. Dixon answered your questions truthfully and to the best of his knowledge. It's not his fault if Mr. Dixon didn't say what you wanted to hear."

Hartley fires back. "I'm sending another invitation that Mr. Coppi appear before us."

"Senator, that'll be a complete waste of this committee's time," Raymond debates. "Mr. Coppi's answers will be no different than what you heard from Mr. Dixon today."

"We'll see about that! Tell Mr. Coppi to expect an invite."

"Yes, I'll be sure to relay your message, but any appearance will have to wait until Mr. Coppi returns from his holiday in France. That won't be until the end of summer."

After the meeting is adjourned, Raymond turns to Vernon. "Good job! James couldn't have done better."

• • • • • • • • ● • • • • • • • •

A few days after Vernon's testimony in Washington, James is unpacking the van that he rented for the day. The family and his maids Gilda and Guadalupe are at the foot of the Alps. They are inside a national park some five miles from the village of Aix les Bains in France. James is setting up the bassinet.

"Are those legs strong enough?" Sam asks.

"Yes." James pushes the bassinet down with his hands. "See, it's fine! And it's in the shade, so the sun won't be a problem for the baby."

Sam places the baby in the bassinet and tucks the blankets around her. Despite being the middle of July, the temperature is a little cool this morning. Sam has a look around after Deborah is situated in the crib.

"This is nice—you picked a beautiful spot for our picnic," she says, staring up at the mountains. "The mountains look different than ours back home."

James stops setting down the blankets and looks around. "That's because the Alps are millions of years younger than the Rockies. Our Rockies are rounded from rain erosion. The Alps are more jagged—they're a lot like the Tetons in Wyoming."

Michael tucks at his leg. "Daddy, I need to go to the bathroom."

"Just go behind the tree."

"I have to do number two!"

James turns to Sam. "Can you take care of this? I have to unpack the car."

"No! I'm sure Michael would prefer his father. I'll unload the car."

James sneers at her. "You know, we wouldn't be debating about this if you'd taught him how to properly wipe his ass."

"Well, here's your chance to teach your son how to do it correctly." Sam smiles and heads for the car.

"Bring me the roll of toilet paper and a bag," James calls to her.

"Come on, let's go," he says to Michael when Sam hands him what he needs. "You're doing the wiping," he barks at his son. "And you'll keep wiping until you're absolutely clean!"

When James comes back, Sam smiles slyly. "How was it?"

"None of your business," he snaps. "If you cared so much, you should've taken care of it."

James turns to his older children. "All right, gather around. Here's the plan. You guys will go with Gilda and Guadalupe to pick flowers to bring home with us tonight to put in our vases. No yellow or white flowers. Only red, blue, or purple. You got that?"

"Yes, Daddy," the children reply in unison.

"Aren't you and Mommy coming?" Molly asks.

"No, we need to stay here and look after Baby Deborah," he answers. "You listen to Gilda and Guadalupe." He points to Michael. "And no wandering off like you did yesterday at the lavender fields."

"Yes, Daddy."

"Molly, you help Christopher; he's too young to do this on his own." James turns to the women. "Please have the children back in two hours for their lunch."

"This is nice," Sam repeats once more as she looks around. "This whole month in France has been wonderful, I'm glad you insisted on the trip, it was so delightful to have you around and not travel." She turns her head to the bassinet as Deborah starts fussing. "She must be hungry." Sam gets up to get the baby. She sits back down, opens her blouse, and frees one of her breasts, placing the baby in position to suckle. "You never told me. How did Vernon make out at the hearing yesterday?"

"Just as expected, Vernon didn't tell them a thing." James says, omitting the threat made by Echeveria. "Completely frustrated Hartley. Apparently, Hartley threatened Marr and demanded that I show. Hartley was thrown for a loop when Marr informed him that I was away for the summer."

"Won't you still have to testify when you get back?"

"Who knows? Two months is like an eternity in the political world. Anything can come up between now and then."

"What about the investigation on who shot Cardiz and Billy?" she asks. "Do you have any leads?"

"No, nothing. We hit a dead end—all we were able to determine is that they were shot by a Colt 1903 .32 caliber revolver

"How's Cardiz doing?"

James looks away for a moment. "The same," he says, and turns back to her. "He's still paralyzed from the waist down. The poor guy is stuck with two bad solutions. If he does the surgery, he might die. If he doesn't, he'll stay paralyzed."

"I feel awful," she says. "Is there nothing that we can do?"

James shrugs. "No, nothing. It's up to the doctors. I'm continuing to pay his salary so that the family won't be hurt financially. Other than that, there's nothing to do. It's up to the doctors and the man upstairs."

James stands up. "I've got to take a leak!"

Sam is putting the baby back in her crib when James gets back. James sits back down on the blanket and pulls her to him, kissing her neck softly. Sam pulls back.

"What are you doing?" she asks.

"What do you think I'm doing? I want to make love to you. This spot is perfect."

"What if the children get back?"

"The kids won't be back for another two hours."

Sam turns to look to where the children headed off—there's no one in sight. "All right," she says.

Sam is on her back, breathless, as they've just finished. James has just fallen off her and is also on his back, gasping for air. She turns to him. "Wow!" she says. "That was intense."

James looks at her and smiles. "You're not kidding."

Sam leans over and gives him a kiss. Through the corner of her eye, she catches a glimpse of the kids from a distance, running toward them. She shoves James. "Hurry up, get dressed. The children are coming."

James sits up and starts putting on his clothes. "What the hell are they doing back so soon?"

Molly comes running over first. "Daddy, look at all the flowers that I picked."

"They're beautiful, dear," he says, looking over at the bouquet of red and purple flowers.

Michael runs up. "Look at mine, Daddy!"

"Your flowers are beautiful too, Michael."

Little Christopher runs up with three flowers in his hand. James walks over and lifts him up. "What have you got there, Chris?"

Christopher smiles. "Flowers."

"They're beautiful." James reaches out. "Can I have the flowers?"

The boy pulls the flowers away from James. "No! Mommy!"

"I'm sorry to be back so soon," Gilda says when the two women arrive. "The children wanted to show you the flowers."

James puts Christopher down. "That's all right, Gilda. You and Guadalupe take a break; Sam and I will take over from here." He turns to the children. "Come on, guys, put the flowers down on the blanket and let's head back out. There're a lot more flowers out there that need picking."

"Daddy, I'm tired," Michael lets out.

"Come on, hop on. I'll give you a piggyback ride."

Christopher stretches out his arms. "Me!"

"You go to Mommy; you gave her your flowers. Let her carry you!"

"What about me?" Molly yells out.

"You'll have to walk for now. You can switch with your brother Michael in a while." James turns to the women. "We should be back in about an hour."

James is looking up at the regal mountain range as they walk off, and a huge smile spreads across his face.

"What are you smiling about?" Sam asks.

"This is such a perfect day," he replies. "Making love to my one and only and picking flowers with my children at the foot of the Alps."

As they are walking James catches a glimpse of a black Peugeot with two men pulling up about a quarter mile from where he left his car. The Peugeot has stopped and the engine is turned off. A few steps later, James has another look. The car and the men have not moved. He takes Michael off his back and turns to Sam.

"You guys keep going. I've got to do number two and I need to go back to the car and get toilet paper."

Sam turns to him. "How will you know how to find us?"

James points. "Just keep walking in that direction, I'll catch up with you."

Gilda and Guadalupe are sitting on the blanket next to the bassinet.

James smiles over at the ladies. "I need toilet paper."

James looks back at the two women when he gets to the car. They don't appear to be paying any attention to him. He opens the front passenger door and unlocks the glove compartment. There behind a stack of papers is the old faithful Smith and Wesson Model 52 semi-automatic. James pulls out the pistol and the magazine clip that is lying next to the piece. As he is loading the gun, he has another look back at the women on the blanket. The ladies are still not paying any attention to him. He lifts up the back of his shirt and tucks the gun in his pants.

He walks to the back and opens the trunk, taking out the roll of toilet paper. As he closes the hood, he has another peek at the two men in the car. The men are still parked in that same location; they have not moved at all. James walks past the women, smiling and waving the roll of paper. He keeps walking into a wooded area and turns to look at the Peugeot—the vehicle has not moved. The men are still sitting in the front seats. Casually, he strolls into the woods, circling his way to the back of the car.

A few hundred yards further, he emerges at the edge of the tree line—behind the car, as he had hoped. This will be the hard part: he will eventually have to come out of the woods. If the men notice him, there could be trouble.

James is beginning to doubt his plan. His baby Deborah and his household staff could be in danger. Finally, summoning up his resolve, he tosses away the roll of paper he still had in his hand and begins walking along the trees toward the vehicle. When he gets to about a hundred feet to the back of the Peugeot, he unfastens his gun from his back and decides to crawl the rest of the way on his belly.

With the gun pointing at the car, he crawls slowly toward the Peugeot. His plan is to take both men out if they come out of the car. He can feel his heart pounding in his chest. When he arrives in the street directly behind the vehicle, he lifts himself up on one knee. The men inside the car are talking in French. Crouching, he makes his way to the passenger side of the car. If the men are armed, it will be harder for the driver to pull his piece out. There's an elbow sticking out of the window, James puts the gun to the man's head.

"You move and I'll blow your fucking head off!" he orders.

The man peeks at him sideways but says nothing. The driver looks over at James.

James commands. "You try anything and your partner is dead and you will die right after him. Do you understand?"

The man nods.

"Do you speak English?" James asks.

"Yes," the guy answers.

"Good," he says. "Put your hands on the dashboard and kneel on your seats, facing forward toward the windshield."

After they comply, James starts patting the passenger down.

The driver turns to James. "We are not armed."

"Where are you guys from? You're not French."

"We are from Mali," he answers.

James smiles. "What are two handsome guys from Mali doing in this park?"

The men look at each other.

"You don't have much time. You better speak up, my finger on the trigger of this gun is getting itchy."

"We were hired to follow you," the driver says.

"Who hired you?"

"Zalenga."

"This Zalenga is from Mali?"

"No," the man shakes his head. "Zalenga is from Zaire."

"What does he want with me?"

The man removes his hand from the dashboard. "We don't know. We were to follow you and report back to Zalenga. That's all."

"Slowly, get out of the car," James says.

The passenger turns to James. "What?"

"I said, get out of the car!"

"Give me the key," James says when they are outside.

The driver gives him the key. James rolls up the windows, and locks the car.

He motions with his pistol away from the car. "Start walking, it's a long way back to town."

"It is very far," the man says.

"Yes, I know, and I don't care. When you get back tell Zalenga to come to my house tomorrow if he wants his car key back." He motions with the gun toward the road, away from where his women are sitting on their blanket. "Get going. If you start now, you should make it to town well before dark."

The next day, Sam walks in the study. "James, a man named Zalenga is in the waiting room. He came to see you."

James gets up from his desk and walks toward the door. Sam grabs his arm. "Who is he?"

"He's from Zaire. He asked for this meeting."

"Does he work for us?"

James shakes his head. "No. I don't even know who he is or what he wants. The only thing I know is that he's from Zaire."

James is walking down the hall to the waiting room. Sam is walking behind him. He turns. "Where do you think you're going?"

"With you. I want to hear what he wants."

"Sam, that's not a good idea. These men don't speak freely in front of women. I'll tell you everything when I get done."

She looks at him with a suspicious gaze.

He smiles, walks over, and gives her a kiss. "Everything, I promise."

James walks into the waiting room where a large man is standing. The man is wearing typical African dress that is Liputa style, which means 'bright colors.' In this instance, a red, orange, and long yellow, dashiki-style shirt.

A smile broadens Zalenga's face. "Mr. Coppi, it is a pleasure."

He can't figure out why the man is acting so happy to see him. "I wish I could say the same. Maybe after you tell me why you are tailing me. Who is your boss?"

Zalenga continues to smile. "As to the first, it's quite simple. I was hired to report on your movements while in France. As to the latter, I'm not at liberty to reveal my patron."

James is getting annoyed. "Did your men tell you what happened yesterday? They came very close to getting shot. Zalenga, I can promise you that if you don't tell me everything that I want to know, you won't last a week."

Zalenga takes a long look at James. "Mobutu," he lets out. "Mobutu is the one who hired me."

"Why does Mobutu want to know my affairs?"

"I don't know. My assignment was to tail you and report back where you went. Mobutu didn't tell me the reason, and I'm in no position to force him to reveal his motives."

James reaches into his pocket and pulls out a car key, handing it to Zalenga. "After you pick up your car in the park, tell Mobutu that you were discovered. Let that fat bastard know that if he wants to know what I'm up to, he can ask me directly."

Zalenga is about to reach for the key when James pulls it back. "Your assignment is over, am I clear? There'll be no more following me or my family!"

"It is understood."

James hands Zalenga the key.

Sam walks into the room after the man leaves. "Well?"

"He was hired by the President of Zaire to follow me." James starts to walk out.

Sam grabs his arm. "Why?"

"Zalenga didn't know why, he was just following orders." He releases her grip and walks away.

She runs after him and clutches his arm once more. "How did you know that he was following you?"

"I noticed his two men in the park yesterday."

"What?" she yells out. "There were men at the park? Where? Why didn't you tell me?"

James smiles. "There was nothing to worry about—I had the situation under control the whole time. No one was ever in any danger." He releases her grip and walks away quickly.

"Get back here!" she shrieks. "You've got a lot more explaining to do!"

CHAPTER 19

AN ATTEMPTED MURDER

A month later, the summer vacation is over and James is back in his office. He has been in a meeting all day with his management team. The last meeting is with Vernon, who once again is giving him a recap of his testimony in front of Hartley's committee.

James laughs. "You totally frustrated Hartley. I would've loved to have been there and seen his face when he saw that I didn't show."

"Don't look so glad, James. Hartley says he'll subpoena you." Vernon leans forward. "James, why are you taking this so lightly? Hartley is very powerful politically and he's out to get you."

James stands up and rubs the back of his neck. "You did a good job, Vern, really good." He looks over at Vernon. "Vern, I know what I'm up against with Hartley. I'm not being casual about the threat—I know just how ruthless and heartless guys like Hartley can be. Unfortunately, with my lifestyle, making enemies comes with the job. Hartley is another menace that I need to handle."

He looks at the clock on his desk 3:15. "I'm calling it a day. I'm tired—I guess I'm experiencing the effects of jet lag."

He is walking out of his office building. His bodyguard Max is holding open the back door of the limousine. James crouches down to get into the limo when Max shoves him forcibly into the car and sends him flying face down onto the back seat.

Gunshots ring out. James peeks up from his position and sees that Max is firing his revolver. When the shooting stops, James gets up on his knees and looks out into the parking lot. He sees no one.

"Are you okay, sir?" his driver asks.

"Yes, Marvin, I'm fine," he says. "How about you?"

"I'm okay, too. A little shaken up, but otherwise okay. What the heck just happened?"

James doesn't answer. He gets up and out of the car. "What happened, Max?"

"I saw this car drive up slowly and noticed that the guy had a gun in his hand."

James notices blood on Max's left side. "You were hit," he says. "Come on, get in the car. I'm taking you to the hospital." He reaches for Max and pulls him into the back seat.

"Marvin, hurry to the hospital. Max was shot."

The limo peels out.

James looks over at Max, who has his bloodstained hand on the wound, trying to stop the bleeding.

"Marvin, do you have a towel or a cloth?" James asks.

Marvin reaches into the glove compartment, pulls out a small towel, and hands it to James. "Will this do?"

James reaches over and grabs the towel. "It'll have to."

James turns to Max and removes Max's hand, which is covering the wound. He folds the towel in two and applies pressure to the spot that's oozing blood. "How do you feel?" he asks as he continues applying pressure on the towel.

"I'm fine."

James looks into Max's eyes. "You're not lightheaded or anything, are you?"

"No."

"Good." James looks down at his hand holding the towel, which is now soaked in blood.

"We're here, sir," Marvin says a few minutes later.

Max tries to get up, but James shoves him back down. "Stay here. You may be too weak." James turns to Marvin. "Run inside and get help. Make sure they bring a gurney."

Two paramedics dressed in blue scrubs come running out, pushing a stretcher. James turns to the men. "He has a gunshot wound to his side."

One of the men leaps into the vehicle and takes over holding the cloth from James, who climbs out of the limo. The other orderly hands his partner a medical bag that is on top of the gurney. Another man in a blue scrub suit comes out of the hospital and walks up to James.

"Are you all right?" he asks James.

"I'm fine." James points to the car. "Take care of Max."

The fellow looks inside the vehicle, where both of the orderlies are tending to Max. "What do you have, Felix?"

"It's a deep flesh wound, Doc," Felix answers. "It's a big gash."

"Can we get him inside?" the doctor asks.

"In a few minutes, Doc. I'm trying to stabilize the bleeding."

Marvin walks up to James. "How's he doing?"

"I don't know. They're working on him."

Marvin points to James's clothes. "That suit is done for. The cleaners will never be able to get rid of all that blood."

● ● ● ● ● ● ● ⬤ ● ● ● ● ● ● ●

That night, in his study, it takes ten minutes to calm Sam down before James can get into what happened. As soon as she saw James's bloodstained clothes, she freaked out. The only sentence that she heard was that a gunman shot at James, and Max was hit.

"Are you okay now?" James says when there's a pause. "Can I tell you what happened?"

Sam lets out an exasperated breath. "No, I'm not okay. How's Max?"

"Finally," he sighs. "Maybe we can have a decent conversation. Max will be fine. He was grazed by a bullet. It was a deep flesh wound that required stitches. They kept him at the hospital overnight for observation."

"Who did this, James?" she asks. "Was it the African people that were following you in France? I thought you said those people were harmless."

"No, it wasn't the Africans. That's the one thing that's absolutely certain. If it had been them, I'd be dead right now. They wouldn't have missed. Those guys wouldn't have come at me with a cap pistol."

Sam raises her voice. "Then, who did this? The people from Bolivia? James, this is the second time this year that someone tried to kill you."

James throws up his hands. "I don't know! I've got Charlie and everybody at the firm looking into the shooting. It could've been anyone. We do business around the world, and our affairs create a lot of enemies. Or maybe it was a disgruntled employee—I just don't know. There may also be a connection to the shooting of Cardiz and Billy."

"Is all this worth it?" she says. "Why don't you give it up?"

James furrows his brow. "What the hell are you talking about? Give what up?"

"All the businesses that we have. Sell everything! Who needs these headaches? We have plenty of money."

James shakes his head and raises his voice. "What the freaking heck are you talking about? And what would I do with my time? I'm only thirty-five!"

"You can devote your time to the ranch and the horses. You always said you wanted to spend more time on the ranch business."

James shakes his head and smiles warmly. "Honey, I know this episode is upsetting and frightening. But you're not thinking about this rationally. The companies that we own are not just about us. The firms employ thousands of workers that rely on these enterprises for their livelihood. The workers rely on us to manage the operations well and provide them with a future."

"Yeah, but we're the ones that have to face the consequences when something goes wrong."

James smiles. "I think Max would disagree with you."

"What are we doing about what happened today?"

James clears his throat. "Well, as I said, Charlie is investigating who did the shooting. As for us, we both will double our bodyguards. One of us will accompany our children back and forth to school every day."

A worried expression comes across Sam's face. "You think the children are in danger?"

"No, I don't, but it's better to play it safe. I'll let the school know about the possible threat. I'm posting a security guard at the school to keep an eye on things."

Sam shakes her head. "What a way to live." She looks over at James. "Are you sure that we can't just sell the businesses?"

James stands up. "Yeah, I'm sure. I've got to get these bloody clothes off and take a shower." He walks over and gives her a kiss. "We'll get through this crisis. Just like we always do."

The phone rings, and James picks up.

"James, it's Charlie. We've interviewed just about everyone that was at our building. No one saw anything unusual. The spent bullets that were recovered came from a .32-caliber pistol. That's all I've got right now."

"Are these the same bullets that were involved with the Cardiz shooting?"

"I'm not sure, they're running ballistic tests. It's the same caliber, so it's possible." After a pause, Charlie says. "James, you have someone working for you in your household that's Cuban, right?"

"Yeah, Guadalupe. Why do you ask?"

"Do you know that she's dating a Cuban fellow?"

James lets out a breath. "So, who cares! Guadalupe is dating one of her own." James gets louder. "Charlie where the fuck are you going with this?"

"When I was looking into who shot your ranch hands, Billy and Cardiz, the name of this Cuban fellow Herbie came up. Herbie was at the lumber yard when the men were shot. Herbie is Guadalupe's boyfriend."

"Charlie, you got this all wrong. Guadalupe has been with us for years, she's completely trustworthy."

"I'm not saying Guadalupe is involved but she may be inadvertently giving this guy Herbie information about you and the ranch. It's Herbie that I suspect. You've got to admit that it's quite a coincidence that Herbie was at the lumber yard when the shooting of your ranch hands happened. I've looked into Herbie and it turns out that he takes a trip to Cuba every year. He gets into Cuba by going through the Dominican Republic."

There's a period of silence before James speaks up. "Put someone on Herbie's tail. Follow him to Cuba if you have to."

"All right, James, will do."

CHAPTER 20

SAM PUTS HER FOOT DOWN

The next morning Marvin, James' chauffeur, and Regis, the bodyguard, are holding the door open as James comes out of his house. There's an early meeting at the office.

"Not yet, guys. Sam isn't ready," James says.

James looks down the road and notices Mattie coming out of the bunkhouse. He walks down and calls to her. "Mattie, what are you doing here?"

"I dropped the boys off, for today. They don't have school. Jeff agreed to keep an eye on the kids for me."

He plucks at her arm. "How's Cardiz doing?"

Mattie looks away.

James turns her to him. "Is everything all right?"

Her eyes moisten. "He's still paralyzed from the waist down. The doctors now want to do the surgery to remove the bullet."

James looks into her face. "You don't agree?"

A tear makes its way down her face. "The doctors say that he could die. It's a very complicated procedure. And there's no guarantee that he'll walk.

"There's a doctor in Boston, at Brigham and Women hospital," she says. "He specializes in spinal surgeries. I spoke to Gabby in HR, but she said we can't use him because our insurance doesn't cover that hospital." She looks into James's face. "James, what are we to do? We just bought a house before the shooting. If something happens to Antonio, I can't afford the payments. And how long will you keep paying Antonio's salary? You've been more than kind so far, but you can't do it forever."

James puts his arm around her back, and in a comforting voice says, "Stop worrying; just concentrate on getting Antonio better. I'll speak to Gabby at the office later—I'll find out the problem with the health plan and see what we can do."

James looks up the road and notices Jessica, his Vice President of Public Relations, getting out of her car. He turns to Mattie. "I'll see you later."

James hustles up to Jessica. "What are you doing here? You're supposed to be at the office. We may have a big press announcement."

"Sam called last night and said she needed help with the autumn party."

James has to use all of his will to stop the anger from bursting forward. "No, she doesn't need your help. I'll have a talk with Sam—you're needed at the office," he says calmly.

"Are you sure? Sam sounded pretty desperate."

"Yes, I'm certain. Get to the office and tell everyone that I'll be a few minutes late for the meeting." James walks into the house and heads for the study.

"Are you ready?" he asks Sam, who is sitting behind her desk.

"I'm almost done." Sam stands up and walks to the window, pulling back the curtain.

"Who are you looking for?" James asks. "Are you expecting someone?"

Sam continues looking out the window.

"We need to leave," he says. "Everyone is waiting for us."

Sam still has no response.

James walks up to the window and takes the curtain out of her hand. "I told Jessica to report back to the office."

Sam's face turns red. "Why did you do that?"

"Because she's needed at the office today. You know, Sam, we've had this discussion before, but apparently, you refuse to listen."

Sam extends her arms out wide. "What am I supposed to do, James? Take care of the arrangements for this party all by myself? Do you have any idea on how much work is required?"

"Yes, I do, but you can't use our Vice President of Public Relations; it's just not right. You won't to get tough with Helen, your assistant, who refuses to come to the ranch. So, I now have to step in. I'll get you the help that you need."

Sam grabs his arm. "You're not firing Helen, are you?"

James turns to her. "No, I'm not firing Helen. But Helen won't be your assistant anymore—I'm getting someone that'll be of help to you. I'll transfer Helen to Vernon. Vernon's assistant is leaving, and he's looking for someone else. If I know Vernon, he'll straighten out Helen. He won't put up with any of her crap." He begins walking out.

"Who do you have in mind for me?"

"You'll see."

"I hope she's good," Sam says, following behind him.

James turns to her. "Whoever I come up with has to be better than what you have now, which is no one. But don't worry, you'll be very happy. The person that I have in mind will be perfect for you."

"What's on the agenda today?" Sam asks on the ride to work.

"The railroad. The guys from Drexel are coming in to make a presentation. Henry Greenwald will be there, too. By the way, on another matter, I just wanna let you know that I'll be away next week. I'm traveling to Zaire for a meeting with Ernie."

Sam sits up in her seat. "I thought you said you didn't have to go back to Africa. Why are you traveling to Zaire?"

"Why are you getting so upset? It's a quick meeting. No more than two days—Ernie and I need to settle an important problem."

Sam points a finger at him. "When are you stopping this crap, James? You have a family, and four children who need you. Why are you taking up these dangerous adventures? Yesterday, somebody shot at you, for heaven's sake. Do you have some sort of death wish?"

"There's nothing dangerous about this trip. It's in and out—it's in Kinshasa, the capital city. There's nothing risky about the visit."

Sam shakes her head. "I don't know what's worse: your lack of regard for your family, or that you think I'm an idiot. I know exactly what's happening in Zaire. The fellows that you're planning on meeting are the same people who tried to kill you the last time you were there, aren't they?"

Sam turns to him. "How easy will it be for those people to get to you this time? You're in a major foreign city. A lone assassin can take you out, just like the lone gunman in front of our office tried to do yesterday."

"Can we drop this African trip for now? We'll talk about it some more tonight. There're very important meetings today. Can we just concentrate on that program, for today?"

"We'll drop it for now, but you haven't heard the end of this." Sam sits back in her seat. The rest of the ride is silent.

"All right, let's settle down." James calls the board of directors meeting to order a little later, in one of the conference rooms. "Everyone take your seats, please."

After they take their seats, James turns to Vernon. "Are we ready to begin?"

"We're waiting for Kathy, who'll take the minutes of the meeting." he answers.

"Before we begin, I'd like to bring up a matter that I don't want on the record," Sam says. Sam smiles at the assemblage. "I'd like to pass a resolution that our chairman, James Coppi, be curtailed from taking any more dangerous excursions abroad. It's my understanding that James is planning a trip to Zaire to meet up with one of overseas operatives, Ernie Bauer.

"For what reason, I don't really know. This adventurism by James must be stopped. James is the chief executive officer and is too valuable a part of our organization to continue venturing out on these hazardous assignments."

James turns to Sam. "What are you doing?"

Sam puts up her hand and smiles. "I'm proposing a resolution, dear. I'm well within my right. I'm on the board of directors."

Sam looks around the room. "We received a big scare when someone tried to kill James right in front of the office. We were fortunate that Max foiled the attempt. Can you imagine what would've happened if Max hadn't been successful? I can assure you that this meeting wouldn't have been necessary.

"Now James is galloping off on another risky escapade, refusing to delegate the task to an underling. A voyage to an area where he was also attacked, if all of you remember."

Vernon, from across the way, smiles warmly at Sam. "Samantha, we can't really tell James how to run his business. The board can't put on this kind of restriction. It would be too limiting."

"No, I don't agree, Vern. I believe we can," Sam says. "It's simple. The board can pass a resolution today that says, 'Before James takes on any overseas travel, he must obtain the board's approval.'"

"Mrs. Coppi, do you really want to place that kind of restriction on your husband?" Another of the board members speaks up.

Sam peeks over at James through the corner of her eyes. He's glaring at her; his pupils have become smaller, he's tapping his right index finger on the desk, and Sam knows exactly what he's thinking.

"I would prefer to not put on any constraints, but if James insists on these risky excursions, we have no choice. We, as members of the board, need to take action to protect the stockholders, employees, and creditors of our company. The directors at this meeting would be derelict in their duty if they didn't stop this type of activity by the head of our company."

Sam lets out a breath and points to the group. "By the way, I'm giving the board notice that if you fail to pass this resolution, I'm prepared to take the resolution to a proxy."

Jack, the company's financial officer, speaks up. "Samantha, a proxy fight won't do any good. You and James each own 41 percent of the company. You'd need 50 percent plus one to carry the stockholder's resolution that you're proposing."

Sam looks over at Jack. "What percentage does Kathy own?"

"I believe she owns 5 percent," Jack replies. "But that still only comes to 46 percent. Not enough to carry."

Sam smiles. "Yes, Jack, but I'd be a lot closer. Also, it's my understanding that it's 50 percent of the shares that are voted, not necessarily the shares outstanding. That means that if some stockholders abstain from voting because they don't want to take sides, I could still win with just my shares and Kathy's. Am I right?"

"Yes," Jack answers, "that's correct."

"James, can't you and Samantha reach an arrangement on this point?" Vernon voices. "A proxy fight will hurt the image of our company. We have a lot of important matters that we're working on. One of the matters is the primary reason for this very meeting. The last thing that we need is a battle between the two top stockholders."

James smiles at the people in the room. "You're quite right, Vernon. Since this matter appears to be so important to my wife, I'm willing to back down and cancel my trip to Africa." James looks over at Sam. "Are you satisfied?"

Sam smiles smugly. "Yes, we can proceed with the meeting."

"Now that I've been completely emasculated and whipped down by my wife," James stands up, "I'll get Kathy so that we can discuss what we really had on the agenda."

As he is about to leave, he mutters, "Maybe I can regain some of my dignity."

Kathy enters just as he's about to walk out. "I'm sorry that I'm late."

James looks at Kathy and scowls. "Thanks a lot for throwing me under the bus, you traitor!"

Kathy squints and stares into James's face. "What are you talking about?"

"You agreed to vote your shares with Sam against me."

Kathy shakes her head. "What vote? I don't know what you're talking about?"

James looks over at Sam, who smiles shrewdly. "Kathy never agreed to vote with me. I simply asked Jack how many shares Kathy owned. You jumped to that conclusion on your own. Now that your travelling matter is settled, can we proceed with the other company business? I believe we're to discuss the railroad?"

• • • • • • • • ● • • • • • • • • •

"I want to thank you for participating today," James says as the board of directors meeting closes. "I'll keep you updated on the negotiations on the initial public offering." James stands up. "Let's take a short break. After the break, Vernon, Jack, and Maxwell will return, as you'll be needed. The rest of you are free to go. Once again, thanks for your participation."

James turns to Kathy. "Do me a favor, get Henry and bring him to the conference room. I believe he's in my office." He turns to his wife. "Sam, can I speak to you in your office?"

In the office, he says. "I hope you're happy. That was one of the worst stunts that you've ever pulled on me."

"You left me no choice."

"No, Sam, I did—I told you in the car that we'd discuss this later. You know that I would've eventually have given in to you. I always do."

Sam shakes her head. "No, James, I'm sorry, I don't agree. Not when it comes to Ernie. You like hanging out with that man. Some sort of macho adventure. But it's time that you start putting your family first. I've been very patient with you through the years, but it's come to the point that you need to think about us." Sam walks up to him and cups his face. "Please try to see this my way. Please." She gives him a kiss. "Come on, let's go back and finish this project."

As they're about to leave the room, he grabs her arm and turns her to him. "I'm sorry."

Sam smiles and gives him another kiss. As he's holding her in his arms, he says, "Thank you for your support through the years. I know it hasn't been easy on you."

Henry Greenwald is with Kathy when they are back in the conference room.

"Henry," Sam calls out to the slim, silver-haired, mustached elderly gentlemen.

The man smiles warmly. "Samantha," he hails back, and walks up to give her a hug and a kiss. While holding on to both of her hands, "It's been a while," he continues, smiling broadly.

"Not my fault, Henry. I've invited you at least a dozen times just in the last year."

"I know, I'm sorry. But please keep inviting me. I'll come around; you'll see." He looks over at James. "How was your meeting this morning with the board? Any problems?"

"None concerning what we'll be discussing next." James turns as Vernon walks in.

"Am I too early?" Vernon says.

James looks over at Kathy. "Have the people from Drexel arrived yet?"

"They're downstairs in the lobby."

"Good," James says. "Call Maxwell and Jack and tell them that we're ready to begin, then fetch the people from Drexel and escort them here." James turns back to Henry. "Why don't we take a seat?"

"Mr. Greenwald, how did you and James meet?" Vernon asks, once they're sitting. "You guys go way back, but I've never heard the story of how you guys met up. I mean, it seems kind of odd; James being from New York and you from New Mexico."

"Henry was our first client," Sam speaks up. "He gave us our start."

"Yes, I've heard that before," Vernon says. "But what matter was it?"

"My granddaughter Penelope was kidnaped by this fiend," Henry reveals. "The police had arrested the wrong man and given up the search. James found her—he and Samantha hunted this animal down and freed my baby."

Vernon smiles. "That's quite a story."

Maxwell and Jack walk in, and a moment later, Kathy walks in with two men from Drexel.

"Henry, I don't believe you formally met Symon Willoughby," James points to one of the men, "and his associate, Peter Fries."

Henry smiles at the men. "No, James, I haven't. I've spoken to these gentlemen a few times on the phone, but never met them in person. It's a pleasure to finally meet you two."

James points to the chairs. "Why don't we take a seat and get right into the discussion. I'm anxious to learn what you guys came up with." James turns to Kathy. "Thank you; you're free to go, we won't need you."

It's Symon who begins the talk. "James, we took your idea to dozens of high-powered investors and venture capitalists. All embraced your project enthusiastically. There wasn't any negative feedback whatsoever. Everyone that we spoke to saw the value of providing low-cost railroad freight service. The investors immediately grasped your belief as to why rail freight hasn't been profitable. And all were impressed with your plan to streamline the operations."

Symon smiles over at James. "These financiers are ready to back the project. The investors are eager to move forward." He turns to his partner. "Peter will explain what we came up with, as a proposal that will work."

Peter clears his throat. "We're suggesting an IPO spinoff of 40 percent of the railroad company to outside investors. Right now, you and Samantha own 80 percent and Henry owns 20 percent. After the offering, you and Samantha will own 48 percent and Henry will have a 12 percent stake."

"Doesn't that mean that we'll lose control?" Sam asks. "At 48 percent, we'll no longer have a majority ownership."

"That's not quite true, Mrs. Coppi," Peter replies. "With Henry's shares, you still control 60 percent of the company."

"Besides, Mrs. Coppi, none of the new investors want to run the railroad," Symon cuts in. "At 48 percent, you have effective control. All you'd need is to buy 2 percent of the railroad's stock on the open market if it ever came to a proxy fight. No one would dare take you on."

"What do we get for giving up some of our ownership?" James asks.

"It's a two-part transaction," Peter continues. "The first is to spin off the real estate properties owned by the railroad. We'll create a realty company owned by the Coppis and Greenwald at the same eighty/twenty formula as the current ownership.

"The railroad owns some very valuable properties in the heart of many major cities. We estimate that the value of these assets is somewhere between four hundred to six hundred million dollars."

"Does the real estate spinoff create a taxable event?" Jack asks.

"We've spoken to our tax people, and we're confident that it's a tax-free exchange. You may want to discuss this deal with your own tax attorneys."

Peter turns back to James. "The remainder of the railroad, without the real estate, we value between 12 to 15 billion dollars. The public offering of 40 percent will raise $4.8 billion for the company."

"Excuse me, Peter, but 4.8 billion dollars for 40 percent of the company means that the railroad is being priced at 12 billion, the low end of your estimate," Vernon brings up.

"Yes, that's true," Peter says. "But in today's high-interest environment, it's hard to find investors to back any sort of project. Remember, you can get 8 percent on your money at the bank. To get this deal done, and done quickly, we need to incentivize the investors."

"How much of that $4.8 billion comes to us?" Henry asks.

"None," Peter replies. "That money is for working capital. Capital to be used to modernize the existing rail lines and for acquisitions of other railroads, as James envisioned in his plans."

Symon cuts in. "Remember, Henry, you and the Coppis are getting the real estate properties."

Henry turns to James. "What do you think? You haven't said much."

"We need the money. If we're to make this business a success, we have to bring in the cash. It's a good deal." James turns to Sam. "How about you? What's your opinion?"

"You and Henry know more about this stuff than I do. If you guys think it's good for the railroad, I'm all for it."

Henry gives Sam a fatherly smile. "Samantha, do you fully comprehend what this transaction will do?"

"Yes. It'll raise much-needed money for the growth of the railroad."

Henry's smile gets broader. "Yes, that's true. But, I meant what this transaction will do for you, personally."

Sam creases her brow. "What do you mean, Henry?"

"After this offering, the railroad will be a public company, traded on the open market. The entire country will know that you and James are billionaires."

Sam bursts out laughing. "Have you totally lost your mind, Henry? James and I are well off, but billionaires? Not even close."

Henry presents Sam another warm smile. "Did you not hear what these gentlemen said about the value of the railroad? These men value the business at 12 billion dollars. You and James will own 48 percent of that company after its public. That means the value of your share comes to more than 5 billion dollars, and that's just for the railroad—that's not counting any other businesses or assets that you guys own. The whole world will know that the Coppis are billionaires. One of the richest families in the country."

Sam turns to James. "What is Henry saying?"

James smiles. "I believe what Henry is trying to say, dear, is that you and I may need more bodyguards."

CHAPTER 21

SAM GETS AN ASSISTANT

"Will you need me for anything else?" Sam asks James after the meeting. "I need to get home and continue planning for the upcoming party that we're having." She gives James a scornful stare. "I've got a lot of work to do, now that you took Jessica away and I'm left to do everything all by myself."

James smiles. "You wouldn't be doing the work by yourself if you were tougher with Helen." He stands up and walks over to give her a kiss. "I'll have a new assistant for you before the day is out."

"Yeah, who?"

James smiles slyly. "It's a surprise. She'll be at the ranch as soon as I've worked out the details. She'll be perfect. Come on, I'll walk you to the elevator."

"Kathy, please call Miles and Gabby and have them come to my office right away," James says when he gets back. "You join the meeting, too, when they get here." He's about to walk into his office when he turns. "Oh, by the way, have Gabby bring Mattie Cardiz's personnel file."

"I learned something very disturbing this morning," James says to the people when they're sitting in his office. "One of our employees, Antonio Cardiz, is very ill and can't get the care that he needs. Apparently, our health plan doesn't cover this particular hospital."

"I'm sorry, James, I'm not familiar with this matter." Miles says and looks over at Gabby. "Do you know anything about this?"

"Yes. Antonio wants to be treated at a hospital in Boston. This facility isn't in our health plan," Gabby answers

Miles turns back to James. "I'm sorry, James, but there's nothing that can be done for Antonio. We don't have any employees in Boston, so there wasn't a need to include that region in our coverage."

"Doesn't our plan cover nationwide?"

"No, it doesn't," Miles answers. "To save on money, Jack left out areas where we had no employees. Up to now, there wasn't any reason to cover these other parts of the country."

"How about our railroad workers? Do they have the same plan as we do?"

"No, I believe the railroad's health plan may cover Boston," Gabby speaks up. "But Antonio isn't on their payroll."

"Well, transfer Cardiz to the railroad," James says.

"James, that wouldn't do any good," Gabby explains. "There's a ninety-day waiting period before the medical coverage kicks in at the railroad. That'll make matters worse. Antonio would be without coverage completely for ninety days."

"And, James," Miles cuts in, "you have to remember that Antonio has used up his sick leave and you're still paying him. The unions wouldn't tolerate that at the railroad. The unions wouldn't allow you to make an exception for just one person. They'll want the same treatment for all the employees."

"Here's what you'll do," James says. "Transfer Cardiz to the railroad and make the transfer paperwork retroactive to ninety days ago. That'll take care of his health insurance. Don't worry about paying him sick pay any longer, I'll handle that problem."

James turns to Miles. "You can go, Miles; we won't need you for the rest of this meeting. Make sure you take care of transferring Cardiz ASAP."

"Did you bring Mattie's file?" James asks Gabby after Jack leaves.

"I have it right here." Gabby shows him the file. "Do you want to see it?"

"Is there anything in that folder that says that Mattie can't do Helen's job?"

"You're firing Helen?" Kathy calls out. "Why?"

"I'm not firing Helen. I'm transferring her to Vernon. He needs a new secretary, and Helen isn't working out for Sam. Mattie will be Sam's assistant." James turns back to Gabby. "So, answer my question, Gabby: can Mattie do the job?"

"Yes, of course. Mattie is way too qualified to be a receptionist. She ran the entire office at her previous company. We were waiting for an opportunity to move her up."

"Good, then let's bring Mattie in and see if she'll take the job. How much is Helen earning?"

"Sixty thousand a year," Gabby says.

"Sixty thousand?" James sits up. "Are you freaking kidding me? Is that what all the secretaries make around here?"

"No, James," Gabby says. "Helen was Samantha's assistant. An executive assistant. That's a lot more responsibility."

"A lot more of nothing. Jessica was doing Helen's job!" James turns to Kathy. "How much am I paying you?"

Kathy smiles slyly. "None of your business!" She turns to Gabby. "And don't you dare tell him." She turns back to James. "And you and I both know that I'm worth every last penny."

"Let's get Mattie up here," he says.

"Mattie, do you like your receptionist job?" James asks when she's in his office.

"Yes," she answers faintly.

James recognizes the look of concern that's come over her. "There's no need to worry, Mattie, your job isn't in jeopardy. We're looking for an assistant to replace Helen and work with Sam. Everyone in here agrees that you'd be perfect."

"How about Mrs. Coppi?" Mattie asks. "How does she feel?"

"Sam doesn't know anything about this decision, yet—I wanted to get your reaction first. Of course, Sam will have the final say."

"This is quite a promotion," Gabby says. "A lot more responsibilities, but with that promotion comes a nice raise."

"How much does the job pay?" Mattie asks.

"Sixty thousand a year," James answers.

Mattie gulps. "Did you just say sixty thousand?"

"Yes, sixty thousand," James answers. "What do you say? Do you want the job?"

Mattie puts her hands to her chest. "Yes, of course, that's more than triple what I'm currently making."

James smiles. "Good. After we're through here, go to the ranch and have a talk with Sam. I'm sure that you won't have any problems. You can start right away. Sam needs help with an affair that she's planning."

"What about my current job? Who'll be the receptionist?"

"Don't worry about that. Gabby and Kathy will get someone to fill in." James turns to Gabby and Kathy. "Okay, we're done. I want to speak to Mattie alone."

After they leave, James turns to Mattie. "I want to speak to you about Cardiz." He clears his throat. "I managed to get Cardiz on the railroad's health plan. That new plan covers the cost of treatments at that hospital in Boston that you mentioned this morning. Now all you have to do is convince Cardiz to go. Unfortunately, because of the switch in companies, Cardiz will lose his sick pay."

"I guess that's okay," she says. "My new pay scale is way more than both of our current salaries combined." She stops for a moment and looks at James. "Oh!" Mattie gets misty-eyed. "Thank you, James; thank you for all your help—I don't know what we would've done without you. I hope that someday we can repay you in some way."

James stands up. "You can repay me by helping Sam with her work and keeping her from borrowing my Vice President." James stretches.

"What if Sam doesn't want me?"

James smiles. "Oh, I'm sure she'll snap you up. You better get going." He writes something on a slip of paper, folds it and hands it to Mattie. "Hand this name to Sam—tell her to make sure she invites this guy to the affair that she's planning."

• • • • • • • • • ● ● ● • • • • • • • •

Sam is in the study, trying to outline a plan of action on the upcoming party. Billingsley knocks and looks in. "Excuse me, Mrs. Coppi, but Mrs. Cardiz is here to see you."

"Uhm, I wonder what she wants," she mutters, and looks up. "Please send her in, Billingsley."

Sam stands and walks up to greet Mattie. "Mattie, what a surprise. Why aren't you at work? Is everything all right?"

"Yes, everything is fine! Mr. Coppi sent me over. I'm supposed to be your new assistant, replacing Helen."

Sam eyes widen. "You're the replacement for Helen?"

"Yes," she says. "That is, if it's okay with you. Mr. Coppi said that you had to approve."

Sam smiles broadly. "That sneak! Wait until I get him."

"Mrs. Coppi, if you don't agree with his decision, please let me know."

Sam shakes her head. "No, of course I agree. You're perfect! I'm sorry that I never thought of you for the job myself." Sam walks behind the desk.

"Thank you, Mrs. Coppi."

"You can call me Sam."

"No, thank you," Mattie says. "While at work, I'll address you as Mrs. Coppi, if you don't mind."

"Why is that?"

"Two reasons. The first is that you deserve the same respect as Mr. Coppi." Mattie looks at Sam and smiles. "The second is that I want everyone to know that I work for the most important person at the company. There'll be no one addressing you in the familiar except for maybe the top executives. Not when they're around me."

Sam let's out a laugh. "Okay, have it your way. Come, put down your pocketbook and let's get started. There's a party that I'm planning, and I desperately need help."

Mattie places down her bag and reaches in to take out the note that James gave her earlier. "By the way, Mr. Coppi wanted me to tell you to make sure you invite this person to the affair."

Sam reaches over and takes the slip of paper. "Umm, that's weird. Him? Why him?"

CHAPTER 22

THE PARTY GUEST

Two weeks later, Kathy looks up from her desk and smiles. "What are you doing at work? Shouldn't you be at home, helping Sam prepare for the party tonight?"

James lets out a laugh. "Believe me, the best help that I can provide Sam is to stay out of the way. The ranch is a madhouse right now with all the arrangements. There's a television crew that's set up. Jessica is at the ranch talking to the newspaper reporters.

"This pain in the ass party of Sam's has become the social event of Colorado Springs. Sam is talking of expanding our house so that we can fit more people next year. What a calamity! I just want to stay away."

He's about to go into his office, but turns back. "By the way, Ernie Bauer is coming in this morning."

Kathy looks down at her book. "Ernie Bauer? He's not on my schedule. What time is he coming?"

"I don't know. He should be here sometime this morning. Get Phil Eisley on the phone, please."

A few moments later, Eisley is on the line. "What's up, James?"

James's voice is blunt. "Phil, I've been very patient with you, but my patience has run out. I'm asking you for the last time: are you delivering that information on the Hartleys, or not?"

"Yes, James, I've got people working on it. We want to make sure we have everything that you asked for—we don't want you to come back and telling me that we held out."

"How much more time do you need?"

"A week?"

"All right, one week but no more!"

Kathy buzzes in. "James, Ernie is downstairs. I'm going to get him."

James looks upon the rugged body and the sun-worn face of the Afrikaner in front of him. He's known the soldier of fortune for nearly ten years now. He first met Ernie in Angola when James was on assignment for a European oil company. Ernie was leading a battalion of soldiers from his native South Africa.

His men were so ruthless that, after the campaign, his government court-martialed him. James used his influence to have the charges dropped. Colonel Bauer was booted out of the South African army—he's now a mercenary, available to anyone that will pay his price. James has used him countless times.

"So, what happened to you?" Ernie smiles. "How come you didn't make it to Kinshasa?"

James laughs. "No more fun for me, old friend. Sam laid down the law. I've got four kids that need me. From now on, you're on your own."

Ernie smiles broadly. "I was wondering when that sweet lady would put her foot down. She let you get away with a lot all these years."

"Yeah, she did. How about you, Ernie? When are you giving this up and settling down? You've got two daughters, don't you?"

"Yeah, but my kids are older and have families of their own—I don't know what I'd do if I couldn't do this anymore."

James changes the subject. "How was your meeting with Benga?"

"It was a good meeting and we worked out a suitable agreement. Benga's sole preoccupation is to overthrow Mobutu. Since we couldn't care less who runs Zaire, it was easy to come to an arrangement. Benga will stay out of the territory we control and leave the mines alone. We agreed to let him have access to the rest of the country."

James looks at the door and turns back to Ernie. "What about the other matter that I asked you to look into? Was I right? Do the arms shipments to Mobutu in Zaire have something to do with Colonel Chase and the money that's buying arms for the Bolivians?"

Ernie nods. "Yeah, you're right. This guy Chase is running the operation. He's ripping off the US."

James leans forward. "How's he doing that?"

"Chase is doing it through arms purchases for Mobutu." Ernie leans forward and puts his hands on the desk. "Here's how it works. Let's say the US authorizes the purchase of a piece of equipment destined for Zaire. Chase tells the US that the equipment costs $1 million, when in actuality it's only 500 grand. Chase transfers the remaining money to this company in Chile that's assisting the Bolivian rebels. In turn, the Chilean company pays you for the military gear that you're supplying."

James shakes his head. "Damn! So, in reality, it's American taxpayer money that's supporting the rebels?"

"That's right."

"How hard is it to find out what Chase is doing? How hard was it for you?"

"Not hard at all, James. I just had to spread around a little loot—and not very much cash, at that—bribes don't cost much in Africa. James, I'm warning you—this is getting out."

"Yeah, I know. I better prepare for the fallout. On that note, can you handle another assignment? Can Gary run the Zaire operation without you?"

Ernie sits back in his chair. "Yes…I'm sure he can. As I said, there's not much happening. What do you need from me?"

"You need to travel to Chile and Bolivia."

"What do you want me to do there?"

"You're to report on this group, the Guerreros, I'd like to know firsthand if the rebels have a shot at winning this war."

James looks over at Ernie. "But the most important guy I need you to meet is this fellow Gaytan in Chile. He's the mastermind behind this affair. I need to know if he'll hold up if things get tough. When this money movement affair with Chase gets exposed, I need to make sure that Gaytan won't fold when our government comes around asking him questions."

· · · · · · · ● · · · · · · · · ·

"I don't know why you do this affair every year," James says to Sam that night at home. "And it's bigger every time. How many people are we having, over two hundred?"

Sam smiles warmly. "The autumn party at the Coppis is the toast of the town. Everybody hopes to be invited. It gets the whole city in a festive mood. And, besides, look how much money it raises for charity."

"As much as this affair is costing, we'd be better off just donating the money directly to charity and forgetting the party. It'd be a lot less of a hassle, that's for sure. And a lot less work for me. Do you have any idea how exhausted I'll be after this evening?"

"I might have a little inkling of how tiresome the affair might be, since I'm the hostess. And don't forget that I had to put this gala together." Sam walks up to him, fixes his tie, and gives him a kiss. "Are you livening up, or are you pouting all evening?"

James gives her a kiss back. "I'll be good."

"I have to dress and finish putting on my makeup. Why don't you start greeting the early birds?"

James stands there with a lost look on his face. "Without you?"

Sam shakes her head. "Yes, without me. I can't believe how shy you are." She pushes him toward the door. "Go!"

James walks into the parlor where a half-dozen of the guests are milling about. The string trio hired for the occasion is playing its music. Later, a dance band will take over the festivities. The guests notice James and walk his way. *Oh crap,* James says to himself when he notices the guests coming his way. He lifts up his head and smiles broadly, walking toward the people.

"Oh, hi. I'm so glad that you could make the party."

James has been greeting the visitors by himself for a half hour. Sam is still getting dressed. Kathy walks through the door.

"Hi," she says to James. "How's it going?"

"Awful," he says brusquely. "Sam is still getting dressed and I'm stuck out here as a greeter all by myself."

Kathy lets out a laugh. "Yes, and I know how much you love making small talk."

"Hello," a voice comes from behind Kathy.

"Hello, Richard," James says. "I'm glad you could make the party."

"No problem at all, James," Richard answers. "Thanks for the invite."

"My pleasure." James extends out his arm to the room. "Enjoy the party, please."

After Richard leaves, Kathy turns to James. "Why did you invite him?"

"You know the saying by Sun Tzu, 'keep your friends close and your enemies closer.'"

James notices a couple entering. "Good evening, Sheriff Wilde, I'm so glad you could make the party. You look quite striking in your tux."

The sheriff pulls at the collar of his shirt. "I feel like a stuffed penguin!"

James turns to the matronly woman and smiles broadly. "And how are you, Mrs. Wilde?" He gives her a kiss on the cheek. "I love your dress, it's beautiful."

"It should be," the sheriff says. "It cost me a small fortune."

James smiles again and holds the lady's hand. "It's worth every penny. You are stunning."

The sheriff leans over and whispers in James's ear. "That matter we spoke about is all set."

"Thank you, Sheriff." James motions to the floor. "Please, enjoy the party."

James turns to Kathy. "Take my place. I'm going to find out what happened to Sam."

James walks into the bedroom and knocks at the bathroom door. "Are you ever coming out?" he shouts.

"Wow," he lets out after Sam opens the door.

Sam is wearing a red, low-cut gown. The white pearls around her neck, which are hanging down to her cleavage, accentuate her bountiful breasts. The strawberry blonde hair draped down to her shoulders appears to be shimmering.

"You like?" She extends her arms out wide to give him a full view.

James walks up to her and holds her in his arms. "Like? I love. Why don't we get rid of our guests?"

She gives him a shove. "Let's get started."

"Started? There's nothing left to do. I've already greeted everyone. They're all here."

Sam smiles. "Good. Now I can make my grand entrance."

Three hours into the party, Sam strolls up to James. "Hello, stranger."

"Hello, gorgeous. It's nice to see you again—I see you've been busy."

"Just making sure I hit everyone," she says. "How are you doing?"

"I'm hanging in there." He nods his head toward a man. "Did you get to him?"

"No, I didn't. Why did you invite him? At our last party, he got drunk and annoyed the heck out of you."

"Well, he's behaving a lot better. Hasn't come up to me all night—I haven't seen him with a drink."

Sam looks away from James. "I'll be right back. I just noticed a couple that I haven't spoken to."

James walks up to the man. "Hello, Richard, are you enjoying the party?"

Richard turns to him and smiles. "Yes, very much. Thanks again for the invite." He pauses for a moment. "May I ask you why you invited me? You know that I'm investigating you, right? If you're trying to influence me, it won't work."

James offers a broad smile. "I wouldn't dream of ever thinking that you could be swayed. This is my way of showing you that I'm not worried. If you're fair in your investigation, you won't find anything wrong. You will be unbiased, won't you?"

"Yes, of course."

James places his arm over Richard's shoulders. "Good. Let's head to the bar and let me buy you a drink."

"No thank you. I'm getting ready to leave."

James laughs. "Good idea. In a few minutes, Sam will start hitting up everyone for the contributions to the charities that we're sponsoring. She can be very persuasive, and is a good arm-twister. Come, let's head to the bar and have a nightcap before you leave."

Richard looks over at the bar. "No, I'd better not. At the last one of your parties, I had a little too much and made a complete fool of myself."

James places his arm over Richard's shoulder. "How many drinks have you had? You don't look drunk."

"That's because I haven't had anything to drink."

James pushes Richard toward the bar. "Then I insist. Come on, just one for the road."

"What'll it be, Mr. Coppi?" the bartender asks when they get to the bar.

James turns to Richard, who says, "Jack Daniels, neat."

"How about you, Mr. Coppi?" the bartender asks. "The usual, mineral water?"

"No, Frank, I'll have a beer, please."

After the bartender has poured the drinks, James lifts up his glass to make a toast. "Here's to a fair and honest investigation."

Richard lifts up his whiskey. James bangs his beer into Richard's glass and the whiskey and beer spills all over Richard.

"Oh, I'm so sorry," James calls out, putting his now empty glass of beer on the bar. He reaches over for the bar towel and starts wiping Richard's shirt, but instead of helping, the smearing is making it worse.

Richard grabs ahold of James's hand. "It's all right." He looks down at his drenched clothes. "Well, this makes it absolutely certain that the party is over for me."

"Don't leave yet." James grabs Richard's arm and calls the bartender over. "At least have that drink before you go. That's the least that I can do." He signals to the bartender to pour another drink.

"No, it's quite okay."

"Here." James reaches over and takes the glass from the bar, which the bartender just poured.

Richard looks at the glass and, after a moment, takes the drink out of James's hand. He points the glass toward James. "Here's to us." He chugs the entire drink down. "Thank you, James. Now I'd better get going."

James smiles. "Good night, Richard, thanks for coming. Sorry about spilling the drink. Drive safely."

Richard is driving home slowly, and he's almost home. It's a dark, moonless night and it's hard to see. Looking in his rearview mirror, he notices the flashing lights. He pulls over. When the trooper marches over, he cranks down his window.

"Anything wrong?" he asks the deputy.

"Are you okay, sir? You're driving a little erratic." The deputy points a flashlight at his face.

Richard puts his hand in front of the light. "Yes, I'm fine. It's very dark tonight, and hard to see."

"Have you been drinking?"

"Not really. You probably smell the drink that was accidentally spilled on me."

"May I please see your license and registration?"

"Why? I didn't do anything wrong."

"Please, sir, your license and registration."

Richard lets out a breath and reaches into his glove compartment. "Here." He hands the deputy the registration and pulls out his wallet to take out his license.

"I just want to let you know that I'm also in law enforcement. I'm an assistant district attorney."

The deputy looks at the papers. "Can you please step out of the car?"

"Why?"

"Please, sir. Out of the car."

Richard shakes his head and opens the door. "You see, I'm fine," he says, standing outside with his arms outstretched.

The deputy steps backward away from Richard. "Please walk toward me."

Richard shakes his head once more. "This is ridiculous."

"Walk towards me, sir," the officer commands in a stern voice.

Richard walks toward the deputy.

"I'm placing you under arrest," the deputy says.

"What?" Richard shouts. "For what? There's nothing wrong with me!"

"Are you coming peacefully, or do I have to cuff you?"

"This is preposterous. I'm not drunk. Give me back my license and registration." Richard grabs the deputy's hand and tries to take back his papers.

The officer snatches Richard's arm and shoves him face down on the hood of the car. Richard breaks free and pushes the lawman away. After a brief struggle, the deputy has Richard face down on the ground. He has a knee in Richard's back and grabs ahold of his arm, locking a cuff on his wrist. The deputy snatches Richard's other arm and locks the wrists together. The officer lets out a breath and stands up, raising Richard up by the collar. He shoves Richard into the back seat of his cruiser.

"You sit there and shut the fuck up. I'm getting your car keys."

At the police station, the deputy sits Richard in the interrogation room. "If you promise to behave, I'll take the cuffs off you."

"I'll be good!"

"Listen," Richard says in a much calmer voice after the deputy takes off the cuffs. "I'm sorry that we got off on the wrong foot. But please let me explain."

The cop looks at Richard. "All right, go ahead."

"I was at the Coppi party. The sheriff, your boss, was also there. Mr. Coppi accidently spilled a drink on me. I swear, I didn't have more than one drink." Richard looks straight into the man's face. "Please call Mr. Coppi. He'll vouch for me." When the lawman doesn't move, Richard pleads and motions to the door. "Please, just make the call. Mr. Coppi can clear everything up."

"All right, I will," the deputy says, and leaves the room.

A few minutes later, the deputy comes back.

"Well?" Richard asks. "Did Mr. Coppi clear up everything? Did he repeat what I told you?"

"Mr. Coppi and Sheriff Wilde will be down to the station house as soon as the party is over."

"Coming here? Why? Did you ask him if he spilled the drink on me?"

"As I said, Mr. Coppi and the sheriff will be here when the party is over." The deputy leaves the room.

A few hours later, Richard looks up at the clock on the wall, 4:25. There are voices in the hall, and the door to his room opens. James and the sheriff walk in.

"Finally," Richard lets out. "James, please tell these people that you spilled a drink on me. They've got me for driving drunk." Richard points to the sheriff. "Go ahead, James, tell him that I had only one drink."

James looks over at the sheriff. "Can you give me a few moments?"

"Yeah, sure." The sheriff hands James a folder that he's holding and leaves the room.

James takes a seat across from Richard. "What happened to you?" James motions to Richard's shirt, which is all full of mud.

"I had a little trouble with the deputy." Richard leans forward in his seat. "James, what the hell is this about?" Richard whispers. "Just tell them that I wasn't drinking so I can get the heck out of here."

James leans forward and lowers his voice. "What about the car in the ditch? How did your car end up in the ditch?"

Richard sits up and raises his voice. "What? What the hell are you talking about?"

James opens up the folder and takes out a photograph. He slides the picture in front of Richard. "Isn't that your car in the ditch?"

Richard looks at the photo and looks up at James, a puzzled expression is on his face. "That's my car, but I didn't drive it into the ditch."

"Then who did?"

Richard shakes his head. "I have no fucking idea!"

"What about the young girl?"

Richard furrows his brow and shakes his head. "What girl? What in the world are you talking about?"

James goes back in the folder and takes out another photo. "This girl—she's sixteen. She said that you picked her up."

Richard looks at the picture and looks up at James. "I've never seen this girl in my life." Richard looks at the door and back at James. "James, I think I'm being framed."

James leans forward. "Who would do that to you, Richard? Who in this stationhouse has any reason for framing you?"

Richard pauses for a moment and then glares at James. "You?"

James smiles slyly.

"You son-of-a-bitch!" Richard lets out.

"That's right, Richard, I am."

Richard's face turns beet red. "You're a no-good motherfucker." He stands up. "I'm getting outta here."

"Sit down, Richard, before you do something really stupid."

Richard continues standing. "If you think you're intimidating me into fixing the investigation that I'm doing on you and your wife, you got another guess coming."

"I don't want you to fix anything."

Richard looks over at James, who smiles. "Come on, Richard, sit down and listen to what I have to say."

After Richard sits, James says, "Just calm down and hear me out—I can leave here, now, and your career is pretty much over.

Even if somehow you manage to beat the rap that you're facing, which I don't think you will, you'll still be fired from your job. Now, I won't propose anything that will compromise your integrity—I just need a little help."

"What do you want?"

"You can keep on with your investigation of me and Sam. I'm not worried—you'll find nothing. As long as you're fair and don't try to make a name for yourself, Sam and I will do just fine."

"If you don't want me to fix the investigation, what do you want? Why pull off this stunt?"

James leans forward. "In a very short time, I'll be handing you evidence of another high-profile person's wrongdoing."

"You want me to investigate him?" Richard shakes his head. "James, you don't know how this works. I can't go around investigating anyone that I choose."

James smiles at Richard. "I don't want you to investigate anyone. What I want is for you take the proof that I hand you to your boss. Tell your boss that while conducting your examination into the Coppis, you uncovered another crime. You'll hand your boss the file and ask him what he wants you to do. That's it! Once you've done that, this matter that you're involved in tonight will disappear."

"Who is this high-profile person?"

"That's not your concern right now. You'll find out in due time."

"What do you expect my boss will do with the information?"

James smiles. "I hope he does the right thing and investigates. But I doubt it. In any event, it doesn't make a difference what your boss does. Your part of the assignment will be over."

"That's all you want—just hand in the file, and nothing else?"

"That's it, Richard. You agree to hand the evidence to your boss just as I outlined, and you can leave with me tonight. Now, that's not so bad, is it? No one is asking you to compromise your principles."

Richard looks over at James. "You're not asking me to do anything on my investigation into you?"

James stands up. "No, nothing on your investigation. As I said, if you're fair, I've got nothing to worry about. Well? Do we have a deal? Are you leaving with me tonight?"

Richard stands up. "It's a deal. When can I expect this evidence?"

"I don't know, but it shouldn't be long. Come on, I'll give you a lift home." James smiles. "Send me the bill for the car in the ditch."

CHAPTER 23

BOLIVIA AND HARTLEY

Ernie is bouncing around his seat as a passenger in a Toyota pickup. He is travelling on Carretera de los Yungas, also known as *Carretera de la Muerte*, Death Road. And it gets its name for a very good reason. Nearly three hundred people perish on the road every year. The road seldom gets any wider than 10 feet. There are no guard rails to protect the vehicles from the drops into the valley. Loose rocks are strewn all over the path. Rock slides are not uncommon. There are deep pot holes formed from the torrential rains. Ernie is just happy that he is on the passenger side that's facing the mountain and can't see down the deep canyons that's on the opposite side.

The car turns a corner near La Cumbre Pass the highest point on the road at a height of nearly 16,000 feet. The driver stomps on the brakes. A semi coming the opposite way blows its horn. There's no way that both vehicles can fit. The semi also screeches to a halt. The driver of the semi sticks his head out the window and with a contemptuous toothless grin hollers. *"Muévete cretino!"*

The Toyota immediately begins backing up. Ernie is clutching onto his seat because his vehicle is slipping and sliding on the gravel. Ernie's breathing becomes labored not only from the lack of oxygen but also from the concern that the pickup might slide off the road and fall into the abyss. It's about a quarter of a mile before the driver finds a safe crevice to get out of the way and let the bigger truck through. The driver of the semi smiles and waves as he drives by. Ernie glances at his driver who appears not to have any problem with his breathing.

The Toyota starts back on its journey. This is the descent down the mountain, which is no less dangerous than the climb. About an hour later the car pulls off to a dirt road leading to a valley. A few minutes later, Ernie looks to the top of a hill to his right and a young boy with a Kalashnikov strapped across his chest appears. The youngster looks down at the truck and puts his fingers to his mouth to whistle twice. A little further down the valley another youngster appears on a rocky prominence. The lad is also armed and again whistles twice. The process is repeated a third time and eventually the road opens to what appears to be a small village.

Youngsters, all armed with Kalashnikovs, begin to surround the truck. Ernie looks around. Many of the houses are just huts. Some are just shacks made of cardboard or plywood.

The driver turns to Ernie. "*Estamos aquí.*" He opens the door to get out.

Ernie gets out of the vehicle and one of the youngsters gets closer. "*Gringo?*"

Ernie smiles. "*No, Africano.*"

"*Fuera!*" His driver driver yells at the youngster.

The driver dashes into one of the better-looking houses. That is, a two-story house with stucco walls, a wooden door, and shutters on the windows. A half-dozen fighters come out of the place. One of the men and a young woman approach Ernie.

"Señor Ernie," he says.

"Yes, are you Rivera?"

"*Sí! Bienvenidos a nuestro mundo.*"

"Do you speak English?" Ernie asks.

"*Poquito,*" he replies and points to the young woman. "*Margarita habla Ingles.*"

Ernie smiles at the young woman. "I'd like to get cleaned up, it's been a long day."

Margarita smiles back. "*Sí*, right this way." She leads him to the house.

• • • • • • • • • ● • • • • • • • • • •

It's been nearly four weeks since he arrived at the camp, and Ernie is beginning to consider heading back. Not much has been happening. A couple of patrols that went nowhere. The youngsters held up a meat warehouse in Coroico. They celebrated the robbery with a barbecue. A few other small robberies to get food supplies not much other action.

A lot of target practicing—those young boys like shooting their rifles. An armored personnel carrier and two deuce-and-a-half trucks have arrived, and a shit load of ammo. James is doing his job keeping the rebels well supplied.

Four 85mm mortars and two 3.5 bazookas are also here. Nobody at the camp had any clue as to how to use the equipment. It was a good thing he was here: when the rebels went to try out the bazookas, a half-dozen men stood behind the weapon. The men did not realize that the back blast could have killed them all. Ernie showed the rebels how to properly use the 3.5 and also showed them the damage the piece could do both in front and in back.

This early morning, the men are loading bales of hay onto the trucks. *Well,* Ernie thought to himself, *if you're not going to use the vehicles for fighting, you might as well put them to some sort of use.*

Rivera, Margarita, and two other men come out of the house. They all have rifles strapped to their shoulders. Magazine clips are attached to the front of their vests.

Rivera smiles. "*Hoy va a ser un buen día, Africano.*" (Today is going to be a good day, African.)

"What do you have planned?" Ernie asks.

Rivera's smile broadens. "You will see. *Toma un rifle y súbete al truck.*" (Grab a rifle and hop on the truck.)

Men are beginning to mount onto the trucks. The bales of hay on each side shield the passengers. Ernie begins to understand the reason for the hay. He picks up a rifle and jumps on one of the trucks. When everybody is on board, they load up the last of the hay to screen the back of the truck. Ernie sits down on the bed of the truck, and with him are some twenty fighters. A couple of hours later, they come to a stop. The gate at the back of the deuce-and-a-half opens.

"Señor Ernie," Margarita calls.

Ernie gets up and makes his way to the back. He pushes away a couple of bales.

"Jose wants you," she says.

He jumps off the truck and looks around. They are stopped almost in the middle of the road. Oncoming traffic would have to really squeeze to get by. One of the men is jacking up the back of the truck.

"Over there." Margarita points to the other side of the road, where Rivera is standing with four men.

Two of the men have bazookas on their shoulders. Ernie walks over with Margarita.

Rivera looks at him. "*Te quedarás escondido detrás de esos arbustos con estos hombres. Por si acaso tienen un problema con las bazucas.*"

Ernie looks over at Margarita. "He wants you behind those bushes, to help the men with the bazookas, should they need you."

"Before I do that, he needs to tell me the plan. Who are we fighting?"

Margarita explains, to Rivera, Ernie's request.

Rivera turns to Ernie. *"Dos autobuses llenos de policías vendrán de la academia en aproximadamente una hora."*

"He said two busloads of policemen will be coming from the academy in an hour," Margarita says.

Rivera smiles broadly. *"Estamos aquí para dar la bienvenida a esos cadetes."*

Margarita turns to Ernie. "We are here to welcome those cadets."

Ernie looks at Rivera. *"Bueno."* He walks over to be with the men with the bazookas.

From his perch behind the shrubs, Ernie looks down the road. One of the trucks is up on a jack with a tire lying flat on the road. He's been camouflaged behind the bush in that same position for almost an hour. Only two cars have passed by the entire time. He's beginning to wonder if Rivera has the schedule right, or if this is another of Rivera's missions that never happens.

A green and white bus comes into view around a far turn. Another bus soon makes its appearance. The men next to him begin to stir. They mount the launchers onto their shoulders. The other men load the rocket into the rear of the bazookas.

Ernie looks over at the men. *"Paciencia."* He wants to make sure the men don't fire too soon and miss their targets.

"Esperar (wait)," Ernie says.

The moment the busses get within range he yells out, *"Ahora, fuego."*

Each rocket hits one of the buses. The blast stops the buses in their tracks. When the dust clears, Ernie sees a huge hole in each vehicle. One of the buses has caught on fire. Rivera's men have leapt off the trucks and have opened fire. There is no return fire from the busses.

• • • • • • • • ● • • • • • • • •

James is sitting in his attorney's office sipping on his coffee—he's delayed as long as he can, but he is finally testifying in front of the Senate Intelligence Committee, headed by Hartley.

"How was your time in France?" Raymond says.

"Just great." James sets down his cup. "If our children didn't have to start school, I'd still be there. We could've delayed Michael's start—he's only in kindergarten—but Molly is starting the third grade, and we didn't want her to fall behind."

"What do you need from us to prepare for today's hearing?" Raymond asks.

"Nothing. It's the same old crap. I've done these hearings dozens of times—I know the drill."

Raymond smiles. "Yeah, I guess you do. What about Hartley? James, this man could be a real pain in the ass for you."

James laughs and picks up his cup. "What do you mean, could be? Hartley will be a real pain in the ass. But I got Hartley covered—he won't be trouble."

There's a knock at the door and Ted Gibbs walks in. "There's a problem! It just came over the news that the rebels in Bolivia executed eighty-seven of the Federales. The government is claiming that the men killed were unarmed."

Raymond sits back in his chair. "No shit!" He kooks over at James. "Well, your day just got a lot more interesting."

James sips his coffee. "That's an understatement!"

"Is there anything that you want to discuss?" Raymond says. "This might be a huge problem for you."

James puts down his cup and stands up. "No, this doesn't change a thing." He stretches. "It'll just get a whole lot louder. If I were you guys, I'd bring along earplugs."

• • • • • • • • ● • • • • • • • •

At the steps of the capitol a television crew notices James and his lawyers coming their way. The reporter runs up to James and sticks a microphone in front of his face.

"Mr. Coppi, I'm Amada Gibbons of NBC. Can you tell me why Senator Hartley dragged you in front of his committee today? Does your appearance have anything to do with the killing of the unarmed policemen in Bolivia?"

James pushes the mike back from his face and smiles. "First of all, Amanda, no one is dragging me—I'm here voluntarily. As you know my company does a lot of government work and I regularly appear to update the Senators. Since this hearing was arranged several months ago, I doubt very much that it has anything to do concerning what happened in Bolivia today."

James is about to walk away when the reporter grabs his arm. "What about the fact that Senator Hartley may ask your wife Samantha to testify? Why would the senator want her to testify?"

James's face flushes and turns back to her "Where did you get that news?"

The reporter smiles. "I have my sources."

James composes himself and smiles. "I don't know what Hartley is doing; you'll have to ask him. I don't see any reason for calling my wife. I can answer all his questions."

James takes Amanda's arm away. As he is walking away he whispers to his lawyer Raymond. "Find out what that weasel Hartley is up to! He better not involve my wife!"

Inside that chamber, James reaches over and lifts the pitcher of water in front of him after he's sworn in. He pours himself a glass and has a drink. Marr and Gibbs are situated on each side of him. The senators are seated opposite him behind a long bench four feet above where he is sitting.

James is quite sure that the height of the bench is done on purpose to make sure that the senators are looking down on the person testifying. Probably an intimidation ploy to let a witness know who is in charge. After more than a dozen times of testifying at these hearings, he can honestly say that he has never been unsettled by this tactic. Indeed, he sees this trick as a challenge. How many of these senators can he cut down to size?

"Mr. Coppi, are you aware of the news coming out of Bolivia this morning?" Hartley asks.

James places down his glass and looks up. He smiles slyly. "What news, Senator?"

"The news about the killing of eighty-seven unarmed policemen," Hartley barks. "What do you have to say about that?"

James smirks. "War is hell!"

"Is that it?" the senator yells down at him.

James shrugs. "What do you want me to say? I had nothing to do with the killings, nor do I know whether the story that you're citing is even true."

"Aren't you supporting the rebel group known as the Guerreros, who are behind the killing?"

James shakes his head. "No, I personally don't support anyone in Bolivia. And I'm not aware of any evidence that backs your insinuation that the Guerreros were behind this alleged attack."

"What's your involvement in Bolivia?"

"Not much—I don't believe my company has any direct dealing with Bolivia, and I certainly don't."

"What about indirectly, Mr. Coppi? Do you have any indirect dealings with Bolivia?"

"I'm objecting to that question," Raymond cuts in, and leans forward. "That question is much too broad. If you have any transactions that you'd like Mr. Coppi to address, please bring them forward."

Hartley looks over at Marr. "All right, Mr. Marr, I will." He turns back to James. "Have you or your affiliated companies sold any arms to the rebel forces in Bolivia known as the Guerreros?"

"Once again, I'm objecting to your question, Senator," Raymond speaks up. "There's no reason why Mr. Coppi needs to reveal his business transactions to this committee."

"Mr. Marr, you must be aware that there's a law forbidding the use of taxpayer dollars for the purpose of supplying arms to the Guerreros. As such, I'd like to know whether or not Mr. Coppi's enterprises are in violation of this law. I believe my questions are germane to this end."

"Senator, if that's what you want to know, you need to rephrase your question. And, may I add, you need to be specific as to the transaction that you want Mr. Coppi to comment on."

"All right!" Hartley looks back at James. "Mr. Coppi, are you supplying arms to the Guerreros in violation of this act?"

"To my knowledge," James clears his throat, "my companies have not billed the United States government for any arms that may or may have not been shipped to rebels in Bolivia. Nor have any of my organizations received any taxpayer dollars for that purpose."

The questions continue from Hartley and other senators on the committee. Hartley is unmerciful in his inquiries into James, but except for Hartley, the other legislators' queries are relatively mild. As the inquiry is about to conclude, Hartley tries again, using a different approach.

"Mr. Coppi, I'd like to move on to your involvement in Zaire."

"Zaire?" Raymond yells out. "This hearing is supposed to be about Bolivia. We're not prepared to discuss Zaire."

"Hartley, what's this all about?" one of the senators of the opposing party cuts in. "Mr. Marr is quite right; this hearing was supposed to be about Bolivia. Why are you bushwhacking the witness with Zaire?"

Hartley turns to the senator. "I'm not ambushing anyone. There are events happening in Zaire that I'd like Mr. Coppi to elucidate. If Mr. Coppi doesn't have the knowledge to answer my questions, he's free to say so."

"This is a terrible waste of time," the senator fires back. "I'm far too busy with other matters. We should stick to the agenda."

"As the head of this committee, I'll decide on the program," Hartley says. "You're free to leave if you don't want to participate."

Hartley turns back to James. "Now, Mr. Coppi, can we move back to Zaire?"

"All right, what do you wanna know?"

"It's my understanding that your men may be mistreating prisoners and the opposing combatants."

Raymond objects. "Do you have any evidence that this is happening? Is there a particular incident that you'd like Mr. Coppi to address?"

"No, I don't. That's why I'm asking the question."

"In that case, I'm advising Mr. Coppi not to answer," Raymond says.

Hartley looks over at James. "What are the rules that your men are using for the treatment of prisoners in Zaire? Are your men following the rules for the treatment of prisoners specified in the Geneva Convention?"

"The protocols specified by the Geneva Convention don't apply there, Senator," James answers. "We're fighting enemy combatants not subject to those rules."

"Are you saying that you're mistreating the prisoners?"

James takes a drink of water. "I'm not saying that at all. You asked about the rules of engagement, and I answered your question. I know it's quite difficult for a draft dodger like you, who refused to go to war, to understand the correct military jargon."

Raymond leans over and whispers in James's ear. "I guess you decided to go for the jugular."

James simply smiles.

Raymond sits back. "Well, the day just got a lot more interesting."

"I served in the National Guard!" Hartley yells out.

James smiles. "Yeah, that's what I said—you were a draft dodger."

"Are we now discussing your military career, Hartley?" another senator calls out. "Can we move on?"

"One last point, Mr. Coppi." Hartley won't let it go. "Earlier, we spoke about eighty-seven unarmed policemen killed by the Guerreros. Do you remember that conversation?"

"Yes, I do!"

"Your comment to that news was, 'war is hell.' That statement sounded a bit flippant and cavalier. Do you not care about the loss of life that this war is causing?"

"I'm sorry I came across as glib, Senator. Yes, of course I care for the loss of life that is the result of the foolishness of mankind to not sit peacefully at a table and work out their problems. If I had a way of ending these conflicts, I certainly would do so."

"But you don't seem to mind profiting from these conflicts," Hartley debates.

"Senator, I believe Mr. Coppi has cleared up his earlier remark about the loss of life," Raymond cuts in. "There's no need to scold Mr. Coppi on what you perceive to be his business practices. May I remind the panel that Mr. Coppi and his companies work hand in hand with the United States government in protecting our national interests. Those companies owned by the Coppi family provide an invaluable service to the American people."

Outside in the hall, when the meeting is over, Raymond turns to James. "That went rather well. With the way the hearing began, I didn't think it would end up this well."

James smiles. "Don't jump for joy, Raymond, this isn't over. Hartley isn't letting this go. This is Hartley's own private peeve, and he's not giving up easily."

The attorney looks into James's face. "Why don't you just drop the project, James? This can't be that much business for you. It seems to be more trouble than it's worth. Just let it go!"

"And let asshole Hartley get the best of me? No way, Marr! This is personal!" James looks over at Raymond. "I've got to get going; my daughter Molly has a soccer game today and I want to be there. Call me tomorrow to let me know how we made out but most of all, find out what Hartley is doing about Samantha."

· · · · · · · · ● · · · · · · · · · ·

The soccer game hasn't yet started when James gets to the field. There are so many parents and spectators that James is having a hard time locating Sam. Finally, James notices her standing on the sidelines with Michael and her bodyguard Regis, at the far end of the field.

Sam walks up to James and gives him a kiss. "You made it just in time. They'll be starting in a few minutes."

James leans down and lifts up Michael. "How's my boy?" He gives Michael a kiss.

"Molly is playing, Daddy."

"I know, son." James turns to Sam. "Where's Molly?"

Sam points to the middle of the sidelines. "Over there with her teammates. Molly is number seven."

James puts down Michael. "I'm walking over to say hi."

When Molly sees her dad, she runs to him with a big smile on her face.

"You made it!" she says.

James bends down and gives her a kiss. "Of course! I would never miss your first game. I love your uniform. Green and white, really nice. You look like a professional soccer player, with your cleats and shin pads."

"Hello, James." A man walks over.

James rises up. "Hello, Marty. Thanks for taking the time to coach my daughter and all these young girls."

"It's my pleasure." The coach turns to Molly. "You need to get with your teammates and do your pre-game stretching. You know the drill."

As Molly is running away, James hollers, "Score one for Daddy!"

"Well, I better get with the team," Marty says.

"Okay, good luck today," James lets out, and walks back to be with Sam.

James looks out at the field, and when Molly's team comes out to take their position, he turns to Sam. "Where's Molly? I don't see her."

"There she is, on the sidelines with some of her teammates," Sam answers.

"She's a substitute?" James's shoulders sag. "Isn't she any good?"

"I guess not."

There's no score ten minutes into the game.

"I don't know why we came. Molly isn't even playing," James says.

"We're here to show support," Sam replies.

"How bad can Molly be?" James motions to the field. "They all stink out there. We've been here ten minutes, and neither side has come anywhere near scoring a goal! All that the girls keep doing is running up and down the field."

"They'll put Molly in soon, I'm sure. The rules are that each player has to play at least two minutes."

"I'm speaking to Marty."

Sam grabs his arm. "Please don't make a scene."

James smiles at her. "I'm not making a scene. I'll be right back."

"Marty, may I have a word with you?" James pulls the coach to the side. "Can you put Molly in for a few minutes? I'd love to see her play."

"I was inserting Molly in the second half."

James puts on his sorrowful face. "Would it be too much of an imposition if you put her in now? It's not like it'll make any difference in the outcome of the game. All that the kids are doing is running up and down the field."

Marty looks around. "All right, I'll get Molly into the game at the next break in the action."

"Thank you!"

"You've become one of those parents," Sam says to him when he gets back.

"What the hell does that mean, 'one of those parents'? What have I become?"

"One of those parents, in that their child always has to shine. Their children take precedent over all the others."

"I am not. All I want is to see Molly play." James points and smiles. "There she is! The coach put her in."

"Go get them, Molly!" He cups his hands and yells out to her. "Score one for Daddy!"

"Can you keep your voice down?" Sam scowls. "You're embarrassing us."

"I don't care. What's the use of coming to watch your child play if you can't root for them?"

Suddenly, Molly intercepts a pass and starts racing down the field. James dashes down the sidelines, shouting.

"Go, Molly, go! Watch out for that defender!"

No need for Molly to watch out, as she scoots by the opponent easily. Keeping the soccer ball a few feet in front of her, she sprints towards the other team's goal net. James is rushing down the sideline yelling at the top of his lungs, rooting her on.

Along the way, he collides into several of the spectators in an attempt to keep up with Molly. There's only the goalie in Molly's way as she nears the net. With just a slight feint, Molly easily avoids the defender and kicks the ball softly into the empty net. James is jumping up and down, cheering. He returns to Sam, gasping for air.

"You just made a complete fool of yourself," Sam says.

James is still breathing heavily. "Did you see her? I thought you said she wasn't any good. Molly ran by the entire team."

At that moment, Molly intercepts another pass and starts her journey down the field. James immediately turns and bolts down the sidelines with her, once again shouting words of encouragement and instructions. The result is the same, with Molly scoring another goal. The breathless James returns to Sam's side, and she shakes her head in disapproval. James creases his nose at her. The referee comes over.

"Mr. Coppi, you need to stop what you're doing. You're scaring the girls."

"All right, I'll behave."

"You're lucky the ref didn't ask you to leave," Sam says after the ref walks off.

Molly scores two more goals. James fights off his instincts and stays quietly on the sidelines.

"They should take that little redhead out," James overhears one of the parents saying as she points to Molly. "She's too good, she's making the other players look bad."

It's as if the coach just overheard the comment, because at that very moment, he sends in a substitute for Molly.

"Why is he taking Molly out?" James asks Sam, shaking his head.

"All the girls need to play, remember? That's the rule."

"Yeah, but he should take out one of the other kids. Molly is the best player that he's got!"

After the game, Molly runs up to her parents.

"You were great out there, Molly," James voices. "Where did you learn to play so well?"

"I practiced with Afonso," she answers. "Afonso is really good; he's on the middle school team."

"Cardiz's son? Where did you practice?" he asks.

"At the ranch, behind the barns."

"Let's get home and clean up before dinner," Sam says.

"No way. We're going out for dinner to celebrate," James lets out. "Any restaurant Molly wants."

"Can we go to Giuseppe's for pizza?" she yells out.

"Yes, of course," he replies. "Any place that you want."

James walks into the bedroom and places his watch on the end table next to his bed. "Well, Molly finally went to sleep," he says to Sam, who is propped on three pillows on her side of the bed, reading a magazine.

Sam puts down the magazine. "What were you guys talking about? You've been in there over an hour."

"Well, we started just talking about the game, and then we moved to a brief discussion of what I thought about her teammates. Then proceeded to a long talk of what she thought about each of her teammates. And then we progressed to an even longer conversation about what Molly thought of her classmates."

"Wow! You must've been bored out of your mind."

James smiles broadly. "No, I loved every second of our talk. It was just great." James opens a drawer and takes out his pajamas. "I'm taking a shower."

Before he goes in the bathroom, he turns to Sam. "By the way, remind me to thank Afonso for helping Molly with her soccer. He really taught her well—she played great."

"Molly's great play had nothing to do with Afonso."

James comes back, sits on the bed, and is taking off his shoes. "What do you mean?"

Sam sits up. "I saw Molly in practice two days ago. She played nothing like she played today. Molly's great play today was because of you."

"What're you talking about, Sam? I had nothing to do with the way she played. I've never even kicked around a ball with Molly."

Sam smiles. "Molly's problem was never that she couldn't play. She was timid and insecure around her teammates. Too afraid of making a mistake and being laughed at. When you ran down the sidelines with her like a crazy man, she got the confidence that she needed. You brought Molly out of her shell. That, and the fact that Molly wanted so much to please you."

James stands up and heads to the bathroom. "Well, I'm still thanking Afonso. I'm sure he had a lot more to do with Molly's play than I did."

Early the next morning, James is on the phone with his attorney. "What's new, Raymond? Any feedback from our source as to what Barrett is doing with Samantha? Was the rumor true?"

"Yes, James, it's true, Hartley wants to subpoena Samantha!"

"Motherfucker," James says under his breath. "Why her?" he says aloud. "Sam doesn't know anything about this Bolivian affair—or Zaire, for that matter."

"You already know why, James. Hartley is ratcheting things up. He's putting the screws to you."

"What if we ignore the subpoena?"

"You ignore the subpoena and Hartley will take it out on your government contracts. James, you'd be risking losing all that business. It's far better if we cooperate. Anyway, let me talk to the other committee members and let me see if I can get them to not issue the subpoena. I'll try to get it quashed, or at least pulled back to an invitation, but it's probably not happening. Hartley won't play ball. Samantha will have to testify under a subpoena."

"All right; try your best, Raymond. Don't make it easy on Hartley."

"Sure thing, James, I'll give it my best shot."

After James hangs up, he utters to himself, "So it's all-out war, Hartley! That's the way you want it! Well, you're getting what you asked for!"

CHAPTER 24

THE SQUEEZE

Early Saturday morning, Richard Faulk is sitting in the backseat of the gray Impala sedan looking at the apartment complex. In the front seat there are two FBI agents who are working with him on the Coppi matter. Richard is worried, James has that arrest report dangling over his head like the sword of Damocles. James promised that he would not interfere in the investigation, but will he keep that agreement if Richard uncovers damaging evidence on him or his wife. Knowing what he knows about James, it is obvious that James will renege on the promise and fight back.

Richard considered asking his boss to relieve him of the investigation into the Coppis. But he has concluded that the only way to be completely assured that James will not use the arrest report is for Richard to get something damaging on James. James is a street fighter and Richard knows that the only way to defeat a street fighter is to get down and dirty, to his level. Once Richard evens the score, he is absolutely certain that James will cave.

One of the men in the front seat turns to him. "Are you ready for us to go in? The lights just went on inside the home."

"Let's give them a few more minutes," he replies.

• • • • • • • • ● • • • • • • •

Inside the apartment, Miles is in the kitchen making Jen a pancake breakfast. Jen is still asleep and he wants to surprise her by bringing her breakfast in bed. The toddler Liz is sitting in her high chair, nibbling on the Cheerios that are on her plate.

"What are you doing?" A voice comes from behind.

Miles turns and smiles. "You're supposed to be in bed. You spoiled the surprise, I was serving breakfast to you in bed."

"The aroma of the bacon frying woke me up." Jen takes a seat at the table. "May I have a cup of coffee?"

Miles reaches for the pot. "You certainly may." He pours her a cup and puts it in front of her.

There's a knock at the door and they both turn.

"Who could that be?" Jen says.

Miles walks over and opens the door.

Two men in gray suits are there. One of the men waves a badge in front of Miles's face. "I'm special agent Floyd Henrathy, of the FBI. Are you Miles Cornish?"

"FBI," Jen jumps up from her seat and goes over to the door. "What do you want with us?"

The agent lets himself in. "I'm sorry to disturb your breakfast. We need to speak to your husband."

The agent looks over at Miles. "Maybe it's better if we talk outside. We have a car parked out front. It shouldn't be long."

"All right," he says and turns to Jen. "I'll be right back."

Jen nervously opens the slat of the blind in the living room. Her trembling hand holds on to the slat as she peeks out the window. She is feeling weak and tries to summon up her strength to continue looking. She can feel her heart beating against her pajama top. An ominous sensation inside her body is telling her that Miles is in trouble, but she can't imagine what. She looks at the clock: 7:42.

Agent Henrathy opens the back door of the car parked out front and Miles gets in. Jen catches a fleeting glimpse of a man inside the vehicle. The two agents stand outside the car and light up a smoke. The baby is fussing and Jen goes back in the kitchen lifting Liz out of the high chair. She walks back to the window with Liz in her arms and again lifts a slat to have a look.

It feels like a like a lifetime that Miles is in the car. The backdoor of the car opens. Jen looks at the clock: 8:18. Miles climbs out, and the men get back in the vehicle. Miles stands there as he watches the gray sedan drive off. Jen lets go of the blind, placing Liz in her playpen and walking back into the kitchen.

"What happened?" Jen asks immediately when Miles is back inside. "What did they want?"

Miles points to the table. "You better sit down."

Jen and Miles take a seat and Jen looks over. "Well?"

"They are investigating the Coppis."

"The Coppis, why?"

Miles shrugs. "I don't know. They didn't say."

Jen leans forward. "What do they want with you?"

"They want my cooperation. They want me to work undercover for them on the investigation. Give them exclusive information on what's going on at the company. They know that I'm writing a book on the Coppis, and are demanding all my notes."

Jen reaches for his hand. "Do they want you to help bring down the company?"

Miles nods. "That's exactly what they want."

Jens voice rises up a notch. "That's horrible. What happens to all the people who work there? What happens to us? Why would they ask you of all people for help? What would lead them to believe that you would assist?"

Miles clears his throat. "Jen, I need to tell you a story. A story of something that I've never told you before. An embarrassment that I experienced before I met you."

Miles clears his throat. "Coming home from my high school prom I was involved in an automobile accident. The convertible that I was driving went flying off the road and into a ditch. My date was thrown from the vehicle and was killed."

Miles pauses for a moment. "They arrested me for drunk driving and the police charged me with negligent homicide. My brother used all his political influence to get my charges reduced. I ended up pleading guilty to drunk driving and did six months of community service and four years of probation. Since I was seventeen, the judge said that my record would be expunged at age 21 if I kept clean and had no more offenses."

"That story is disturbing, but what does that have to do with the men that came to the house?"

"In that car outside was Assistant Attorney Richard Faulk. Faulk said that if I didn't cooperate with the investigation, he was going to reopen the case and charge me with involuntary manslaughter."

Jen lets out a gasp. "Oh, my God, can he do that? I thought the case was over and you were sentenced? You served your punishment."

"Faulk said that he would bring charges on a federal level. The accident happened in a national park." Miles reaches for her hands. "It doesn't matter, Jen, whether Faulk can or can't charge me. If this news gets out, I'm pretty well finished."

"What are you going to do?" she asks. "Are you going to cooperate?"

"No, I'm not. That wouldn't be fair to the Coppis—they have always been good to us. I'm heading into the office first thing Monday and resigning."

Tears are flowing down Jen's face. "Won't they charge you with the crime?"

"No, I don't believe so. Once I'm no longer working for the company, I can't very well provide them with inside information, can I? I believe the DA will just go away." Miles looks into her face. "I'm afraid our Colorado Springs adventure is over. This is a small town. Once word gets out, no one will hire me. We'll have to go back to Massachusetts."

Jen reaches over and lifts up his chin. "You listen to me and listen carefully. The Cornish family are not quitters. We're not going home with our tail between our legs. Nobody is driving us out of town. We did nothing wrong. We'll just figure out a way out of this mess. If I have to, I'll go back to work. You'll find another job but we're not leaving Colorado Springs!"

• • • • • • • • ● ● ● • • • • • • •

Sam is walking out of her bedroom when Billingsley walks up to her.

"Domingo from the gatehouse just called and said that Jennifer Cornish is at the entrance," he says. "Should Domingo let her through?"

"Huh, I wonder what she wants," Sam mutters. "Yes, of course, let her in."

When Jen is at the door Sam greets her. "Jennifer, what a lovely surprise."

"I'm sorry to bother you, Sam, but I need to speak to you and ask for your advice," Jen says. "Can you spare a few minutes?"

"Yes of course. Come in." Sam points to the back door. "Why don't we sit on the patio; it's a beautiful day." As they pass

Billingsley Sam says. "Mr. Billingsley, please bring us some ice tea, we'll be outside."

Sitting outside Jen remarks. "It's beautiful out here. What a lovely view of the Rockies."

Billingsley comes out with a pitcher of ice tea and pours them two glasses.

"Is everything all right?" Sam says to Jen after Billingsley leaves. "You look troubled."

"Thank you for taking the time to speak to me," Jen says. "A problem has come up and I could use your advice."

Jen tells Sam what happened earlier that morning with the FBI.

When she's finished Sam remarks. "I see why you're so upset." Sam takes a sip of the tea. "So Miles's solution is to resign and go back to New England."

"Yes," Jen says shakily. "But I told him that even if he quits, we're not going back to Massachusetts." She looks over at Sam. "I like it here. This is where we're going to make a life." Jen lets out a sigh. "What do you say, Sam? Is there anything that you can do for us?"

"James is at a golf outing with the Sheriff, the Mayor, and our Congressmen. I'll speak to James tonight when he gets home."

Jen smiles. "James doesn't strike me as a golfer?"

Sam laughs. "He's not. He stinks at the game. But those men have invited him a lot and he ran out of excuses."

Jen stands up. "I better get moving, I've taking up too much of your time."

Sam stands up and reaches for her. "Nonsense, you can stay as long as you like, I enjoy your company."

"No, I better get back. Miles will be wondering where I've gone and I didn't want him to know that I was coming to see you. He would've tried to stop me." Jen looks over at Sam. "Do you think you guys can help?"

Sam smiles and winks. "Don't tell Miles until after I speak to James, but I wouldn't be in a hurry to pack my bags yet if I were you—I've got a feeling that you're going to be in Colorado for a while."

· · · · · · · ● · · · · · · ·

That Monday morning Miles is sitting in his car looking at the building of Coppi Enterprises. He lets out a breath as he ponders what will be his last look at the structure. With a heaviness, he gets out of the car and walks to the entrance. He will go directly to see his boss Jack and hand in his resignation. No need to waste time; just get it over immediately. The weekend at home had been quiet. For some reason, Jen wasn't in a particularly sad mood.

He barely acknowledges the greeting from the receptionist as he walks into the lobby and toward the elevators. At his floor he walks quickly to Jack's office, knocks at the door, and peeks in.

"Jack, have you got a minute?"

Jack stands up from behind his desk. "Oh, Miles, I'm glad you're here. We can't talk now, James just called and wants to see both of us right away."

"Jack, just a minute please, it's important—I really need to speak to you."

Jack walks past him. "It'll have to wait until we finish with James. Come on."

They walk up to Kathy's desk.

"James wants to see us," Jack says to her.

"Go right in, he's expecting you," she says.

Inside, James looks up when he notices the men. "Come in guys, have a seat."

James looks at Miles. "What can you tell me about the book you're writing about me and Samantha?"

Jack sits up in his chair and looks at Miles. "What? Is that true? Are you writing about the Coppis?"

"Yes, it's true," Miles answers.

Jack yells at Miles. "Why would you do that without speaking to me first? How could you be so foolish?"

"Jack, can you please let me conduct the meeting," James says.

Miles turns to James. "I'm sorry, sir. I didn't mean to cause any trouble. I'm so fascinated by what you and your wife have accomplished that I thought it would make a great story." Miles leans forward in his chair. "Please believe me that I wouldn't have ever shown the contents to anyone without first getting your approval."

"How did Richard Faulk find out about the book?" James says.

"Who is Richard Faulk?" Jack asks.

"He's an Assistant District Attorney for the Justice Department," James answers.

Jack looks over at Miles. "You're talking to the Justice Department, why?"

"Jack, if you keep interrupting I'll have to ask you to leave," James says. He turns to Miles. "Go ahead."

"I believe Richard got the information from my brother. My brother called me a while ago just to chat and asked me how I was doing here in Colorado Springs. During our conversation I mentioned that I was writing a book on you to pass the time." Miles leans forward. "Writing is a hobby of mine and I find what you and Samantha have accomplished amazing. The background check that I did on you guys was so fascinating that I thought it would make a fantastic story."

"Tell me about this meeting you had on Saturday," James says and looks over at Jack. "And don't interrupt!"

When Miles is finished, Jack speaks up. "James, I know you don't want me to speak but I feel it's incumbent on me to warn you that we need to terminate Miles immediately. He is a danger to our company. Not only did Miles lie to us when he applied for the job by not disclosing his criminal record, but he showed a complete lack of judgment. Writing about you and Samantha without your consent. And I don't believe for one minute that he revealed the book to his brother just by happenstance. James, Miles can't be trusted, he has to go."

Miles turns to Jack. "That's all right, Jack, no need to say anything." Miles reaches into his suit jacket. "This is my resignation, this is what I wanted to speak to you about before coming into this meeting. My resignation is effective immediately."

Miles turns to James. "I don't intend on cooperating with the FBI. There's no way that I would agree to turn against you James."

Miles stands up.

"Sit down, Miles!" James states firmly. "No one is quitting, he looks over at Jack, "and no one is getting fired!"

James lets out a breath. "You can leave, Jack. I want to speak to Miles alone."

After Jack leaves, James smiles at Miles. "Let's talk! You and I have a lot to discuss."

$$\bullet \; \cdot \; \cdot \; \cdot \; \cdot \; \bullet \; \bullet \; \bullet \; \bullet \; \bullet \; \bullet \; \cdot \; \cdot \; \cdot \; \cdot$$

That night when Miles gets home, Jen immediately comes over to him.

"How did it go?" She says. "I've been praying for a miracle all day. I'm hoping that you coming home at a normal time is a good sign."

Miles smiles. "Your prayers worked. I still have my job."

Jen looks up at the ceiling. "Thank you!" She grabs Miles's hand. "Come on, sit, tell me all about it."

Miles sits next to her and reaches for her hands and begins. "After Jack left, James and I had a talk. He apologized to me."

Jen stares at Miles. "Apologized to you, for what?"

"He was sorry that he hadn't sat with me for any extended time until now. 'I like to get to know all my managers,' James said. 'I've just been so damn busy.'"

Miles smiles wryly at Jen. "There was a sad look in his eyes as he said, 'I need to get my act together. I'm ignoring a lot of people close to me that need my attention.'" Miles looks into Jen's face. "Jen, for that brief moment, I saw James in a different light. That tough, no-holds-barred image of him was gone. He appeared vulnerable. How easy it is for us to forget that behind that strong facade that we see, is a man who's only human."

Letting out a breath, Miles continues. "James smiled at me and said, 'There's no schooling for my job, is there? You have to learn as you go. I'm still in training, so please forgive me for not getting to you sooner.'"

Miles shakes his head. "Can you imagine that, Jen? The man was apologizing to me. We spent the rest of the time talking about me. He wanted to know how I liked my job. How was I adjusting to Colorado?"

Miles reaches for her. "And we also talked about you, Jen. Talked about you a lot, James particularly wanted to know how you were getting on with life here. He knew all about your volunteer work and your house hunting."

Miles smiles. "He said, 'Sam tells me that she's quite a character. I can't wait to meet her.'"

"At the end of our talk, he said, 'Don't worry about Richard Faulk, I've got that under control. It should be over soon. If Faulk puts any pressure on you, let me know. Go home and have a nice evening with Jen.' James smiled. 'I'm looking forward to reading that book of yours, when it's finished.'"

Miles looks into her eyes. "Jen, that man isn't firing me. While my boss Jack was freaking out, James already had a handle on the problem."

Jen let's out a breath, leans over and gives Miles a kiss. "You have no idea how relieved I am."

"Me too!" Miles laughs. "I guess you praying to that Higher Power worked for us."

"Yes it did!" Jen stands up. "That Higher Power is truly amazing. I even gave her a name—I call her Samantha."

CHAPTER 25

BOLIVIA BLOWS UP

It's early morning, two days later. Ernie is back from Bolivia and is sitting in James's office. Before Ernie gets started on giving James his report, there's a knock at the door and Rodney peeks in.

"James, may I interrupt for a minute?'

"Yeah, come in. What's up?"

"We have a problem. Colonel Chase got caught moving money around."

James sits up. "What happened?"

Rodney looks over at Ernie before turning back to James. "I was talking to a source that I have at the agency. He told me that they caught Chase trying to move money that was intended for us to another venture in Central America."

"Can the government trace this back to us? We don't have anything to do with Central America."

Rodney shrugs. "I don't know; it all depends on how sloppy this guy Chase is. Frankly, he sounds like a loose cannon. He seems to have his hands in every covert operation. You better be ready in case it does land on us. I'm sure Hartley will drag Colonel Chase in front of his committee."

James rubs his chin. "Get in touch with Ian wherever he is, have him come here immediately. We need to sit down and discuss this latest event."

After Rodney leaves Ernie smiles. "Things have just gotten a lot more interesting for you."

James forces out a laugh. "Yeah, I'll say. Tell me what you uncovered in Bolivia. Can these two guys, Gaytan and Rivera, be trusted to keep their mouths shut if someone from the US goes down there and starts asking a lot of questions? Especially now, when things are about to heat up."

Ernie nods. "Yeah, both of the men are really good at feeding bullshit. You shouldn't have any problems."

"Good. How about Rivera's troops? Do they really stand a chance of overthrowing the government?"

"They're getting better. Rivera just established another rebel base outside of Santa Cruz. They've got a lot of firepower, thanks to you. Two Sherman tanks arrived last week. The problem is that Rivera's men are young and extremely undisciplined. To these men, all the military gear is like toys. The largest attack they've mounted so far is the assault on the policemen. Rivera is fortunate that the government troops are also in disarray and the morale among the Federales is low. The Federales haven't been paid for months. The only thing keeping the Bolivian government from falling is the Cubans."

James looks over at Ernie. "Um, so it's true that the Cubans are involved?"

"Yes, the Cubans are involved. And not just as advisors. They're participating in the fighting." Ernie sits forward in his chair and lowers his voice. "James, I want to make you aware of another potential problem. When I was in Santiago meeting with Gaytan, another fellow was there. I asked around and I was able to learn that he was Colonel Morales. He's very high in the Bolivian military."

"What's your take on this meeting, Ernie? Do you think Gaytan is getting ready to switch sides and double-cross Rivera?"

"Yeah, it's possible. I don't believe Rivera and Gaytan like each other much." Ernie moves forward in his seat. "Remember, James, Gaytan is part of the old guard. Gaytan is in with the rich old families that want to return Bolivia back to where the country was before the socialists came to power. You know, keep the status quo that says the old families stay in control. Gaytan only went to Rivera in desperation. Gaytan and the old family hierarchy will dump Rivera the minute they get a chance."

James lets out a breath. "Listen, Ernie, have you got a little time for me? You're not needed in Zaire, are you? Gary can handle Zaire without you?"

"That's right, James, I'm free. Since we made peace with Benga, there's not much going on in Zaire. There are other warlords in the country, but they're not very powerful. What do you need?"

"I'd like you to go back to South America. Go to Santiago first and see if you can find out more about the association between Gaytan and Morales. After that, head back out to Rivera. Tell him that he needs to get busy and intensify the fighting. Impress on Rivera that the money may be drying up, and if that happens, so will our support."

After Ernie leaves, James makes another call. "James Coppi for Phil Eisley," he says to the receptionist.

"What's up, James?" Phil says on the line.

"Do you have what we agreed on?"

"It'll be done by the end of the week."

"Good." James says. "What about the IRS audit into my father in laws church? Has that been stopped?"

"I thought it had—do you know for sure that this examination is still happening?"

"No, but I don't know that it's over either? Find out and call me back."

"I'll see what I can do."

James makes another call. "Richard, can you come by the office next week? I've got that information that we talked about."

After Richard, he buzzes Kathy. "Have Miles come to my office."

"Tell me what's happening with the IRS investigation into my father-in-law's church," he says to Miles when he's sitting in the office. "Has that ended?"

"I'm afraid not James," Miles says. "The agents are on another assignment but they'll be back." Miles leans forward. "It's that check drawn on a foreign account that's the problem. By law all American citizens have to report money held in foreign banks, you and Sam did not."

"What's my liability? What are Sam and I facing here?"

Miles thinks for a moment. "If it were just this one transaction probably not much of a liability. What worries me is that the auditors will want to know of other foreign accounts that you may have." Miles looks over at James. "I'm assuming that you have other overseas accounts?"

When James doesn't answer, Miles adds. "That's the risk James, the IRS is going to dig into all your overseas transactions. Both you and Sam are not only facing financial liability but also criminal charges. Who knows about these foreign accounts?"

"Me, Sam and Kathy."

"That's it?"

James nods. "Miles, tell me how to get out of this mess. How about if I get someone to stop this audit?"

"I'm not sure you can get these field guys to back off. Stuff like this can make their careers. The higher echelon would be too afraid to cover up a criminal activity. Especially activity that concerns defrauding taxpayers." Miles looks at the door and turns back to James. "If you want this problem to go away, we have to give these field auditors a plausible, harmless, explanation of why the check was issued. Some sort of evidence that what they've uncovered isn't serious and a waste of their time."

"Like what?"

"Here's what I'm thinking," Miles smiles. "It's a little shady but I believe it'll work. I'd like to treat the transaction as an error."

James shakes his head. "How can it be an error? The contribution was made and the check was cashed."

"What if the check was drawn on an empty account?"

James laughs. "Are you losing it Miles. The check was honored. Money changed hands."

"I know James. But think about this for a minute. Let's say you guys opened an account overseas but never funded that account. Sam inadvertently wrote a check from that unfunded account. When the check was presented to the Cayman bank what would the bank do?"

"Bounce the check!"

Miles nods. "Yes, probably. But what would Cayman bank do if you are a good customer." Miles leans forward. "That bank would call you before bouncing the check. And, if after that call, you worked out an arrangement to pay back the proceeds of that error. That bank would honor the overdraft. Am I right?"

James rubs his chin. "I see."

Miles smiles broadly. "All we need is evidence that you had this arrangement with the Cayman bank. Evidence such as a promissory note signed by you and the bank dated at the time the check was honored."

"Do you think the IRS auditors will go for this?"

"Maybe. We also need a letter from the bank that the checking account was never put in effect. An account was started but there was never any money deposited into the account. When Sam wrote the check, she didn't realize that the account wasn't active. We'll claim that it was just a simple oversight on her part. This will make it difficult for the IRS to prove fraud."

Miles pauses for a moment. "James the auditors will probably not buy this excuse fully. They'll still be a doubt. But if you use your political connections to apply pressure to stop the audit, it may work. We'll supply just enough evidence to cast a doubt that there was any criminal activity. We will claim that it was just an honest mistake. The field agents won't be able to justify to their superiors that it's worth allocating more extensive man hours on the audit. At that point, the auditor's bosses at the IRS can easily justify bringing to an end the examination. What do you think?"

"Yeah, I see your point."

"Can you get the overseas bank to play ball and work out this note?"

"Yeah, I can."

"How about terminating the audit?" Miles asks. "Can you get that done? You'll have to get someone really high up at the government—these audits aren't easy to stop."

"That's going to be a little harder," he says.

"That's important James. The examiners won't end the audit unless they get pressure to stop. They smell blood. You and Sam's blood. No amount of money or influence will get you off the hook with the IRS once the auditors find something. You need to end the examination before it gets that far."

James stands up. "OK, I get the picture."

•••••••••●•••••••••

James is in his office, talking to his men Ian, Rodney, and Vernon three days later.

"So, what do you want me to do?" Ian says. "How do you want me to play this moving forward in Bolivia, now that Colonel Chase was caught using US funds and there'll be no money coming from the United States?"

"Ernie called earlier, he met with this fellow Gaytan in Santiago," James answers. "Gaytan told Ernie that both Chile and Argentina have agreed to come up with money to make up the shortfall."

"James, you're missing the point," Rodney speaks up. "Congress can put sanctions in effect against the Guerreros and Gaytan. There'll be no way to funnel the money through the international banks. No bank will handle the transaction. The banks will be too afraid to touch any deal that involves Gaytan or the rebels."

James looks over at Ian. "Put into effect the same methods that we did in South Africa."

"You want couriers to hand-carry the proceeds?" Ian says. "James, that's quite a task. We'll have to set up a whole network. Ernie will have to get more involved."

"What about personal liability, James?" Rodney brings up. "Don't forget, this act also bars American citizens from helping the rebels. You and any employee of this company can be held criminally liable."

"The act doesn't really bar US citizens from helping the rebels. We just can't use taxpayer dollars." James turns to Ian. "Just to play it safe, use my Italian company. I'm a dual-citizen, since I was born in Italy. The Italians have no laws about helping the rebels."

"Why are we doing this, James?" Rodney says. "Why not just drop this? We did our part. It's not our fault that Colonel Chase screwed everything up. Our firm can get out of this very clean. Let's just drop the whole thing."

"Yeah, that's probably the smart way out," James says. "But that's not the way we do business. We took on a client, and we just don't leave the client high and dry because things get tough."

James looks back at the men. "Ian, get that network set up as soon as possible. Contact Paolo Rizzi, the head of my company in Italy. Let him know what we need from him."

"James, shouldn't we wait until we can figure out the political fallout?" Rodney says. "If what I read in the papers is correct, this could be quite a mess. We're surely getting dragged into this quagmire."

"Yeah, I know. Raymond Marr is coming over to update me. He met with the President's chief of staff, Jack Dalrymple."

James looks at the clock on the wall. "In fact, he should be here any time now. Rodney, I know there'll be problems, but you're not thinking this affair all the way through. It's not just keeping our word to a client.

"Right now, we have no cards to play. If we stop what we're doing, there's no reason for anybody at the government to play nice with us. We've already surrendered. If we keep going, we can negotiate a cease to our activities, in our favor. We'll still have a hand to play."

Vernon speaks up. "James, have you taken into consideration what impact this will have on our initial public offering of the railroad? You and I are scheduled to travel around the country over the next month to attract potential investors. These investors won't take too kindly if you become embroiled in a scandal. Your face will be plastered all over the news if you get dragged in front of a congressional committee regarding this Bolivian matter. This isn't exactly the kind of news that will entice these money men to part with their money."

James stands up and arches his back. "All right, guys, thanks for your input. For the time being, let's stay the course until I can get a better gauge on this affair. Meanwhile, Ian, contact Ernie and give him the news that he needs to be more involved with the movement of funds and arms to the rebels. Let me know when the new network with our Italian company is up and running."

"James, Raymond Marr is in the lobby," Kathy buzzes in.

"All right, Kathy, I'm done here. Please get Raymond and bring him to my office."

"OK, Raymond, what have you got for me?" James asks the lawyer when he's sitting at his desk.

"It's a real mess, James. This thing with Colonel Chase is about to explode. Many of the opposing parties are even using the word 'impeachment' again."

"You know, Raymond, these politicians have some nerve. This is the same party that got us into a mess in Southeast Asia, which cost the country over 50,000 of our best young citizens. This is the same party that continuously lied to the American people. Suddenly, they find the high moral road. These hypocritical politicians make me sick."

Raymond waves his hand. "Forget the politicians, James. Let's worry about us. What do we have at stake here? Remember, you went in front of the Senate and told that committee that you weren't involved."

"I'm not involved. We sold merchandise to a company in Chile. What they did with the equipment isn't my problem."

"James, in this political environment, that reasoning isn't going to fly. That's just being cute, and Congress won't let you get away with it."

"What law did I break, Raymond? None at all. The Hartley amendment said that we couldn't use taxpayer money to purchase the arms. To our knowledge, we didn't use taxpayer money. We had no idea where Chase was getting the funds. Unless Chase lies and said that I knew, they can't connect me to this scandal. Secretary Reichwald and Zeist both assured me that this affair was on the up and up.

James smiles. "By the way, for your information, we're still selling military gear to this Chilean source."

Raymond sits up in his seat. "What? Are you crazy? If the Senators find out that you're still doing business, they'll crucify you."

"Maybe." James smiles slyly. "But I don't think so. You see, Raymond, if I stopped, I'd be admitting that I was doing something wrong. This client is still buying, and the client most certainly isn't using taxpayer money anymore."

James leans forward. "Don't you see my point? If the government wants me to put an end to what I'm doing, they'll have to negotiate with me. That means they'll have to offer me something. Something like a free pass in this controversy. If I stop on my own, I'll have nothing to negotiate with and no card to play."

Raymond shakes his head. "I sure hope you know what you're doing."

James smiles. "Yeah, I believe I have a handle on the affair."

• • • • • • • •● ⬤ ●• • • • • • •

Kathy comes walking in when he's done with Raymond. "James, Richard Faulk is downstairs in the lobby. He's been waiting this entire time while you were talking to Raymond. He wants to see you for just a minute."

"All right, have him come up."

"May I ask what you're doing with Richard?"

James smiles. "You can ask, but I'm not telling you, nosy. Please bring him to my office."

"Well, James, I handed in the file just as we agreed," Richard says when he's in the office.

"What did your boss say?"

"Just as I predicted, he asked where I got the information? And I told him, like you said, that I got the file from you. And then I asked him what he wanted me to do. Should I expand my investigation?"

"What was his answer?"

"He'll get back to me."

James smiles. "Just as I thought."

"So, am I done? I kept my end of the bargain."

"Yes, Richard, you're done."

"And that police matter concerning me will disappear and will never be brought up again?"

"Yes, Richard, that other problem is no more, just as we agreed."

"And you will not interfere with my investigation into you and your wife?"

"It's just as I said, Richard, we're done." When Richard doesn't get up, James says, "What now? What's the matter?"

"You know, James, I never figured you for a blackmailer."

"Blackmailer!" He almost loses it with that remark. "You got some fucking nerve calling me that!"

He takes a moment to collect himself. "Don't you dare try and feed me that pious, sanctimonious crap, you lousy son of a bitch," James shouts. "You were ready to destroy me and my wife."

James shakes his head. "What did you say to Kathy? 'This investigation could make my career; the orders came directly from Washington.' And just exactly how would investigating Sam and me help your career? If your investigation found us innocent, your career wouldn't have moved forward at all."

James folds his arms on his chest. "So, now tell me, Mr. Pious, what outcome are you seeking in your investigation that would advance that career?"

When Richard doesn't answer, James smiles. "Yeah, exactly! Destroy the Coppis. The only way to move your career forward is to find us guilty—innocence is not an option. Did you ever give it any thought on why Washington was asking you to investigate me and my wife?"

When Richard doesn't answer. "No, of course not. You just saw an opportunity for advancement. Because of your greediness, you were ready to bring on the unlimited might of the US government against Sam and me. It didn't matter that you might be destroying the lives of two innocent people. Four innocent people if you count Miles and Jen Cornish."

He lets out a breath and spits out. "Some of you government people make me sick—you walk around with your holier-than-thou attitude. You are supposed to be public servants, working for the public good, but all you care about is your careers. I wonder how many innocent people are in jail because of your appetite for career advancement?

"And when someone like me has the audacity and capacity to fight back, using the same tough, no-holds-barred tactics that you use on your victims, you have the chutzpah to call me a blackmailer.

"Blackmailer!" James shakes his head. "I could've just as easily destroyed you. But, unlike you, I have a conscience, and I gave you a way out."

James points to the door. "Get out of my office!"

As Richard is about to walk out, "Richard, one final thought," James says.

Richard turns around.

"Aside from my wife, Kathy is the most wonderful lady that I have ever had the pleasure of knowing. Kind, warm, smart, caring, loyal, and absolutely flawless. But you'll never know that, will you? Your avarice for career advancement cost you the opportunity to get to know that wonderful woman. Because, unlike you, Kathy knows the meaning of fidelity."

CHAPTER 26

SETTLING SCORES

Secretary of State Reichwald is on his way to the White House. The president called and asked to speak to him in the Oval Office. This Bolivian matter is completely consuming everyone's time and is screwing up all the plans. The secretary had such high hopes when he came into office. He and the President were embarking on a bold mission to stymie the expansion of communism and the Soviet influence around the world.

This Bolivian arms scandal is threatening to derail those goals. Kind of foolish, when you really think about it. Why did everyone in the administration feel a need to get involved in a small country like Bolivia? Probably because everyone thought that Bolivia would be an easy task. A quick success at the very beginning of the presidency to establish momentum. The public would know that this president and his staff could be relied on for much bigger victories.

Instead, the entire episode has backfired, and they are scrambling to recover. No matter; now that the box is opened, a strategy must be devised to extricate the administration from the Bolivian mess.

Reichwald is ushered into the president's office as soon as he gets there. Sitting on the sofa alongside the president's desk is the campaign manager. This confuses Reichwald, who wonders why the president felt a need to include that man in the meeting. He nods to Drew.

The President looks up and points to a chair. "Have a seat, Henry. There's an important matter that we need to address."

Henry takes a seat. "About Bolivia?"

"Yes, Bolivia," the President answers. "In particular, James Coppi."

"What about Mr. Coppi?" Henry asks.

"Both Drew and I believe that Mr. Coppi can cause a lot of trouble for us. We're quite sure that Hartley will drag Coppi in front of his committee. We need you to speak to Mr. Coppi and find out what testimony he will provide at the hearing."

"And not just about Bolivia." Drew sits forward on the couch. "Also about Phil Eisley, if that name comes up."

Henry turns to Drew. "What about Eisley?"

Drew smiles nervously. "Coppi did an investigation on Eisley a while back and discovered some sensitive and damaging material." Drew proceeds to tell Henri about what James uncovered.

"I see," Henry says when Drew is finished. "What makes you think that Eisley's name will come up during Coppi's testimony in front of the Senate committee? Bolivia has nothing to do with oil wells."

"We don't know if the name will come up," the President says. "But if Eisley's name does, we need to know what Coppi will say."

The secretary stands up. "All right, Mr. President, I get the picture, I'll have a talk with Mr. Coppi right away."

James is at the window of his suite at the Parker House, knotting his tie and staring out onto downtown Boston. The large clock of the Custom House Tower, which he can see from his window, says 11:42. Billingsley is brushing off his suit jacket. He arrived this morning and went right to a meeting with a Boston brokerage house. This is the beginning of the dog and pony show to attract investors into putting money up for the initial public offering of the railroad.

Travelling with him are Vernon, Maxwell, and Jack. Not that anyone will be paying any attention to those three men. All the money men will want to hear from James. The investors want to know exactly what he has planned. The financiers understand that it is James that makes the final decisions in his companies, it's not the supporting players that he brought along for show.

Earlier that day, they had lunch with the Bank of New England, and tonight he will have dinner with State Street Bank. Two more meetings tomorrow and then it's on to Providence to dine with Fleet Bank. James will be meeting with two or three banks or brokerage houses a day, around the country, until they are finished, about a month from now. He's getting exhausted just thinking about his schedule. He turns to look as the phone rings.

"Do you want me to get that, sir?" Billingsley asks as he lays out James's jacket on the bed.

"No, I'll get it."

"James, this is Secretary Reichwald," the caller says when James is on the line. "I'm sorry to bother you while you're traveling; your assistant at your office said that you're very busy. However, I need to speak to you—I was hoping that you could squeeze me in sometime tomorrow. It's my understanding that you're in Boston. I could fly up in the morning."

"I'm sorry, Mr. Secretary, but my schedule is really tight. I won't have any time."

"James, it's extremely important that we meet. Please, can you make some time for me? It shouldn't be more than half an hour."

"Why can't we discuss it on the phone? Tonight, when I get back from dinner."

"No, James, this needs to be discussed face to face."

"How about tomorrow, late afternoon?" James offers. "But it'll have to be in Providence."

"Okay, Providence it is. Where are you staying?"

"The Hotel Providence."

* * * * * * * ● * * * * * * *

Sam is in the office while James is traveling. She buzzes Mattie. "Mattie, do me a favor. Call Miles and have him come to my office right away."

There's a knock at her door and Miles looks in. "You wanted to see me?"

"Yes. Miles, come in and take a seat." She looks over at him. "Can you tell me why you're snooping around the office and asking a lot of questions about me and James?"

Miles tells her about the book that he's writing. "Sam, it's just like I told James. I will never publish the piece without you and James reading and approving what I wrote."

"James knows that you're writing a book about us?"

"Yes, he said he's looking forward to reading the story when I'm done. Quite honestly, the book is coming out pretty good. You and James lead quite an exciting life. So, what do you say? Can I continue? I swear, you guys get the final say."

"As long as James and I get to approve the final piece, you can continue. Please stop asking about me and James around the office, it's creating a lot of unnecessary gossip. If you need anything go through Kathy. In fact bring in what you've done so far and let Kathy have a look."

After Miles leaves, the door opens and Ano Hiawalah looks in. "I'm sorry to bother you, Mrs. Coppi, but will you be speaking to James anytime soon?"

Sam looks up. "I don't really know his schedule, Ano, but I'm sure he'll call me sometime today. Why? Is it something important? Is there anything that I can help you with?"

"No, nothing urgent—I just wanted to find out if he had that check for Mendoza's family, as he promised."

Sam points to a chair. "Come in, Ano." After he sits, she asks, "What check?"

"Mendoza, a fellow soldier that served in 'Nam with your husband, was shot and killed a few months ago. James agreed to donate two grand to help the family."

"Who is Mendoza? Why does that name sound familiar?"

"Mendoza was one of the three men that testified against James at the Camby trial."

Sam sits up in her chair. "What? When was he killed?"

"A couple of months ago, as he was heading to work in Los Angeles."

Sam buzzes Mattie. "Mattie, go into James's office and get me all the files on the Camby trial." She looks up at Ano. "There were two other men who testified against James. Who were they?"

"Garcia and O'Farrell."

"Do you know where the men live now?"

Ano shrugs. "No, I don't."

"Is Charlie in today?"

"Yes, I saw him earlier."

"Do me a favor. Find Charlie and tell him that I want to see him when he has a moment."

After Ano leaves, Mattie brings in the files.

"Please get in touch with Kathy. I want to know how to reach James," Sam says.

"Oh, I know where he is," Mattie says. "I spoke to Antonio a few minutes ago. Mr. Coppi will be visiting Antonio this morning at the hospital in Boston."

"Call Antonio and tell him to have James call me when he gets there."

About twenty minutes later, Charlie knocks and looks in. "You wanted to see me?"

Sam looks up. "Yes, Charlie. Please come in."

"What's up?" he says, after taking a seat.

Sam looks over at the middle-aged man whose once-solid physique is now showing signs of softness. The most striking feature on his face are the tiny purple bumps on his nose, which are the result of his drinking. Charlie was the first detective hired by James. He was an ex-cop that had been kicked off the force because of his alcohol abuse. Down and out, Charlie had tried to commit suicide.

James found Charlie in a desperate situation and took a flyer on the man. She remembers the speech James gave Charlie. 'I might be crazy but I'm going to take a chance on you, Charlie. I'm the only person in the world who will gamble on you. This is probably your last chance, so straighten up.'

Since that day twelve years ago, Charlie has fallen off the wagon twice. Each time James has given the man, who he fondly nicknamed The Big Palooka, the same speech. 'This is your last chance, Charlie, you better straighten up.' And he promptly sends Charlie to a rehab facility for alcoholics. She's pretty convinced that there's no way that James can ever fire The Big Palooka, no matter how many times he falls off the wagon.

Sam smiles. "What's happening with the investigation into the shooting at James that took place in front of the office? Do you have any suspects in mind?"

"Not really. We were looking into this Cuban fellow, Herbie. He's dating your maid, Guadalupe. Early on, we thought this fellow could have been involved, but we haven't been able to tie the guy to the shooting."

Sam frowns. "Guadalupe? Whose idea was it to investigate her?"

"We weren't investigating her," Charlie says. "It's her boyfriend, Herbie. We thought that maybe she was unintentionally giving this fellow information on James. But we could never prove there was any connection between this guy and the shooting. We even tailed Herbie to Cuba. He didn't do anything suspicious while he was there—only visited his family."

"I might have a solid lead for you," she says.

Charlie sits up. "Really? Who?"

"Ano just told me that, a couple of months ago, this fellow Mendoza was shot and killed."

Charlie shrugs. "What's that got to do with our case?"

"Mendoza served in Vietnam with James. He was one of three men that testified against James in the Camby trial two years ago. Do you remember?"

Charlie thinks for a moment. "Camby was the sergeant killed by his own men?"

"Yes, that's right. Mendoza and two other men pled guilty to killing Camby. They were offered a plea deal if they were willing to testify that James was part of the conspiracy."

Charlie nods. "Yeah, now I remember. What's that got to do with our case?"

"There was a fourth man involved in the Camby murder, Antonio Cardiz."

Charlie sits up. "I'm beginning to see where you're heading. You think that the Mendoza murder and the Cardiz shooting are connected?"

"Yeah, I do. Camby had two boys, ages 15 and 17. I remember seeing them in the courthouse during the trial—I suspect that they're out to get revenge for the killing of their father."

Sam leans forward. "Charlie, there are two others out there that were involved in the Camby affair—Garcia and O'Farrell. I need you to locate the men. Those two men are probably next on the target list if they haven't already been killed. Also, I need you to send men to find the Camby children. Two years ago, they lived in Utica, Kentucky. Send someone to find these youngsters. We need to stop the boys before they kill anyone else."

"All right. I'll put Frank Gurney on the case."

"Good. Report back to me as soon as you have something," she says as Charlie stands up to leave. "One last thing: call the LAPD and see if you can match up the ballistics with our shooting. Let's tie this down."

Just before he leaves, Charlie says, "It's very impressive, how you put this together."

Sam smiles broadly. "James is a good teacher."

Charlie smiles back. "I do believe the student has outgrown the teacher."

• • • • • • • • ● ● • • • • • • • •

A little later after the time Sam is speaking to Charlie, James is walking down the hallway at Brigham and Women's Hospital to look in on Cardiz. When he gets to the room, Cardiz is sitting up in his bed. A wheelchair is nearby. James notices crutches against the wall.

The Cardiz smile widens across his face. "Well, it's about time, Coppi—I was beginning to think you'd forgotten your old buddy."

"I'm sorry, Cardiz. I would've gotten here sooner, but I'm sure Mattie filled you in on what I'm going through."

"Yeah, you've had your share of problems," he begins, trying to move himself on the bed. "Come on, give me a hand. I want to get out of bed and sit up."

259

"Are you sure that it's okay?"

"Yeah, I'm sure. Move the wheelchair closer to the bed and give me a hand."

After they're done, James points to the crutches. "You're able to walk with those?"

"Not too far. I've only been working with the sticks for three weeks. The therapist says that I'm doing good."

"That's good news. What do they say about your chances of a full recovery?"

"They don't say. They're taking this one day at a time." Antonio clears his throat, and his eyes moisten. "Listen, Coppi, I want to thank you for all that you've done for me…"

"Stop it, Cardiz. You don't need to thank me. Just get better."

James sits down. "Is there anything else that I can do for you?"

"Nothing; you've done enough. It's up to me, now. I've got a lot of work ahead of me." Antonio lets out a breath. "I'm determined to walk again."

"If anyone can do it, it's you, Cardiz. I'll be rooting for you."

"Coppi, Mattie called earlier. She said that Sam needs to speak to you. It sounded important."

"Do you mind if I use your phone?"

"No, go ahead."

James gets Sam on the line, and she tells him everything that she's uncovered on the shooting.

"What about Garcia and O'Farrell? Were you able to locate the men?" James asks.

"Garcia is in Tucson, and O'Farrell lives in Brooklyn," she tells him. "I've got Gurney and Hiawalah heading to Kentucky to see if they can catch up to the Camby boys."

"All right. Good job, Sam. I'm stopping off in Brooklyn to look in on O'Farrell and warn him as soon as I get a chance. Have Charlie try and get in touch with Garcia."

"What's up, James?" Cardiz asks when he's off the phone.

"Sam thinks she found out who shot you and tried to kill me," he says. "It was Camby's boys. They were avenging their father's killing. A few months ago, they shot and killed Mendoza."

Antonio scowls. "They were the ones that put me in this condition."

"I'm afraid so." After a moment, James says, "You can't really blame the boys, can you—we did kill their father."

"Yeah, but their old man was a real son of a bitch. You know that, James. He got a lot of men killed and would've gotten a lot more guys hurt if he wasn't stopped!"

James gives him a wry smile. "Yeah, but Camby's kids don't know that. They think their dad was a hero."

James shrugs. "I'm afraid that nothing good came out of 'Nam."

• • • • • • • ● • • • • • • • •

That afternoon, James is sitting with Secretary Reichwald in his hotel suite in Providence. Earlier, he received a report from Ernie Bauer. Events in Bolivia were moving fast. Just as Ernie had suspected, the strongman, Colonel Morales, organized a coup and overthrew the Federales.

Gaytan, his Chilean client, switched sides and is also behind the takeover supporting Morales. Rivera and the rebels, Guerreros, are completely left out of the new regime. The arms shipment deal his company had with Gaytan ended abruptly. James advised Ernie to make his way out of the country.

If that were not confusing enough, Senator Hartley had called this morning and wants to meet with him, too. James will fly down to Washington tomorrow morning to meet with the Senator. The scandal over the use of taxpayer money to back the rebels is all over the news.

Both General Farnwell and Colonel Chase have been summoned to appear in front of Hartley's committee. Some newscasts are even mentioning impeachment. James knows that he's knee-deep in this affair and needs to extricate himself out.

His attorney Marr called earlier and warned him to be very careful about what he says to these fellows at the upcoming meetings. "Everyone is running for cover, and they're looking to pin this on some poor dupe."

James doesn't need the warning. He already knows how the game is played. That's why he set his plan in motion long before this affair blew up. He had assessed, from the very beginning, that Colonel Chase was a loose cannon and didn't know what he was doing. It's surprising to him that no one else was able to see Chase's shortcomings.

James looks over at Reichwald and grins. The past five minutes have been mostly idle chatter. "I'm sorry to be rude, Mr. Secretary, but I'm on a very tight schedule. What can I do for you? What's this all about? Why did you call for this get-together?"

The secretary smiles. "James, I'm pretty sure that you know what I want to talk about—it's all over the news."

James lets out a laugh. "Yeah, you're right. That's all the news will cover." James gives Reichwald a sly look. "It's a good thing for me that you've got my back, eh?"

"James, can we cut the jokes and get serious?"

"I am serious, Mr. Secretary. Isn't that what you told me when we first started this project? You gave me your assurance that everything was on the up and up. I've got nothing to worry about."

Reichwald clears his throat. "James, I just want to know what you'll tell the Senate committee when you testify. I simply want to make sure that our stories align. All of us, including the President, were every bit as surprised as you were as to what Colonel Chase was doing and how he was getting the money."

James shakes his head. "Oh, come on, Reichwald, cut the crap. You knew exactly what was happening."

"No, James, we had no idea. This was Zeist's department. Zeist was in charge of supervising Colonel Chase."

James has a grin on his face. "So, I guess Zeist is being sacrificed? He's the one taking the hit for this mess?"

"I don't know what you mean by sacrificed, but Zeist certainly owes everyone an explanation as to what happened. After all, Chase worked for him. Which gets me back to the reason for my visit. What will you say when you are asked to justify your actions?"

"Go back and tell the President that he has nothing to worry about as far as my testimony. His name will be kept out. Isn't that why you're here? The President sent you, didn't he? They're bringing up the 'I' word again. Impeachment is being bandied about. So, report back to your boss that he's got nothing to worry about when it comes to me. My testimony won't hurt him one bit."

The Secretary looks up at James. "What about Phil Eisley?

James furrows his brow. "What about Eisley?"

Reichwald clears his throat. "What will you say about Eisley if his name comes up while you're in front of Hartley's committee? You know, that audit you did on his oil holdings."

"Don't worry, Eisley's name won't come up!" James states firmly.

"How do you know?"

"I just know." James smiles. "Listen, Reichwald, just report back to your boss that nothing I say or do will hurt him whatsoever. I can't vouch for what some others involved in this affair might say, but my testimony will not cause him any damage."

Reichwald stands up. "All right, James, thank you; and the President thanks you. Keep me informed if anything changes."

"Hold on a second Reichwald, we're not done."

The Secretary looks over. "What?"

James smiles. "I need a favor from the President. There's an IRS audit in process at my father-in-law's church in Texas. An audit that began by the urging from someone on the President's staff. This examination needs to end."

"James I'm not sure we can stop an IRS audit," Reichwald says.

James smiles. "I'm sure you can." James places his hand behind Reichwald's back and escorts him to the door. "Tell the President and everyone else on the staff, the audit stops."

• • • • • • • ● • • • • • • • •

It's early morning when James enters the restaurant of the Willard Hotel in Washington two days later. It's so early that the place isn't really open yet. The staff is removing the chairs from the tables in order to set up for the breakfast shift. There's no host in front to greet James. He looks around and notices the lone figure sitting way in the back.

"I guess you wanted to make absolutely sure that no one would notice our talk." James smiles at the man and takes a seat.

The man looks up. "I'm sorry, James, but there wasn't much time in my schedule. This Bolivian affair has me going nonstop."

A waiter comes over and pours water in a glass in front of James. "Would you like coffee?" the waiter says.

"Yes, please," he answers, and turns back to Hartley after the waiter leaves. "What do you need, Hartley? Why did you ask for this meeting?"

Hartley smiles. "I believe it's time that you and I have a frank and honest discussion."

"Go ahead, let me know what you've got in mind."

"Let's begin with Bolivia. You must have heard about the latest developments. You can see now why I was against getting involved in that affair from the very start. This president is in a lot of trouble. He'll be lucky to survive."

"You know, Hartley, I'm not here to discuss Bolivia or the President. As I previously told you, I don't get into politics, and as far as I'm concerned, Bolivia is all about politics. If you need to know about my affairs concerning Bolivia, you can wait until I'm in front of your committee. Why don't we discuss the real reason you asked for this meeting, the file that I have on you?"

The waiter comes over and pours James a cup of coffee. "Are you ready to order?"

"I'm just having coffee," James answers.

After the waiter leaves, Hartley leans forward. "Okay, let's discuss the file. What do you intend to do with that information?"

"What I do with the information is entirely up to you."

Hartley looks around before answering. "James, I can't stop the committee from calling you, if that's what you're looking for. Your knowledge of this affair is an integral part of the investigation. The remaining senators won't stand for you not appearing. All I can do is have the hearing conducted behind closed doors, and not open to the public."

Hartley clears his throat. "I'll cite that what you know may be considered classified and impacts national security. I can also promise to go easy on my questions to you. If anyone else on the panel gets a little too hard, I can shut them down. Beyond that, I can't do very much."

"What about my wife and my controller, Miles?"

"What about it?"

"Will Sam and Miles have to testify?"

"No, I'll withdraw the summons. Neither Samantha nor Miles will have to appear. I'll tell the committee that since you're cooperating, there's no need to call anybody else." After a pause, Hartley says, "Well, is that it? Are we settled?"

"No, there are two more demands. The first is that your wife, Abigail, immediately resign from the board of Regis Petroleum, and that she'll have nothing further to do with that company."

"All right, I'll arrange for her resignation. What's your other request?"

"When your term is up, you agree not to run for reelection."

Hartley's eyes widen. "Is that really necessary? What good will that do?"

James smiles. "It'll get rid of a corrupt hypocrite from the government. That's one less slime ball that the people of this country have to deal with."

"Are you sure you want to take this route?" Hartley leans forward and smiles skillfully. "You know, James, I could be a very useful ally of yours in the Senate. Your company gets a lot of government work. You could use someone like me on your side."

"I'll pass on the offer. Do we have a deal?"

"Why be so obtuse? Except for this last affair, we always got along. Don't you believe in second chances?"

"It was all business until you took on Sam. Once you included her, it became personal. You had no right to go after my family. So, what's your answer? Do we have a deal?"

Hartley lets out a gasp. "I guess I have no choice."

James stands up. "Good! I'll see you at the hearing. Please don't schedule me to attend for at least the next three weeks; I'm very busy."

• • • • • • • • • ● ● ● • • • • • • •

The black limo is moving deliberately up the street in Brooklyn that afternoon. The driver turns to James in the back seat.

"Are you sure this is the right place? There's nothing on this block except auto body repair shops."

James turns to a sign on one of the buildings, 'Viola Pigeon Club.' Could that sign be an omen? He turns back to the driver. "Yeah, this is the right street. The house is on Stillwell, and this is the avenue. Just drive slowly so I can see the numbers on the buildings." James looks up. "Stop, I think that's the house right over there!"

"Where, sir? I don't see a house."

"A little further back up the driveway, in between those two auto body shops. I'll get out and have a look."

"Do you want me to come with you, Boss?" Max asks.

"No, I'll be fine," James says as he gets out of the car.

He climbs the three steps of the porch and knocks.

"What do you want?" O'Farrell says harshly when he answers the door.

James smiles. "I thought you'd be happy to see me. You can at least invite me in for coffee."

"I'm getting ready for work. What do you want, Coppi?"

"There's something important I need to speak to you about. It'll only take a couple of minutes." James pushes his way in.

O'Farrell motions to a sofa. "Make it fast."

James takes a seat, and O'Farrell sits across the way. "Well?"

James looks over at him. "Mendoza is dead! He was shot heading to work. Cardiz was partially paralyzed when someone shot him. And a little while ago, somebody tried to kill me." James pauses. "Do you see where I'm going?"

"No!"

James lets out a laugh. "You were never very bright." He lets out a breath. "I think you might be next."

O'Farrell shrugs. "Next? For what?"

"They'll try to kill you!"

O'Farrell turns pale. "Who is trying to kill me?"

"The same people who tried to kill me, murdered Mendoza, and shot Cardiz—the Camby boys. Camby's two sons. They're out to avenge the killing of their father."

"Don't move, and drop the gun!" they hear Max shout from the backyard.

"You make any kind of move and I'll blow your heads off," they hear Max repeat. "Now, drop the gun." There's a sound of a pistol dropping. "Lay flat on the ground and put your hands behind your head."

James walks to the window and lifts the blinds. Max is pointing a gun at two men who are face down on the ground.

James heads out the door. "What've you got, Max?"

"I saw these guys snooping near the window," Max answers.

"Good thing you were paying attention," James says, and turns to O'Farrell. "Call the police."

After the call, O'Farrell comes outside where James is with Max, who is still pointing the gun at the men.

"These are Camby's sons," James says to O'Farrell. "Had I not been here today, you'd be dead." James lifts his head as he hears the sirens. "That must be the police."

When the police arrive, James gives them a report and turns over the boys.

"We may need you to give a further statement," one of the cops says.

"No problem, but I don't think you'll need to do much work. These guys should be easy to break."

· · · · · · · ● · · · · · · · ·

Three weeks later, Max sets down the glass of mineral water as James stares out at the darkness from the window of his jet. "Can I get you anything else, Boss?"

James turns. "No, Max, I'm good. Why don't you get some rest? It's two-thirty. We still have a few hours before we land."

"All right, Boss, will do."

A few moments later, Mary comes over. "Can I get you anything Mr. Coppi?"

James looks up and smiles. "No, Mary, I'm fine. Did you get to the rest of the party?"

"They're all sleeping—I can't believe you're up; you must be exhausted."

James points to a seat across from him. "Have a seat, Mary. Keep me company—I don't feel like sleeping."

"How about you?" he asks after she sits. "You must be tired, too. After all, you and the flight crew traveled with me."

"At least we rotated with the other crew," she replies. "One week on and one week off. You didn't stop. I don't know how you handled all those meetings. Was your trip successful? It had to do with the railroad, didn't it? The rumor is that you're selling stock in the company—is that true?"

"Yes, probably; if everything goes as planned."

Mary smiles. "Is it a good deal? Should I buy some?"

"Mary, I'm not at liberty to discuss the transaction with anyone. What I might say may be construed as insider information, and we could both get into a lot of trouble.

"When the prospectus comes out, you can read it over. If I were you, however, I'd wait before committing any money. If the offering is successful, we'll make the stock available to employees at a discount. Beyond that, I can't tell you very much."

James takes a sip of the water. "Let's talk about you, Mary. How does your daughter Marcie like her new school? How is she doing?"

Mary smiles. "She's doing just fine. Her grades are good. I still can't believe Marcie is in the same exclusive private school as your daughter Molly—I don't know how you pulled it off."

"I told you, Mary. The school makes available need-based scholarships for deserving children, and you'd be hard-pressed to find anyone more deserving than your daughter Marcie. She's a wonderful young lady. All the members of the tuition committee were impressed by her when she came in for the interview. How is Marcie doing socially? Is she fitting in?"

"Marcie struggled, at first. A lot of the other kids looked down on her. You know, because of her social status. Thank goodness for Molly. Molly took Marcie under her wing and looks out for her. Marcie was at your daughter's birthday party yesterday at your house."

James looks out the window of the jet before turning back to her. "I know. I feel terrible: yesterday was the first time that I've missed one of my children's birthdays. I didn't even get a chance to wish Molly a happy birthday. Every time I called, the phone was busy. I'm so guilt-ridden right now."

• • • • • • • • ● • • • • • • • •

Sam's limo pulls up to the front of her office building and she looks out the window at the row of black limousines parked in front.

Her driver turns to her. "What's going on, Mrs. Coppi? I can't even get a space. Who are all these people?"

Sam smiles. "Money men! We're announcing that the railroad is going public."

Her bodyguard Regis gets out and opens the back door for her. "I guess Mr. Coppi will finally be home," he says.

Sam let's out a breath. "Yes, finally—he's been away over four weeks."

This is the longest James has been away from her since he came back from Vietnam. She really misses him and didn't realize how much he's become a part of her life 'till this last parting. She stills remembers that first night that she walked up to him and introduced herself. It was an instant attraction; she loved him immediately.

Her dream after that first meeting was to marry that young man and live in a modest home on a quiet cul-de-sac here in Colorado Springs. To raise a family of four children and live happily ever after. A modest, quiet, and unassuming life.

Sam looks up at the building and shudders. That young man had other plans—he wanted a ranch. If he had stopped at getting that ranch, she would have been perfectly content, but he didn't.

He also got her a castle in France. She shakes her head. *When will it end, James? When will you have enough? After this transaction, the world will know we are billionaires. Will this be the final piece?* She begins walking into the building; she already knows the answer.

Sam looks down the hall when she arrives at her floor. James is in front of his office speaking to a group of men. He smiles broadly when he sees her and scurries over. James grabs ahold of her hand and pulls her into a nearby office. James closes the door and pins her against the wall.

"You have no idea how great it is to see you." James says, and plants a kiss. "I've missed you so much."

"Wouldn't you guys be more comfortable in a hotel?" Jessica says.

They turn and burst out laughing. Jessica gets up and walks to the door. "I'll leave you two alone."

James reaches for her arm. "You don't have to leave, we'll go."

"That's ok, I need to go to the conference room and see if Kathy needs any help."

James points to a chair. "Come on, let's get caught up before someone comes in to get us. How've you been? How are the children?"

"As I told you this morning when you called, everyone is feeling better. That flu bug that was flying through the house appears to be over. How are you? You must be happy. The offering is done, and you'll probably own all the railroads in the Southwest, soon."

"What do you think of the deal now?" he asks. "Last time we spoke, you seemed concerned about this transaction."

"'Concerned' is putting it mildly," she answers. "I'm scared stiff. This is one monster of a deal. What about you? Any regrets?"

"I'm a little frightened, too," he replies.

"You are? You know, James, it's still not too late. We can still back out. If you believe that for any reason the venture will fail, we shouldn't do the deal. This is a lot of money."

"Sam, I'm not worried about the money. The deal is a good one. I've done my homework. The railroad will be a success."

"Well, what's worrying you?"

"Sam, yesterday was Molly's birthday. The first birthday that I've ever missed. Yesterday was the first time that I wasn't with you guys. I was alone in my hotel room. Alone with just my thoughts. Sam, when this deal is done, we'll be considered one of the richest families in Colorado, if not the United States.

"That's what's scaring me, Sam. What will happen to my family, and how in the world did I get here? A little over thirteen years have passed since we met, Sam, and I'm right back where I started. My life is spiraling out of control."

"You don't have to do this, you know," she says. "We're fine without the money."

"Yeah, I know, but you know me. I can't stop. It's another mountain, and I can't resist a good climb." James stands up. "Come on, let's see if Kathy is finished."

• • • • • • • • ● ● ● • • • • • • •

That afternoon, after the meeting, James is back in his office, looking through the messages that are piled on his desk.

"What are we doing with all this money?"

James looks up. "Uh! What money?"

"The money that we have from the railroad. We'll be billionaires once the company goes public."

James laughs. "Don't be in such a hurry to spend the cash. We don't have any money. We're rich just on paper."

"What do you mean?"

"That's the value of the stock we own—it's not money. To turn it into money, we'd have to sell the stock. Who knows what we'll get if we sell? And don't forget, we'd have to pay taxes."

Sam walks up to him and places him in her arms. She looks into his face and smiles. "But even after all that, we're still billionaires, aren't we?"

"Yeah, I guess you're right."

She looks over at his desk. "I can't believe you still have the same desk that you had when you first started the business." Her hand slides down and caresses his crotch.

James smiles and looks into her face. "I'm guessing someone has something in mind?"

"I want you to fuck me right over that desk," she whispers in his ear. "Fuck me right there on that desk where all those billions were made." She lifts up her dress and begins pulling down her panties.

• • • • • • • • • ● • • • • • • • • • •

Kathy opens the office door just as Sam is letting out her climatic cries. She shakes her head as she sees James's back and him kneeling on the desk with the bottoms of Sam's feet on his shoulders.

James hops off Sam and pulls up his pants. "Can you close the damn door! What the hell do you want?"

Kathy smiles. "I heard these unusual shrieks," she says. "But I should've recognized the shouts. Those cries sounded just like the yells I used to hear coming from your bedroom years ago when we shared an apartment. Nothing has changed." Kathy shakes her head. "Couldn't you horny guys have waited until you got home?" She slams the door.

Sam gets off the desk and reaches down for her panties. She looks up at James and smiles broadly. "I was right, that is a magical desk. That fuck was worth a billion dollars!"

CHAPTER 27

A TRAGIC LOSS

Two weeks later, James gave testimony on the Bolivian affair in Washington. Hartley, true to his word, conducted the hearing behind closed doors and asked relatively easy questions. James lets out a breath and a smile creases his face. Things were finally shaping up. Bolivia is done. The investigation into him and Sam by the AG came to an end. The IRS audit, which had the potential of a catastrophe, came to a close without any repercussions. He is looking forward to the new year and finally putting all the troubles behind him. He will be able to keep that promise he made to Sam to stop all these activities and stay close to home with her and the family.

When James gets back to Colorado Springs, he decides to stop in his office before going home. There's a knock at his door and Rodney looks in. "James, have you got a minute? I need to speak to you about something important."

"Yeah, come in."

Rodney takes a seat and clears his throat. "I've got bad news. Ernie was arrested in Bolivia."

James loses all color in his face. "What?"

"The new junta grabbed Ernie before he could make it out of the country."

"Oh, fuck." James takes a moment to collect himself. "When did they nab him?"

"I don't know."

James shakes his head. "Damn!"

"What are you going to do? Are you going down there?"

James is looking at the wall away from Rodney. After a moment, he turns. "What? Did you say something?"

"I asked you if you were going to Bolivia and try to get Ernie out? You could send someone else, but I don't think anyone here is capable of getting him released."

"No, I promised Sam that I wouldn't go on any more of these excursions."

"So, what are you doing about it? You can't leave Ernie in prison."

James buzzes Kathy. "Kathy, do me a favor and get Senator Hartley on the phone."

A few minutes later, his speaker goes off. "Senator Hartley is on the line."

"Hello, James, what can I do for you?"

"Senator, I need a favor. The US ambassador to Bolivia, Joe Klaus—he's of the same political party as you, am I right?"

"Yes, James. The new administration's appointment for the post still hasn't been confirmed."

"There's a man who works for me, Ernie Bauer. He's a South African. Bauer was arrested in Bolivia. I need you to get in touch with Ambassador Klaus and have him intercede for Ernie. Ernie is no threat to the new junta—he should be freed and allowed to go home."

"Why should I get involved? What do I care about one of your foreign workers?" The Senator gets louder. "James, the deal we made is done; I've kept my end of the bargain—I don't owe you a damn thing."

"I'd be willing to renegotiate our agreement." James clears his throat. "You know the part of our transaction that discusses you not running for reelection? I'd be willing to withdraw that requirement."

"I see. Well, that's certainly more interesting." There's a period of silence. "What if I try for his release and we can't get it done? I can't guarantee that this new man, Morales, who's running the country, will listen to Ambassador Klaus."

"I'm pretty sure that if the ambassador asks, my man will be released. The new regime in Bolivia will want to stay on the good side of the US. Just have Klaus meet with Morales and try to negotiate in earnest for the release of my man. Whether or not the ambassador succeeds, you'll come out ahead: I'll withdraw my requirement."

"All right, James, let me make a call. I'll see what I can do."

"What was that all about?" Rodney asks when James is off the phone.

"Just calling in a debt."

An hour later, Kathy is on the speaker. "James, Senator Hartley is on line one."

"Any news, Senator?" James asks.

"No news yet, but Klaus arranged to have dinner with *El Presidente* this evening. At the dinner, he'll bring up your man Bauer."

"Okay, Senator, thanks. Give me a call at home tonight as soon as you hear."

"Will do."

James looks at the clock when he gets home that night. 7:15. The ambassador should be having dinner with the Bolivian President right about now. He runs into Billingsley.

"Where's Samantha?"

"Mrs. Coppi went shopping, Dinner is almost ready; what should I do?"

"Serve the children their food and hold mine until my wife gets home."

• • • • • • • • ● • • • • • • • • •

James is resting in bed, reading, and Sam still isn't home. There's a knock at the door.

"Mr. Coppi, there's a telephone call for you," Billingsley says. "It's Senator Hartley."

"Thank you, Billingsley. I'll take it in the study."

"James, I'm very sorry, but I've got some bad news," Hartley says immediately when he's on the line. "Ernie Bauer was killed this morning. The government says he was shot trying to escape."

James shakes his head and bangs his fist on the desk. "Damn," he mutters. His eyes moisten.

"James, did you hear me?" the senator says.

"Yeah, I heard. They're full of crap," he spits out bitterly. "Morales executed Ernie."

"James, what difference does that make now? It won't bring him back."

"Yeah, I know." He clears his throat. "Can you make sure that his body is returned to his family in South Africa?"

"Yes, I will." After a pause. "James, I hate to bring this up now, but this shouldn't change the deal we made earlier today."

"No, Senator, it doesn't change the agreement we made earlier. Thank you for trying. You're free to do whatever you want on your reelection."

"Is everything all right, sir?" Billingsley says when he comes out of the study. "You look distraught."

"Just received some bad news."

"Would you like your dinner now?"

278

"No, I'm not hungry. Please bring me a blanket; I'm going to sit on the patio."

"Are you sure? It's very cold tonight."

James smiles despondently. "Then bring me two blankets."

"Mr. Billingsley, have you seen my husband?" Sam asks when she gets home.

"Mr. Coppi is out on the patio, listening to music."

"Outside? It's freezing out."

"Would the madam like something to eat?

"Not right now." Sam heads for the patio. She opens the door and looks out. "James, what are you doing out there?"

James turns to her from the lounge chair. "Just listening to some music and doing a little thinking."

"It's cold."

"It's not too bad under the blankets." James lifts up the blankets that are covering him. "Come on, join me. It's a beautiful, clear night. There are thousands of stars in the sky."

Sam runs over and lies next to him. James tucks the blanket tightly around her. "Are you comfortable?"

"Yes," she says, and lays her head on his shoulder. "What are you listening to? Is it an opera?"

"The song is 'Va Pensiero.'"

Sam looks up at him. "Go thought?"

"Very good!" He smiles at her. "I thought you said your Italian wasn't very good."

Sam lets out a laugh. "You mean, I'm right?"

"Yes, you're right. The actual translation is 'hasten thought.'"

Sam leans her head back on his shoulder. "It's a lovely song," she says after a few moments. "What's it about? What are they saying?"

"It's about Hebrew slaves, far from home. They're dreaming of their homeland next to the River Jordan."

"So, it's a religious song?" she looks up.

"Maybe," he says. "I don't really know what Verdi had in mind when he composed the piece. My guess it's more of a patriotic song."

"Well, whatever it is, it's beautiful," Sam rests her head back down.

"What have you been thinking about, out here?" she asks.

"Ernie Bauer is dead!"

"What?" Sam sits up. "What happened?"

"He was nabbed before he could get out Bolivia—I don't know how he was killed."

Sam stares at James. "You do know that there was nothing that you could've done to save Ernie?"

James looks over at her. "I know. But I can still feel sad, can't I? Ernie was more than a business acquaintance, to me. He was my friend. Had been for a long time."

He looks at her and smiles wistfully. "Sam, recently, I've had this recurring dream about Vietnam. It's about a house that was near my base camp. It was a nice house with well-maintained grounds.

"There were two teenagers that lived in the home—I'd watch them play in their yard. Happy young kids. I used to wonder how anyone could be so happy with a war happening all around their home. I've been racking my brain as to why, all of a sudden, this house has popped up in my thoughts. A few days ago, I figured it out."

"What is it?" Sam asks.

"Sam, I'm now second-guessing myself as to the life path that I chose."

"Why?"

James looks at her. "Sam, do you remember that just before we got married, you tried to show me this cute house on a cul de sac? That house represented your dream home. You wanted a simple life. A nice home and a family of four children. But I had different plans—I had something to prove, and I wanted to show the world what I could accomplish. I was so resolute that I refused to even get out of the car that day and look at the home that you wanted me to see.

"Now I'm wondering whether I wouldn't have been better off with a much simpler life. Just like those two teenagers that I saw in Vietnam. The surroundings around those kids may have been depressing, but they were happy in their own little world."

James clears his throat. "But I know it's too late. We can't go back."

Sam touches his cheeks gently. "James, I'm thoroughly happy with our lifestyle. There's no reason to second guess yourself on that point. You have built a storied world for me. More magnificent than I could have ever imagined."

"Really? Are you certain?"

"Yes, absolutely certain! But, James, I need more from you than these material things that you have provided." She looks away for a moment. "James, I think that you have drifted away from me."

"What?" James sits up. "What makes you say that?"

"Because, James. Look at the travelling that you do. You're away almost half the time. You go off on these dangerous ventures." She reaches for his face and turns him to her. "James, if you're not happy with me anymore, you need to tell me. I love you so much, and would do anything to keep you by my side. But I wouldn't want to keep you caged in a relationship that you don't want. Letting you go would be unbearable for me, but that's how much I love you, I would let go to make certain that you're happy."

He looks into her eyes. "Oh, Sam, you have no idea how wrong you are. There's no place that I'd rather be than by your side like I am at this moment. I may have gotten carried away with my job. It's my own selfishness in not letting others take over some of my duties. But throughout my travel, my love for you has never waned. Sam, I promised that I'd change, and now that I know how much this problem has upset you, I'll make a greater effort to that end."

He strokes her hair gently and kisses her forehead. "Sam, I'm so sorry that I let us get to where we are today. But it's not just about my travel, it's about letting you look inside me. Letting you see exactly what's down deep. I've always guarded myself from you—but no more. I intend to expose myself completely to you. You may not like everything that's inside me, but there's one irrefutable fact that you'll discover, and that is how much I truly love you."

He leans over and pulls her to him, and their lips touch.

CHAPTER 28

BRINGING HIM HOME

Two days later, Sam sees James off as he heads out the door. "How long will you be?"

"A week, probably," he says.

Sam frowns. "I don't understand why you have to go. Why couldn't you send someone?"

"Ernie Bauer was my friend. I'd like to accompany the body home to his family. That's the least that I can do." He reaches over and takes her in his arms.

Sam looks up at him. "Isn't it dangerous?"

James smiles. "Not at all. The casket is being brought from Bolivia to Buenos Aires. From there, we fly to South Africa. Nothing dangerous."

"What hotel are you staying at?"

"Alvear Palace Hotel in Buenos Aires."

"Will you call me when you get there?"

He gives her a kiss. "Of course. And don't worry, there's nothing dangerous. I better get started."

• • • • • • • • ● • • • • • • • •

Three days later, Sam is walking down the hall at the office. She will be meeting with Giselle to review her ideas for the upcoming fashion season. Rodney is walking toward her.

Rodney stops. "Samantha, have you spoken to James?"

"Yes, he called last night to let me know that he arrived in Buenos Aires."

"Was he successful in getting Ernie Bauer's body released?"

Sam creases her brow. "What do you mean? I thought that detail had already been worked out. James just went on the trip to accompany the casket back to South Africa."

"Err…I guess…I must be all mixed up." Rodney walks away without saying anything else.

Mattie looks up from her desk when she sees Sam. "Good morning, Mrs. Coppi. Would you like coffee?"

"Yes, please," she says.

"Did Kathy come to work today?"

"Yes, ma'am."

"Could you please call her before you get my coffee? Tell Kathy that I'd like to see her."

A few moments later, there's a knock at her door and Kathy peeks in. "You wanted to see me?"

Sam looks up from her desk. "Yes, come in and have a seat. What can you tell me about what's going on with James? I just ran into Rodney in the hall, and he told me that there may be some problems in retrieving Ernie Bauer's remains."

Kathy shrugs. "I'm not aware of any problems."

"You would tell me if there was a problem?"

Kathy nods. "Yes, of course!"

Sam gives her a stern look. "Even if James told you not to say anything?"

Kathy thinks for a moment. "That would be hard, but yes, even if he told me not to."

"All right, thanks."

A few minutes later, Sam buzzes Mattie. "Mattie, do me a favor. I'd like to get my hands on newspapers from Bolivia and Argentina."

"Where would I find such newspapers?" Mattie says.

"I don't know. Call the local libraries or some of the newsstands in town or in Denver. But it's important—I need the papers right away."

A few hours later, Mattie buzzes Sam. "Mrs. Coppi, I found a newspaper dealer in Denver that agreed to stock *La Nación*, an Argentinian paper, and *El Diario*, a Bolivian paper. I had to agree to a one-month subscription. The dealer will mail the first copies to us starting tomorrow."

"Thank you, Mattie, but don't have the papers mailed; have someone pick up the newspapers and bring them to the ranch every day."

"Are you sure? That's over an hour each way."

"Yes, I'm certain."

Mattie answers "All right, will do. You are aware the print is in Spanish?"

"Yes, Mattie. I'll have Guadalupe translate."

Sam has read ten days of papers, and she can't glean any news that may have anything to do with Ernie or James.

Last week, James called and told her that he was traveling to Santiago, Chile, to meet with this fellow Gaytan. He was trying to get to the bottom of why there was a delay in releasing Ernie's remains. James told her not to worry; he would be out of touch for a few days.

The courier just brought today's dailies.

"What's it say?" Sam asks Guadalupe, who is reading the papers. "Any news on James or Ernie Bauer?"

"No, nada," she replies.

Sam points to a headline in the Bolivian paper. "What's this headline? *Seis Prisioneros Muertas en un Motín?* What's that about?"

"It is about a *prisioneros* riot."

Sam has a chill go through her body. "Where did this happen?"

"In Santa Cruz, six *prisioneros* were killed in a riot in the Prisión de Palmasola." Guadalupe looks up. "*Señora, está bien?* Your face *esta pálida.* This news has nothing to do with Señor Coppi. The prison is *muy, muy* far from Buenos Aires."

Sam smiles drily. "Yes, I'm sure it doesn't have anything to do with James." But the coldness running through her system still remains. James has not called in over a week—something is wrong, she just knows it. She goes into her bedroom and throws herself face-down on the bed. Tears are beginning to flow. "You promised, James," she utters. "Why can't you stop what you're doing?"

• • • • • • • • ● ● ● ● ● • • • • •

James is in his suite at the Alvear Hotel when he first arrives in Argentina. He's meeting with Gary Pator and another of his mercenaries, Herman Weld. James is looking out the window as the early morning sun is rising.

"How are we playing this, James?" Gary speaks up.

James turns around. "We're waiting for a call from Ambassador Klaus. He's making arrangements to retrieve Ernie's casket."

"James, I've got to inform you: this is not sitting well with me or the men. They're not happy that Gaytan and Morales are getting away with killing Ernie."

James gets loud. "I'm not happy about Ernie's death either, Gary." He lets out a breath and in a calmer voice says, "Let's bring

Ernie home to his family. We can talk about what to do about Gaytan and Morales after we get this task completed."

The phone rings and it's Ambassador Klaus. "James, there's a problem. Morales is not releasing the body."

"Why the fuck not?" James shouts into the phone.

"I don't know why; he refuses to deal with me. Morales says he's waiting for the new ambassador to be appointed. I'm sorry, James, there's nothing that I can do."

"I'm guessing by the look on your face that there's a problem?" Gary says after James hangs up.

James doesn't answer, but dials the phone. "Ian, can you get in touch with Gaytan? Arrange for me to meet with him in Santiago."

"When would you like to meet?"

"As soon as possible, it's important."

"All right, I'll see what I can do."

"What's going on, James?" Gary asks.

"Morales won't release Ernie's remains."

"What are you going to do?"

James shakes his head and yells. "Gary, I would really appreciate you not asking all these fucking questions. I'm not in the mood. If you got any ideas, speak up; otherwise shut the fuck up!"

Later that afternoon, Ian calls. "James, I was able to arrange a meeting with Gaytan in two days in his office in Santiago. Let me warn you, the guy isn't being very cooperative—I had to call him four times and plead with him before he finally agreed."

"All right, Ian, good job."

James looks over at Gary, who was listening to the conversation. "We'll get there," he smiles. "I'm not leaving until we bring Ernie home." James walks over and gets his jacket. "Come on, let's get something to eat. Some of the finest Italian restaurants are in Argentina. And why not? Italians make up more than 60 percent of the population."

Two days later, James chartered a plane to take them to Santiago. A driver is meeting them at the Arturo Merino Benitez airport to take them to Gaytan's place.

"Where's Gaytan's office?" Gary asks.

James looks over at Herman, who is out cold, snoring. "That guy sleeps more than he's awake." James turns back to Gary. "It's in a warehouse in Barrio Italia, about an hour's drive from the airport."

Gary lets out a laugh. "More Italians? You guys really get around."

James laughs. "Hey, the whole continent was named after an Italian."

"Yeah, who?"

"I can't believe you don't know. Amerigo Vespucci, an Italian explorer."

"What's our plan for Gaytan?" Gary asks.

James shrugs. "I don't know. I hope he tells us something that will help us with Ernie."

"And if he doesn't?"

James smiles. "You said you wanted to avenge Ernie—you can kill the son-of-a-bitch."

There's a driver holding a sign, 'Señor Coppi,' and he's standing in front of a red Skoda Octavia when they get off the plane.

"Do you speak English?" James asks.

"*Poquito*," the driver answers.

"Maybe he speaks Italian," Gary laughs.

"Very funny." James gives the driver a note with an address written on it. "Can you take us here?"

"*Sí, señor, certeventamente.*"

The car fills up with leaded fumes when the driver starts it up. The chauffer turns around. "*Necesito gasolina.*"

"Why didn't you get the gas before we got here?" Gary hollers.

"Because he doesn't have any money," James answers, and turns to the driver and waves. "Go ahead get the *gasolina. Ottenere abbastanza gasolina per l'intero viaggio.*"

"What did you tell him?" Gary asks.

"I told him to get enough gas for the entire trip. I don't feel like getting stuck."

"I didn't know you spoke Spanish," Gary says.

"I don't," James laughs. "That was Italian, I hope he understood me."

James reaches into his pocket and takes out a roll of pesos when they get to the gas station. "*Quanto?*"

"*Quinientos pesos,*" the chauffer answers.

James looks out the car window when they reach the warehouse.

"*Estamos aquí,*" the driver says.

James gets out and reaches inside his jacket, pulling out a revolver.

"Are you expecting trouble?" Gary says

"No, but it's better to be ready," he answers, putting the gun back in his pocket. "You are packing, aren't you?"

Gary smiles. "Of course."

There's a woman typing behind a glass enclosed counter when they get into the building. She slides open the window and smiles.

"*Hola. Puedo ayudarte?*"

"Señor Gaytan," James answers.

"*Tu nombre?*

"James Coppi."

"I think that next time we should bring an interpreter," Gary says.

The lady gets up and knocks at a door of an office behind her. She lets herself in and comes out moments later.

"*Señor Gaytan, te verá ahora!*"

A balding, chubby little man stands up from his desk, walks over, smiles broadly, and extends his hand to James.

"Señor Coppi, it is a pleasure to finally meet you."

James shakes Gaytan's hand. "Thank you."

Still holding onto James, Gaytan smiles even more broadly. "Gracias for all your help."

"You're welcome." James motions to the other men. "This is Gary and Herman, two of my associates."

"They are not Americans," Gaytan says, looking at the men.

"No, they are from South Africa. Ernie Bauer was their commander. They're here to bring Ernie home."

"I see." Gaytan motions to the chairs. "Please, gentlemen, have a seat."

Gaytan walks behind his desk and takes a seat. "What is it that you want from me?"

"Very simple," James says. "Give me the body so I can return Ernie home."

Gaytan fiddles with his handlebar mustache. "There's one problem. I don't have Señor Ernie to give you. *Coronel* Morales is in charge."

James points to the phone. "Call Morales and tell him to release Ernie."

Gaytan forces out a laugh. "Just like that!"

James nods. "Yeah, just like that. You said you were thankful for my help. Here's your chance to repay me."

Gaytan shakes his head and throws up his hands. "If there were any way that I could, I would certainly help you. But you are not understanding the political climate in Bolivia. I don't have that kind of authority."

"So, you won't help me?"

Gaytan folds his hands in a pleading manner. "Please, Señor Coppi, understand, I can't."

"I see," James turns to Gary. "I guess we came here for nothing. This guy is useless to us. Time to start avenging Ernie. Take him out back and shoot the son of a bitch."

Gary and Herman stand up.

Gaytan looks at the men and yells nervously at James. "What are you doing?"

James smiles. "We're going to kill you, you thankless, sniveling, piece of shit!"

Gary grabs Gaytan by the collar and yanks him up.

"Wait a minute; *un momento*." Gaytan is now sweating. "Let's talk some more. Maybe we can work this out."

"Can you get me Ernie?" James shouts.

"I can help," Gaytan says.

James looks over at his men. "Put him down, fellows." He turns back to Gaytan. "Speak fast, Gaytan, I don't have a lot of time."

"Ernie Bauer *está vivo*!" Gaytan says.

"What?" Gary yells out.

"Where is he?" James asks.

"If I tell you, you will not kill me?"

James nods. "If your story checks out to be true, and Ernie is alive, there'd be no reason to kill you."

"Your Mr. Bauer is in a prison in Bolivia."

James furrows his brow. "In prison? Why don't they just let him go? Ernie is no threat."

Gaytan smiles dryly. "Ernie, no, Señor, he's no threat." He points to James. "But you, Señor Coppi," Gaytan wiggles his finger, "you are *mucho peligroso*. Rivera is still alive. What's to stop you from supplying Rivera arms to continue his fight? Morales wants to hold on to your man, to be used as collateral to stop you from helping Rivera."

"So, Rivera is still alive, too?"

"Yes, he's still in charge of a small band of rebels. They are based in Yacuiba, a small town on the Bolivian and Argentinian border. He goes back and forth between the countries."

"What about Ernie? Where's he being held?"

"The Palmasola Prison. It's in Santa Cruz."

James looks down for a moment. He raises his head back up. "All right, contact Morales. Tell him that if he releases Ernie, I'll give him my word that I won't help Rivera. In fact, I'll have nothing further to do with Bolivia whatsoever. I'll stay out of all Bolivian affairs."

Gaytan shakes his head. "*No es bueno.* Morales will never agree; he doesn't trust you. You are not a country that can sign a treaty. Morales is convinced that the only way that he can guarantee your *cooperación* is to hold on to your *hombre*. If you want Señor Bauer back, you'll have to find a way to convince Morales."

James sits there quietly, thinking.

Gaytan leans forward. "Señor Coppi, are we *completo*? I told you everything that I know."

James stands up. "Yes, we're through." James looks at his men. "Let's go."

When they get outside, Gary asks, "Now what?"

James shakes his head. "Again, with the fucking questions."

Four days later, James is sitting in the back of an uncomfortable yellow bus on a bumpy road to Santa Cruz de la Sierra, Bolivia. He chartered a plane and flew to Asunción, Paraguay. From there, he felt it would be better if they drove the rest of the way. Not an easy task, as Santa Cruz is over a thousand miles from Asunción. The trip is mostly over dirt and unfinished roads. He is avoiding main thoroughfares so that he won't raise the suspicions of the police.

For the first time in his life, he's beginning to realize that he may be too old for these operations. The bus trip has taken nearly three whole days, and they're now about 100 kilometers from their destination.

James had unsuccessfully tried to negotiate Ernie's release before starting out. Morales wouldn't even speak to him. This left James no choice but to try the bold plan of breaking Ernie out of jail. James has spent the last few days learning everything that he could about this particular prison.

The Palmasola prison system is unique. The prison guards only monitor the perimeter. The guards don't get involved inside the facility. Inside the penitentiary, the cell blocks are run by gangs. Each cell block has a different gangster running the area. Gang wars over who runs the turfs are not uncommon. To get a good cell or privileges in the jail, you need to either pay or work for the gang leader. These privileges include good cells, food, and visitation by women and family.

For many of the inmates, life in the prison is better than the outside world. If you don't have any money, however, the prison life isn't very pleasant. You can't get a cell, and you sleep on the floor in the common area and eat the prison food.

Each cell block is like a small town run by a gangster in charge. Ernie is in a section called PC4, supposedly one of the better blocks. That area is under the iron fist of a gang leader who goes by the name Macudo.

James had tried to get Ernie out by bribing Macudo. He offered the gangster a lot of money for Ernie's freedom. But the thug wouldn't negotiate—Macudo was too afraid of the repercussions from Morales if he let Ernie go. This left James no choice but to try this breakout. Another six mercenaries were flown from South Africa to help in the rescue.

Gary comes to the back and sits next to James. "I know you don't like me to ask a lot of questions, but I believe it's time we go over your plan."

James smiles and scratches his chin. "Yeah, let's do that. What do you want to know?"

"Let's start from the beginning. How do we get in?"

"When we get to Santa Cruz, we'll be met by Arturo Camacho, a former inmate that I hired to help us with the job. Arturo was able to bribe two of the prison guards to let us in."

"Can we trust Arturo?"

James gives Gary a side glance. "Yeah, Arturo filled out an application for the job and had good referrals from his previous employers."

Gary laughs. "All right, it was a stupid question. What about a layout of the facility?"

James shakes his head. "No, I have nothing on the place. Arturo was a former inmate and knows his way around the prison. He'll be our guide."

Gary reaches for James. "How can you trust this guy Arturo? You don't know anything about him. For all you know, he could be working for Macudo. We may be walking into a trap!"

James frowns. "You can back out if you want, Gary—I won't hold it against you."

When Gary doesn't answer, James says, "Gary, this is our only chance to get Ernie out. The longer Ernie is in that place, the greater the risk that something bad will happen to him."

James pauses for a moment. "Ernie would do the same for us if the situation was reversed."

James smiles at Gary. "Let me finish detailing the plan. Getting in should be easy. The guards have already been bought. We need to get to cell block 9; that's where Macudo has a cell. Since Ernie is an important prisoner, he shouldn't be too far away. Macudo will want to keep an eye on him.

"Getting to the cell block shouldn't be too hard; we're going in at night. Arturo told me that the other prisoners won't put up much of a fuss. There're too many of us. But if anyone gets in the way, they need to be immediately eliminated. We can't afford to get bogged down. In addition to the Kalashnikovs, we'll have pistols with silencers. If a gun is needed, it's better if we use the silencers. We don't want to wake up the entire prison population."

James looks into Gary's face. "We need to be merciless. These are hardened criminals in that jail."

"What happens when we get to Macudo?" Gary asks. "How do we get him to cooperate?"

"We put a gun to his head."

"And if he still doesn't cooperate?"

James smiles slyly. "We blow his fucking head off!"

"Then how do we find Ernie?"

James clears his throat. "Finding Ernie shouldn't be too difficult even if we don't get any cooperation from Macudo. As I said, Ernie's cell should be right near Macudo. We'll just go down the cell block until we locate him."

James looks over at Gary. "It's a flimsy plan, I know, but that's all I can come up with. We'll have to do a lot of improvising as we go. Speed is the main thing. We need to get in and out before anyone has time to react. If we do that, the mission will be successful."

James points to the front. "Talk to the men. Tell them the plan and let them know what they can expect. Remember, no mercy: we can't let our feelings get in the way—make sure our men know that."

• • • • • • • ● • • • • • • • •

James is sitting in the front of the bus with Arturo looking at the two-story brick wall of the Palmasola prison. There's a guard tower protruding tall in the corner of the wall, but he has not seen a guard. He looks at the entrance and up the street, but there's no one in sight.

He turns to Arturo. "Give me a quick lesson on what we can expect."

"Once we get through the gate, we go down a long corridor," Arturo says. "The passageway opens to an area where there will be shops and stands of merchants selling goods. This time of the night, the shops and stands will be locked. There may be people about, but you don't need to worry; no one will pay you any mind. You might also see some prisoners sleeping on the ground.

"After that area, we proceed across another open yard, which in the day is used for outdoor activities and sports. Again, this time of the night, there won't be anyone around. Once we get past that yard, we'll come to PC4. That's our destination."

"Do you know where Macudo's cell is located?" James asks.

Arturo smiles. "His cell will be easy to find, it's the biggest in the entire block."

Arturo points to the prison entryway where a figure is flashing a light. "That's our man giving the signal. We better get going."

James points to the tower. "What about the guard?"

Arturo smiles. "Do not worry, Señor, *El Guardia* is probably sleeping. No one ever breaks out of Palmasola." Arturo smiles at James again. "Not until tonight, that is."

James turns to the rest of the men that are with him. "Herman, you stay in front with me. Gary, put two men to guard our rear. You and the rest of the men will cover our flanks. We don't stop. If anyone gives us a problem, eliminate the threat and keep moving."

James looks at the men. "Make sure your silencers are on." He turns back to Arturo. "Let's go."

James is totally unprepared for the scene when he gets into the penitentiary. The prison looks just like the villages he passed on the bus ride. The street is lined with shops. Fenced-in yards feature greenery and hanging plants. Except for the high brick walls with barbed wire on top, you might not know that it's a prison. The men continue to walk briskly until they get to a cell block.

Arturo points and whispers to James. "There is Macudo's cell."

"How do we get in? Is it locked?"

"No."

James turns to Gary. "Post two men here and two others at the other end of this passage. You, Arturo and Herman, come in with me." He turns to the rest of the men. "The rest of you, wait out here."

The cell is huge. There's a king-size bed in one end, with a man and a young woman sleeping. A television set is on a stand across the bed. A couch and a coffee table and two wing chairs take up the center of the place. The other side is the kitchen, with a huge oven and grill. The floors have marble tiles.

James whispers to Gary, "Go to the other side and cover the woman."

He walks up to the side of the bed where Macudo is snoring belly up and puts the silencer to his forehead. It's the young woman who wakes up first, and she lets out a loud gasp.

James looks at the young girl. "*Silencio!*"

Macudo's eyes flip open, and he stares at the pistol to his forehead. "*No muovi,*" James says in Italian.

Macudo stays still. James grabs him by the collar and sits him up. The gun is still against Macudo's forehead. "*Dov'è Ernie Bauer?*" James is still speaking Italian, but he's sure that Macudo understands him.

"*No conozco a ningún hombre llamado Ernie Bauer,*" Macudo says.

"He says he doesn't know anybody by that name," Arturo says.

James grimaces. "I know what he said. Tell him that he has ten seconds to tell me where Ernie is, or I'll blow his head off."

Arturo turns to Macudo. "*El Americano dice que tienes diez segundos para decirle dónde está el Señor Bauer o te disparará la cabeza.*"

When Macudo doesn't answer, James starts counting. "*Un, dos, tres……*"

"*El hombre está dos celdas abajo,*" Macudo blurts out.

Arturo looks at James. "He says that Bauer is two cells down."

"Good," James says. "Ask him where's the key to Ernie's cell?"

"*Dónde está la llave de la celda?*"

Macudo points to the kitchen counter. "*Está sobre el mostrador.*"

James looks over at Herman. "Get the key."

Herman walks over and gets the key.

"Bring it over here," James says, and takes the key from Herman. "Keep a gun on Macudo. I'll get Ernie."

When he gets into the hall, he motions to one of the men. "Come with me."

James looks into the cell, where Ernie is sleeping on a cot facing the wall, fully clothed. This cell is about a third of the size of Macudo's place and looks more of what he would expect to see in a prison: Three discolored gray drab walls with half the plaster missing. James unlocks the door and walks over to the cot.

He gives Ernie a shove. "Are you getting up, or do you really like it here?"

Ernie turns quickly to James. A smile broadens his face. "*Boet!* It's about time you got here."

"You're lucky I came at all! What a *dompkop*, getting yourself caught. How are you? Can you walk?"

"Yeah, I can walk." Ernie starts putting on his shoes.

"Good, let's get the hell out of here!"

When they come out, they go back into Macudo's cell. Gary smiles. "Colonel!"

"It's nice to see you again, Major," Ernie says.

"Gary, I'm taking Ernie out of here," James voices. "Give us a couple of minutes' head start and round up the men. Make sure you don't leave any of our men behind." James turns to Ernie. "Let's go!"

When they get into the hall, there's the muffled sound of a pistol firing off two rounds.

"That can't be good," Ernie says.

James grabs Ernie's arm. "Let's get out of here!"

Ernie and James move quickly through the prison, not running, keeping a wary eye on their surroundings. James finally lets out a breath when they are outside. They hustle down the street to where the bus is waiting.

James takes a seat in front and is looking at the prison door for his men to appear. He takes a quick glance at the guard tower, but there's no one there. A few minutes later, the men come running out. He's taking a count and is relieved when he realizes that every one of the men is accounted for.

"Is everyone all right?" he asks Gary when the men are on the bus.

"Yeah, everybody is good." Gary answers, still breathless. "We had to fight our way out."

"As long as we're all good." James turns to the driver. "Let's go." He turns to Gary. "Check on the men once more just in case––I'll be in the back with Ernie."

"Did everybody get out safely?" Ernie asks when James sits next to him.

"Yeah, everybody is okay."

"Good." Ernie gets misty-eyed. "James, I want to thank you…"

"Cut it out before I slap you over the head. What happened? How did they nab you?"

"I woke up one morning and the whole camp had emptied out. Rivera and his men had disappeared during the night. I hitched a couple of rides and made it to La Paz. Unfortunately, in La Paz, policemen picked me up at the airport and turned me over to Morales."

Ernie looks over at him and bellows out a laugh. "How did you convince that lovely wife of yours to let you do this latest adventure—I thought she had put her foot down?"

James smiles wryly.

Ernie laughs even harder and gives James a shove. "You didn't tell her, did you? You know she'll find out—the women always do. What'll you do when she learns about this escapade?"

James frowns. "There's an empty cell that just became available in Palmasola."

CHAPTER 29

TIME TO FACE THE MUSIC

Sam is in bed, propped up by three pillows, reading a magazine. It is late, 12:30, and she is expecting James at any moment. He had called from the airport and told her that he had landed and was on his way home. She hears the sound of his limo pulling up outside. She lifts herself out of bed, slides her feet into her slippers, reaches for her robe, and makes her way out to greet James.

As she walks down the hall, tying her robe, Billingsley come outs of his room.

"I heard a car," he says. "That must be Mr. Coppi."

Sam smiles. "Yes, I'm sure it is, Mr. Billingsley, but go back to bed; it's late."

"Are you sure? Mr. Coppi may be hungry."

"Yes, I'm certain. I can take care of James. Please, go back to bed."

James is just coming out of the foyer when she sees him. He smiles broadly, takes her in his arms, and gives her a kiss. "I missed you," he says.

"I missed you, too." Sam gives him a kiss and breaks the embrace. "Are you hungry?"

"No, I ate on the plane."

She takes him by the hand pulling him toward the living room. "Let's sit and talk, you can tell me all about your trip."

James stops her. "Are you sure? It's late. Why don't we wait until morning?"

Sam tugs at him again. "No, I'm too curious—I won't be able to sleep."

She takes him to the couch, and as they're sitting, she asks, "What happened? How did you find out Ernie was alive?"

"Well, when I got to Argentina, I immediately called Ambassador Klaus, and I was surprised to learn that Klaus still didn't know when Morales would release Ernie's remains. After a couple of days of the same old story, I had Ian get in touch with this fellow Gaytan. When I learned that Gaytan was in Santiago, I immediately made arrangements to pay him a visit."

James looks over at her. "It's late; you must be tired. Why don't we continue in the morning?"

"No, I'm not tired at all. Continue."

James clears his throat. "That's when I found out that Ernie was still alive. The strongman Morales was holding Ernie as a hostage in Palmasola prison."

Sam looks over at James. "Hostage? Why?"

"Morales was afraid that I'd continue to supply arms to the rebels. The leader of the rebels, Rivera, is still alive and in hiding."

"But you weren't going to supply the rebels anymore arms," Sam says.

"Yeah, Morales didn't believe that—so I spent my time working out the agreement, and after we were done, I managed to get Ernie released from the prison."

"So, Ernie got out before the prison riot?"

James sits up. "What prison riot?"

"The riot where six of the prisoners were killed."

James furrows his brow. "Where the heck did you hear that?"

Sam sits up. "I read it in the newspaper."

"What newspaper? I never saw that story."

"The Bolivian paper."

James shakes his head. "Where did you get the Bolivian paper? For that matter, why were you reading the Bolivian paper?"

"I had Mattie get me the paper, and Guadalupe translated the language for me. There was a story in the paper about prisoners being killed."

James sits back in the chair and laments. "You were spying on me!"

"No, I wasn't spying. I was just concerned about you."

James sits there, not saying a word.

"Say something," Sam says. When he doesn't answer, she reaches and turns his face to her. "You really can't blame me, can you? You hadn't called in five days."

James smiles sadly. "No, of course not, it's my fault. I'm to blame for how we got here. You lost trust in me."

James pulls her to him and lifts her chin up. "I'll tell you this, Sam. I'll be working real hard to get that trust back."

Sam rubs her chin. "Um… where have I heard that before? Oh, yeah, about four months ago. Someone thanking me for being so patient with him through the years and promising me that there would be no more dangerous overseas excursions. Now we're right back where we were." Sam stands up and looks down at James. "You need to stop fooling yourself. You love the action more than you love me. I'm off to bed." She begins walking away.

"Sam, come back," James calls out. He points to the couch. "Sit down, please. We have a lot more to discuss."

She folds her arms against her chest and looks over at him.

James smiles and pats the couch. "Please, just give me a couple of more minutes."

She comes back and sits next to him.

"Sam, right now you might not believe me, but I don't hold much back from you. I've tried to keep you involved in all our affairs. I take you to all the meetings. You have unrestrained access to any of our employees. The office is open to you anytime that you like, unfettered. Do you know why I do this?"

Sam shakes her head no.

"'*Sic transit gloria mundi*,'" James lets out.

Sam creases her brow. "What? What does that statement mean?"

"It's Latin—an ancient Roman saying. The literal translation is, '*thus passes the glory of the world*.' What it means is that '*all glory is fleeting*.' It's to remind someone who is having success that it won't last forever."

James clears his throat. "Sam, there may come a time that I, too, might stumble and fall. What this year has revealed is that our enemies are growing ever more powerful. They approach us from every direction. Those adversaries have come after you and me—they've come after our friends, our employees, and someday they might even target our children. We must maintain an ever-increasing vigilance. If I should ever fall, you'll have to take over. That's why I include you."

Sam forces out a laugh. "You better never fall; we'll be in big trouble if I have to take over."

James shakes his head. "No, Sam, that's not true. I've watched you closely the past few years. I'm confident that our affairs are in equally good hands with you."

"If that's true, why didn't you speak to me before embarking on the prison break?"

"Because you would've talked me out of it, and I didn't want you to talk me out of it." James looks into her face. "Sam, I may have my faults, but loyalty and duty are not among them. We had a friend in trouble. A dear friend that has always been loyal to us.

Ernie has risked his life countless times in pursuit of our affairs. If I hadn't made an effort to free Ernie from that prison, I couldn't have never lived with myself—I had to try to free him."

James touches her cheeks tenderly. "The only person that had enough sway to stop me from making the attempt is you. I hope I'm never faced with that decision again."

James gives her a soft kiss. "Sam, I know that over the years I have taken precarious undertakings—persuading myself that those tasks were necessary in achieving our dreams. We both know that wasn't completely true. You are right in calling me out and demanding that I stay more grounded at home with you and the family."

James looks into her eyes and smiles warmly. "A beautiful, wonderful home and family that you've created. I gave you my promise to stop this adventurism on my part, and I intend to keep that promise. I've always been cautious on letting you see the real me. Always been afraid that if I let you in completely, you wouldn't like what you saw."

James's face gets tight. "But, no more—I intend to fully let you in, with no more holding back. You'll get to see the real me. Once you get a complete look, you'll appreciate how much I truly love you. And I look forward to spending the rest of my life close to you without going off on my own."

James gets off the sofa and kneels on one knee. He looks up. "Samantha Powers Coppi, now that I've explained myself, will you give me yet another chance and stay married to me?"

Sam stands and pulls him up. "Get up, you lunatic."

James looks into her face. "You didn't give me an answer."

Sam reaches and pulls him tight against her body. "Of course, I'll stay married to you." She taps her index finger into his chest. "And it's lucky for you that I will stay married to you, because as I've always said, the only way out of this marriage for you, buddy, is in a body bag." Her lips touch his and they kiss passionately.

James lifts her into his arms.

"What are you doing?" she asks.

"I just realized that I never carried you over the threshold when we got married."

As they are walking down the hallway, Billingsley peeks out of his door and notices Sam in James's arms.

"I don't even want to know." Billingsley shakes his head and shuts the door.

I'm thankful to Sam and James for letting me write about this chapter in their lives without any revision on their part. And I'm most grateful to Kathy for taking the time to fill the gaps that I was missing in my piece.

There was one requirement made by James. Because of the sensitive nature of my story and that many of the people in the manuscript are still alive, I cannot publish the book for forty years. That means the earliest that my work can go into print is 2022. -Miles Cornish

www.ingramcontent.com/pod-product-compliance
Lightning Source LLC
Chambersburg PA
CBHW060905190726
48286CB00002B/373